ALSO BY NELL STEVENS

Bleaker House: A Memoir

The Victorian and the Romantic: A Memoir

BRIEFLY, A DELICIOUS LIFE

A Novel

NELL STEVENS

SCRIBNER

New York   London   Toronto   Sydney   New Delhi

Scribner

An Imprint of Simon & Schuster, Inc.

1230 Avenue of the Americas

New York, NY 10020

First Scribner hardcover edition July 2022

SCRIBNER and design are registered trademarks of The Gale Group, Inc., used under license by Simon & Schuster, Inc., the publisher of this work.

For information about special discounts for bulk purchases, please contact Simon & Schuster Special Sales at 1-866-506-1949 or business@simonandschuster.com.

The Simon & Schuster Speakers Bureau can bring authors to your live event. For more information or to book an event, contact the Simon & Schuster Speakers Bureau at 1-866-248-3049 or visit our website at www.simonspeakers.com.

Interior design by Wendy Blum

Manufactured in the United States of America

1   3   5   7   9   10   8   6   4   2

Library of Congress Cataloging-in-Publication Data is available.

ISBN 978-1-9821-9094-1

ISBN 978-1-9821-9096-5 (ebook)

For Eley

The sky is turquoise, the sea is azure, the mountains are emerald, the air is heaven. Sunny, hot days; everyone in summer clothes. Guitars and singing all through the night. . . . Briefly, a delicious life.

—Frédéric Chopin

Who amongst us has not, at some time, selfishly dreamed of forsaking his affairs, his habits, his acquaintances, and even his friends, to settle in some enchanted island and live without worries?

—George Sand

Knowing them, I am sure that within a month of being together, they will not be able to stand the sight of one another.

—Marie d'Agoult

NOVEMBER

TWO MEN KISSING

Of course, it wasn't the first time I'd seen two men kissing. It was 1838 and I had been at the Charterhouse in Valldemossa for over three centuries by then. I had seen hundreds of monks arrive, kiss each other, and die, but still, the sight of these two stopped me in my tracks.

The men—slight bodies, bony, both very short, standing amongst rotting pomegranates and flies in the overgrown garden of one of the abandoned cells—were gripping each other's faces, hands like masks. There was a smell of fermentation rising from the ground, and it gave the scene—the lovers, the kiss—a fizzy, too-hot quality. Sweat had worked its way through the shirt and jacket of the smaller one, spreading darkly between his shoulder blades. (It was November but still warm; the weather had yet to turn.)

The taller man trailed his fingers along the other's neck, and let them drape over his shoulder. The hand was very pale, as though it rarely saw the sun, and surprisingly broad below a narrow, snappable wrist. Fine bones pressed against the skin, splayed like a wing; thick muscle curved around the base of the thumb. The fingers looked heavy, the way they hung, faintly blue, from rounded knuckles.

A bird startled in the tree above them and flew off, dislodging a little flurry of feathers and leaves, and both men looked up as though expecting bad news.

Three hundred years earlier, I'd seen Brother Tomás with Brother Mateo in that very same garden, beard crushing against beard and the clatter of rosary beads hitting the paving stones. A decade or so after that, there was the boy from the village who sold bad oranges with the boy in the kitchens who made bad preserves. Around the turn of the sixteenth century there was a complex triangulation amongst Brothers Augustin, Miguel, and Simón. And so on, over the years: countless combinations, differing ages, differing levels of urgency and tenderness, but always more or less the same, the kissing and gripping and so often the very same skittishness, the entirely justified fear of being found out, the creeping sensation that they were being watched.

The point is: I was used to seeing habits fall from shoulders, formations of body hair on chests, backs, buttocks, et cetera. I enjoyed it. It was comforting. These, after all, were not the sort of men I worried about. It was the others, the ones who had fewer secrets, that kept me on my toes.

What surprised me was the presence of these lovers in the garden at all. There had been no monks at the Charterhouse since the government seized it from the Church three years before and sent them all away. The eviction happened quickly: the news, the tears, the goodbye kisses. There was a scramble for possessions they were not strictly supposed to have, and certainly not supposed to care about. Candlesticks stuffed into sacks. Gold crucifixes protruding from the folds of skirts. And then they clinked and clattered off down the hill, and I was left alone. Even the priest, Father Guillem, found the dead atmosphere oppressive. He moved to a house on the opposite side of the square.

I had thought—so funny with hindsight—that perhaps I wasn't needed there anymore. I began to think of moving on, started to fantasize about taking some rooms in the center of Palma, nothing too elaborate, just a vantage point from which I could watch the city happen. I hadn't spent much time away from Valldemossa, the small hillside village where I was born, and the idea of trying my luck in the city was alluring. New smells, new people to worry about and dodge and look out for. But then a sacristan was hired to take care of the Charterhouse in the absence of the monks, and as he swaggered around the place swinging his keys, as he napped in the monks' deserted cots, snoring and smacking his lips in his sleep, as he sold off all the silverware, and then all the gold, as his hands grabbed more and more things that were not his to grab, it became apparent I would have to stay on a little longer to keep an eye on him. In the quiet of the early mornings, I waited for the sound of his heavy footsteps on the tiles. Over time it came less frequently, as the novelty of the job wore off for the Sacristan. Still, I stayed. I was quiet and watchful, became invested in the comings and goings of lizards. I took up bird-watching. Sometimes I threw things. I waited, just in case.

That morning, I had gone into the garden to try my hand at swatting fruit from the branches of one of the taller trees, and after that to sneak up on the starlings and howl, which would send them into the air together like a single giant bird. I had it all planned out and was not prepared, not prepared at all, to come across unfamiliar, uninvited lovers.

Eventually, they stepped back from one another. The smaller one readjusted his jacket and turned his head to the side. My first view of his face: plump lips, dark eyes, long lashes, and glossy black curls pinned back. Cheeks pink in the heat. Sweat on the temples.

Which was when I realized that it was not a man after all. It was a woman dressed as a man.

Which was the second great surprise of my morning.

I FALL IN LOVE

My name is Blanca. I died in 1473, when I was fourteen years old, and had been at the Charterhouse ever since. Over the centuries, I suppose, I came to think of it as solely my domain. I knew more about it than anyone else, that was for sure. I knew the generations of monks, and after they left, the great silence of the place. I knew about all sorts: buried treasure, dead-end tunnels, which doors swelled shut in summer with the heat and which in winter with the damp. I knew where the roof leaked, where the rats nested. And still, for all my expertise, there was no sign whatsoever of where these two people had sprung from: the same old corridors, same echoes, same spiders crawling from beam to beam across the ceiling. I was wrong-footed.

The man-who-was-in-fact-a-woman reached out to brush away a leaf that had caught in the hair of the man-who-was-a-man.

He was pallid, red-eyed, looked exhausted. She was shorter than him but seemed, now I had a sense of her, the larger of the two. They clambered over the low wall at the end of the garden and sat on it with their backs to me, looking out at the tiered fields of almond trees descending the mountain. She dug in her pocket, fumbled with something I couldn't see. When she shifted her head a little I realized she was smoking, which was a tiny thing, the smallest thing, but you have to understand that in all my centuries on earth I had never seen anything like it: this woman—I had taken in the shape of her, collarbones, breasts, hips that swelled below her waist—who dressed like a man, kissed like a man, smoked like a man. She swung a leg back over the wall, straddling it as though it were a horse.

That was it. The bracket of her bent leg against the stones. The way her mouth angled around the cigar in a grimace that was almost a smile. The sight of a woman in a well-tailored jacket and trousers. Unexpected, unimagined. A prickling sensation. A stomach-dropping, blood-fizzing, breath-stopping, knotted lurch-and-swoop that I recognized, by then, as the first faltering step towards falling in love.

And then, behind me, everything started happening. Faint rumbling noises growing louder: grunting, heavy objects being dragged across cobbles, the wheezing and occasional shrieks of a donkey. A child laughed. A man shouted. I darted back to see the Charterhouse doors jerk open, a slab of sunlight fall across the tiles, and chaos tumble over the threshold.

A young woman, very red-faced and sweaty from the climb, attempted to control a girl of around ten years old, who was spinning on the worn-down steps so that her skirts blew out. A young man, or perhaps he was still a boy, was attempting to direct the porter leading a donkey laden with cases.

"It's Cell Three," the boy was saying. "We're to stay in Cell Three."

On the threshold of Cell Three, the strangers stood and surveyed it, panting: its expanse of dust, dust sheets, dust twisting like snow through the columns of light slanting in from the windows. It was a small apartment of three conjoined rooms with high ceilings and thick walls, a smell of damp and firewood. The floor stayed cool in hot weather, its cracked tiles plugged with the dead skin of all the monks who had paced them. There was a small fissure in the plaster above the main doorway where, in 1712, Brother Federico had drunkenly hurled a plate. Each of the three rooms had a doorway that opened out onto the overgrown, half-rotten garden where the lovers were. Tendrils reached inside through the windows and doors as though the plants, like these strangers, were trying to move in.

Cell Three had, in recent years, been the busiest part of the Charterhouse, a place that was, admittedly, not known to be busy at all. The Sacristan, having moved into town and sold what few treasures the monks had left behind, turned his mind to landlording; first, he rented out Cell Three to a political refugee from Spain, who arrived looking harried with a highly melancholic wife and their fourteen-year-old daughter in tow. They were pathetically grateful to the Sacristan, who smirked and lifted his hands in protest and said it was his pleasure. He wasted no time in pursuing that pleasure, leaving little presents for the teenage girl to find under the cloisters' arches, then murmuring sweet things in her ear, then brushing his fingers against her cheek, his lips against hers, and so on. I hated watching it. I screeched after him as he did his rounds; I screwed up pages from Bibles to hurl at his head. He never seemed to care: simply picked up the balls of paper and looked around, bemused, before dropping them and kicking them into corners.

I knew the daughter was pregnant before she did. I snuck inside her body and felt the doubleness, the second heart beating at the bottom of her belly. It was fresh and alarming, the cramping and clenching, the nausea. She started throwing up. I found a bucket in the attic and dragged it to the corner of her room. When she was done, I'd haul it off and dump it out. It took enormous effort for me to make such impact on the world, to move an object from place to place—I am weak, my ability to exert pressure is erratic—but the girl never seemed to wonder what happened to the bucket, how it was that it came back clean every morning; she simply gripped the sides in her shaky, thin fingers and replenished it.

She was almost spherical, mountainous, by the time her parents realized what had happened. They, with their daughter, confronted the Sacristan. (He had barely looked at the girl since she started to show and had not bothered to explain to her that what was happening to her was his fault entirely.) He feigned confusion at first, and then, under pressure from the parents and from me, too—I pummeled his head; he called it a migraine—he shrugged and said, well, yes, it was him, but what of it?

He pointed at the portraits of the Madonna that lined the walls of the Charterhouse corridors: canvas after canvas of broad, white foreheads, beatific smiles, occasional exposed breasts proffered to babies with the faces of old men. Those virgins, he said, were the only ones he was duty bound to protect.

I howled and howled, and the daughter looked up, eyes wide, suddenly afraid. She seemed at last to sense the danger she was in, to understand that the thing she was growing beneath her skin might one day burst out of her so violently and bloodily that she or it or something might die.

The next day the family packed up and left, and I never got to find out what happened.

Over time, the Sacristan became less interested in sex and more interested in food. He moved an old lady called María Antonia into Cell Two. She paid no rent in return for cooking him meals. He told her not to give him bread, and I noticed that whenever he had any, he was overcome with pains and gas. I took to sneaking crumbs into his soup. The bucket the Spanish girl had used was still in Cell Three, and whenever I saw it I liked to imagine her and her baby, wherever they were, together and alive and unmolested.

Now, the newly arrived little girl skidded to the corner, sending up a plume of dust behind her, and peered inside the bucket as though looking for her fortune at the bottom. She tipped it upside down, dislodging a beetle.

"What took you all so long?" The lovers, drawn by the commotion, were standing at the window, the woman leaning into the room with her forearms draped on the sill. Her voice: clear, low.

There was a long silence and then the young man said, somewhat pointedly, "We were carrying things, Mama."

"Amélie," the woman said. "Go and make up Chopin's bed at once. He is exhausted from the climb." The older girl patted sweat from her face and stared blankly as though she were going to refuse. "Now," said the woman, and Amélie hauled herself to her feet.

I ordered the family in my mind: Mama, Chopin, son, daughter, and reluctant domestic, Amélie. The children and servant looked astonished to find themselves there—kept looking around at the walls and ceiling, at their feet on the floor—as though this was as unexpected by them as it was by me. The adults seemed oblivious. They wandered inside.

Mama crouched down beside a suitcase, unfastened and

opened it. Inside was a rubble of oddities that smelled damp and foreign. As she removed a handkerchief, a single moth fluttered up from the case so it looked, for a second, as though the cloth it-self was taking off. A magnifying glass, which she held to her face, turning a giant, augmented eye upon the room, owlish and black. When she blinked, her lashes brushed the lens. She placed the glass on the floor beside her left foot, as though that was where she intended to keep it, but as soon as she did so the little girl leapt forwards and carried it off to examine dust in a crevice by the window. Mama withdrew a pair of compasses, walking them idly along her forearm. The points dug into her skin, leaving white spots that shrank and turned pink.

"What are you doing?" said the boy.

Mama dug the point of the compass under her thumbnail, scraping out a crescent of dirt. She looked up. "Unpacking, Maurice."

And so the foreign family filled the familiar rooms with their unfamiliar things. Mama produced trinket after trinket, clue after clue, from her case, setting them beside her on the floor. Sheet music, scrawled hastily as though it were a lovers' note. Tobacco. Neckties. A sheaf of papers clasped in a worn-out leather folder, embossed with faded letters that read: *From the pen of George Sand.*

"We're really going to stay here?" Maurice, hovering in the doorway from the garden, looked uncertain.

She turned her attention back to her hands and said, wearily I thought, "We really are."

My heart—the place where my heart had been when I was alive—soared.

BEAUTIFUL WOMEN

I should explain: When I was alive, I lived in a time of beautiful men. They were everywhere: big and broad and manly, managing everything mannishly, manifesting whatever they wanted and manhandling what they didn't. I ogled them, it's true. Everyone did. It was normal. They were so beautiful. As my mother used to say: we had two religions; there was the Church, and then there were the men.

After I died, I found myself in a time of beautiful women.

It was a shock, of course, when I noticed this. It was not something I'd considered in my life. Women had represented only safety to me, comforting boredom. My mother, for instance, single-handedly managing the family pig business. My sister. Girls in the village who understood me completely and had their own worries and secrets and fears that were just like mine. I had never seen anything remotely alluring in them. The idea! Like being attracted to a glass of milk.

But then there I was, transported. In the early days of my death, the women of the village struck me as godlike. They moved through the world as though they were distinct from it—crisp-edged, wrapped in their skins—while the men seemed to fade into the earth, revealing themselves to be muddy, boggish, unreliable. I'd had enough of men by then to last a lifetime and longer. I learned too late to be wary, suspicious, to comb through their thoughts for nefarious intent, but I took it up after death for the sake of the women that survived me.

The women that survived me! They stepped out of their houses into the daylight and if I'd had any breath I would have been breathless at the sight of them. The hands of women. The ankles of women. The voices of women as they called to each other across the square. I could have kicked myself for not realizing it before.

I wanted to know everything, wanted to know what a woman smelled like, not just from a distance, but right up close—nose to armpit, nose to foot, nose to crotch. What a woman tasted like. What a woman's mouth felt like when it kissed you. I could only imagine approximations, insufficient and overly poetic. It would be like the wing of a pigeon brushing against your lips. It would be like someone crushing the head of a rose against your tongue. In those early dead days, I was still a teenager after all. I thought like a teenager, concocted similes like a teenager.

What a waste of a body, I thought, not to have found out all these things when I had time to feel them.

Eventually I fell in love. It took me a couple of decades, but when the time came, I couldn't help it. It was with a girl called Constanza, who was always alone, and for whom I would have died a second time. *Constanza, Constanza,* I used to whisper, as she meandered down to the river to wash clothes. She would kick stones out of her path as she walked. She would chew hangnails. She would hum. When the pads of her fingers turned wrinkly in the water, she would rub them together until skin peeled off in little gray rolls. After stringing laundry out on bushes in the sun, she would settle, cross-legged, knees splayed. She always had something in her hands to fiddle with—sticks, food, the loose hem of her skirt—never still. Watching her twist a sprig of rosemary between her fingers: the height of entertainment. Watching her roll an olive between forefinger and thumb, the bright trail of oil it left on her skin: all-consuming sport.

I imagined how it would be to press myself against her, in between her toes, into the crook of her elbow, the crease between her nostril and her cheek, though I never quite dared try. Instead, I placed myself under the drip-drip-drip of the wet clothes on the branches and thought of all that could be done between two women in possession of bodies, what effects could be achieved with fingers and tongues.

She was sixteen when I fell in love with her, and unmarried. Her future weighed heavily on us both. We both knew that she could not spend forever alone in the valley, expertly twirling a feather between the fingers of one hand while clean undershirts and dresses stiffened in the heat. She turned seventeen, and then eighteen, and it felt, sometimes, that I would glance aside at some momentary diversion—a passing bird, a lightning strike cracking open a storm—and she would be a year older.

At twenty, she married a second cousin. At first he was gentle, then less so. She had a baby, and another, and another, and another. Constanza at twenty-five, Constanza at thirty. Her husband drank, became belligerent, raised his voice, and swung his fists around. I was astonished, flabbergasted, offended that he didn't realize how beautiful his wife was, how lovely, how fleeting his chance for happiness.

I stayed close. I did what I could. Tipped over his cup, poured the last of his drink onto the floor, watered down the wine. When he lunged for her in a drunken rage, I would try to trip him up before he could get to her, which sometimes worked and sometimes didn't. He woke up, bruised and bleary. I hissed in his ear, *You will never do this again, you monstrous brute, you will never do this again,* until he found himself repeating it out loud to Constanza: *I will never do this again. I'm a monstrous brute.* He always did it again.

Constanza was stoical. She did not overthink. She understood her husband's nature as well as she knew her own. She knew that he held no interest for her, not him nor any man, and she knew there was nothing to be done about it. I lay next to her at night, trying to drown out his snoring with pillow talk. I imagined closing my lips around the tip of her little finger, running my tongue along the edge of the nail. She imagined the unclothed bodies of women. I imagined gripping her forearm tight enough to feel the crisscrossed bones beneath, muscle under the skin, soft hairs prickling. She imagined that the person kissing her was not her husband but the baker's wife, or one of the traveling women who passed through the village from time to time. When he clambered atop her, I would sing as loud as I could and she would close her eyes.

Constanza at forty, forty-five, fifty, and I felt dread settling over me at the breakneck passage of time. Her flesh loosened from her bones. Her eyes grew paler, hair wiry. Her babies had babies, who had babies of their own. She was a great-grandmother before she turned sixty and she died like this: when her husband came home one night, he pushed her—not much force but just enough—and she toppled backwards; the wall was behind her, uneven stone; her skull was in that moment as fragile as eggshell;

head to rock; a crack. She didn't whimper. Slumped to the floor. Time was fast but this all seemed to happen gradually, a small lifetime in that splitting second, the arc of her body through the space between her husband and the wall, the single clap on impact like aborted applause. The next morning, when her husband woke to find her where he had thrown her, he had no memory of how she got there. If it had been in my power to kill him I would have snuffed him out in an instant.

I loved other women after that, though not many. It happened infrequently and they always died.

All of which is to say that by the time the foreigners arrived at the Charterhouse that winter, by the time I had started to fall for the foreign woman, with her boots and her smoking and her thick, low voice, I knew all about everything. I knew about men, about women, and I knew exactly what I wanted.

NOT A PIANO

Many things had already arrived at Cell Three, one after the other: the lovers, the children, sunlight, luggage.

The next was María Antonia, who came limping in uninvited.

María Antonia, the Sacristan's personal tenant-cum-chef, was usually found crouched by her stove in Cell Two, cooking enthusiastically and horribly. She made big stews of past-their-best vegetables and fish that was surely too pungent to be healthy. The Sacristan didn't seem to mind, and María Antonia seemed to think she had earned the right to be a permanent fixture of the Charterhouse. No matter how many times I told her she didn't even know what permanent *meant,* that she was as temporary as a moth, that she had no idea—she couldn't hear me.

"Señor," María Antonia said now, as she approached the foreign family. "Señora?" Her voice sounded croakier than usual.

Mama looked up from her case and stood. The children turned to look at the old lady. Chopin didn't move.

"Señor," María Antonia said again. "Señora." She seemed to sense, as I had, that Mama was the one in charge, and hunched towards her, eyes lifted no higher than her knees. The overall effect was of a woman on the verge of death.

"I hang my head in shame," she started, without even introducing herself, "because I am your servant and do not speak French." She straightened enough to produce a pot of coffee from amongst the heavy folds of cloth draped around her. "But my dear friend the Sacristan advised me of your arrival today. I bring you some refreshment after your journey, and seek to reassure you that your every need will be met here by me, your housekeeper."

The family's faces were blank. Mama looked panicked, then seized on a small leather purse, from which she withdrew some coins. She offered them vaguely to María Antonia.

"For the coffee," Mama said, in what I supposed was French. It had not, until that moment, struck me that the family was speaking a language that was not Mallorquín or Spanish, something entirely new to me but which I had no difficulty understanding. The insights and abilities bestowed on me by death continued to surprise me.

"Coffee!" María Antonia said, nodding and beaming. The word was the same in both languages.

"Coffee," Mama repeated, and held out the money.

"Oh!" said María Antonia, as though only just understanding that the coins were for her. "No, no payment, no payment at all." She placed the pot on one of the boxes to free up her hands, then covered her face as though the money offended her. "I will serve you for the love of God," she said. "For God!" She pointed upwards and crossed herself. "And for friendship."

What are you playing at, María Antonia? I wondered. I watched her eyes dart between piles of unpacked luggage, calculating what was inside, what it might be worth to her. *Not on my watch,* I said, and I would have commenced driving her out at once had something else not happened: the thud of a man's staff against the cell's open door. It was a day when things would not stop happening.

"Excuse me?" A local man poked his head into the room. "Excuse me but where do you want this?" He looked vaguely from Chopin to Mama to María Antonia.

None of them reacted because none of them could see what "this" was. I went at once to find out. In the corridor, I still wasn't sure what I was looking at: some large item of furniture covered with cloth. The man shuffled backwards, got behind it, and began to push it into the room. It made a confused humming sound as it moved.

"What's that?" said Mama.

Panting, the local man stopped to remove the cloth: a narrow wooden box with rivets and hinges in odd places.

"A piano," he said. "We were told you wanted a piano."

Chopin, who had yet to say a word, stepped forwards. He peered at the box, stroking its top and sides before folding back a wooden panel to reveal yellowed keys like bad teeth. He extended a deliberate finger and depressed one. The sound it emitted was jangling: a bird's disturbed shriek. He stepped back as though burned.

"You think this a piano?" he said. The first time I heard his voice. It was reedy, higher-pitched than I'd imagined. He coughed after he spoke.

The local man, speaking Mallorquín determinedly in the face of Chopin's French, repeated himself. "We were told you wanted a piano," he said.

"How wonderful," said María Antonia, stepping forwards to take control, and in her excitement forgetting to limp. "A piano! We'll have music and dancing with our new foreign friends." She patted the instrument as though it were a prize pig. "Bring it fur-

ther in. Bring it in." Chopin stayed by its side but did not help ma-
neuver it. He seemed uncomfortable with other people touching
it, wincing when a drop of the man's sweat hit its lid, but scared
too of touching it again himself. His fingers twitched at the sight
of the keys, hands hovering like hummingbirds.

María Antonia reached for Mama's palm, which was still
holding the coins she had offered for the coffee, and slid two away.
She passed the payment to the man for delivering the piano—one
coin—and sent him off. The little girl's eyes followed the passage
of the second coin into María Antonia's sleeve; she opened her
mouth to say something but Maurice shook his head and whispered, "Don't, Solange."

María gestured at the piano, at the children, and at the coffee she had brought, as though all were untold and equal joys to
her. Then, at last, she hobbled off, muttering almost unintelligibly
about being back later to serve dinner. When she was gone, Maurice pushed the cell door shut, leant back against it, and slid all the
way down to the floor.

"Who on earth was *that*?" he said. His voice, not yet fully broken, started low and ended in a squeak.

Solange set about pouring coffee, sniffing it suspiciously, dip-
ping a finger into the liquid. "A spider," she said, hunching her
shoulders, making claws of her hands.

"A spider," Chopin agreed, imitating the girl's pose and then
compressing the piano keys with his braced fingers: a shock of
sound.

They all seemed looser in their bodies now that they thought
they were alone, lighter on their feet as they clustered around the
coffee cups. The son and daughter padded out into the garden,
where they sat cross-legged in the shade, lowering their lips to

drink and squinting at the sun. Mama took Chopin's hand, tugging him gently, then more firmly away from the piano, and followed the others into the bright outside.

The day's heat had subsided, though the goats on the hillside below the Charterhouse were still lethargic, bells clanging when they lifted their heads. Birds overhead sagged a little in the air. In one of the cottages below, someone began strumming a guitar and the sound rippled its way into the garden. Chopin took a deep breath as he settled himself near the boy and girl, tilting his face towards the sun, eyes closed. His fingers flickered in time with the music, but the rest of him was completely still. Mama sprawled on the ground with her head in his lap and I sat beside her. Nobody spoke.

After a while, Chopin's breathing turned deep and heavy, his fingers slowed. The little girl put her cup down and fell asleep with her mouth wide open. Maurice blinked and said nothing, and neither did Mama, who was looking up at the sky through the crosshatched branches of the tree. It was as though none of them was waiting for anything; none of them was going to go anywhere.

I looked from Chopin to Mama to Maurice to Solange and saw a tableau of possibility. Pianos to be played! Jokes to be made at María Antonia's expense! Kisses to be kissed beneath the pomegranate tree! And Mama herself, whose name perhaps was George Sand, who kept papers wrapped up in leather and who looked at everything—her children, Chopin, strangers, walls, the places where I was standing (where she did not know I was standing)—with the same lovely black-eyed curiosity. I thought, *This is going to be fun.*

WHAT I COULD DO

It took me a long time to realize I didn't have to be alone. For years after I died, I stalked around the Charterhouse as though I were still in a body, stuck inside myself, cut off from other people's minds as I had been before.

I searched for others like me, people who had washed up on the wrong side of their deaths. I imagined that soon enough I'd turn a corner and find the gathered hordes of the dead, keeping each other company, consoling each other, telling the kinds of jokes that might offend the living, ready to dispense advice to newcomers like me. I scrutinized everyone I came across, looking for signs that they too were dead, though I was unsure what exactly would give them away. To the living I was no longer visible, but I had no concept of what the dead looked like to each other. Would I appear to them as I was in life, and if so, at which point during my life? I hoped my eternal form was not my final living one: blood-smeared, vomit-streaked, and utterly, utterly outraged. I hoped I looked better than that. I hoped too that when I finally met the rest of the dead, they looked healthy and robust. I didn't have the stomach for gore, for mangled limbs and sickened faces.

Sometimes I saw a figure standing alone, far off in a field, or by the ocean, or in the mist, looking as perfectly alone as I felt, and I would rush towards it. But then, in the moment when they should have turned to meet my eye, they always looked beyond me and would have walked right through me if I'd stood my ground.

Was I the only one? Was I unique in not having died when I died? Or was it just that we were invisible to each other? I didn't know which was worse. I pictured the air thick with ghosts, all restlessly searching for each other. Then I pictured the air thin, vapid, ghostless. Both were worst.

I cried daily—eyelessly, tearlessly—and got so angry that I made the whole place colder. But when I realized that my rage in the hot summer months was improving the lives of the monks— they sweated less and seemed more energetic—I decided to calm down. I learned to lower my expectations about corners when turning them. The dead were never there.

I taught myself to enjoy simple pleasures: making people jump, knocking things over, tripping up passersby and particularly my enemies. And I began to test the limits of what I could do. I pushed the boundaries of my new self.

The first time, it was almost an accident. It happened while the man I was stalking, the man I loathed, the man who I held responsible for my death, was sleeping. His name was Brother Ramón, although to begin with he wasn't a brother, just a novice. He was breathing deeply. With each exhale his upper lip swelled into a hillock of splayed hair. I was close to his head, watching him, the glimpse of teeth, the bulging eyelids twitching, and I found myself achingly curious to know what he was dreaming about.

I had done various things to upset him that day. I had tipped wine all over his cot so when he lay down to nap his mattress squelched. I had filched an octopus tentacle from the kitchen and hidden it behind his shelf; the weather was warm and the tentacle was already beginning to smell. When he said his Hail Marys I had shouted as loud as I could: *Mary doesn't like you! Mary doesn't like you!* and hoped that something of the sentiment reached him, just a little bit, enough to make him feel uneasy.

Was he dreaming about me? Did he remember me at all? Did he ever wonder why he felt so much less comfortable than his brethren, why his cell smelled worse than theirs, why he was always so unsteady on his feet, and why, whenever something fell, it always seemed to land on his head and nobody else's? Did he even notice that his food tasted bitter, his bread dry or soggy? Did he wonder why he had this strange and devastating sense that God and the Virgin and all the saints despised him?

I leant closer and closer to his face, and then—

I found myself inside him.

I could see everything.

He was dreaming about water. He was sitting in the garden adjoining his cell, in the rippling shade of the pomegranate tree, and he was drinking water. It was lukewarm. A dead insect that had been floating on the surface caught on the side of the cup when he tilted it to his mouth.

I still thrill to think of the havoc I wreaked on that dream. How I turned the water to piss and tipped it in his lap. How the tree dropped ton upon ton of rotting pomegranates onto him and finally keeled over and trapped him beneath its weight. How I pushed the tilted trunk against his neck until he spluttered and wheezed and then, finally, woke up.

He gasped for air. His heart was pounding. Settled inside him, even as he awoke, I could feel the thrumming anxiety, the itch of sweat under his arms, and knew he was thirsty. When he reached for the cup at his bedside, I withdrew from his body to nudge it further from his reach.

That was how I learned what I could do, how I learned that the boundary between the living and the dead was as easily manipulable as sand. It was a comfort, to say the least. I was no longer alone; I could be a part of things again. If ever I felt a flicker of sadness, grief at the death of a loved one and the recurrent disappointment that they did not, like me, stick around despite their demise, or frustration when I was not heard or could not stop evil things from happening, I settled into the mind of a nearby happy child, felt the sun on her skin, tasted the sweet, sharp shock of juice in her mouth. I felt better then. Other consoling sensations: the rasping tongue of a dog greeting its owner; tree bark against the palms of a young person climbing; the rippling orgasm of a woman who had discovered how to use her fingers for herself; salt on the lips of someone who has been swimming in the sea. I liked to feel the soft, humming fur of a cat being stroked. I liked the taste of wine.

With the arrival of the new family in the Charterhouse, I thrilled to think of the pleasures they might experience, which I could experience through and with them. It would take time—it always took time, I found, to get inside the heads of newcomers—but I was nothing if not persistent, and everything I had seen suggested that they would be happy, would feel only pleasant things, would love each other easily.

That first day, certainly, all the signs were good.

I waited until nightfall to begin my approach. Chopin had a room to himself: a single bed and the new piano. Maurice, Solange, and Mama had three little cots side by side in the room on

the opposite side of the living area. Amélie was to stay next door
with María Antonia—news she had received stonily, as though
she was being told to spend the night outside with livestock or
dogs. As it grew dark, Chopin, who had dozed most of the day,
stretched out like a shadow and faded.

"I'm going to bed," he said.

Mama crossed the floor and kissed him. Her jawbone jutted
to the side as she leant into him and I felt a little giddy at the sight
of it. Their hands clasped each other's backs and lingered there.
Maurice looked down at his feet. Solange fixed her attention directly on her mother. Neither child seemed surprised. It was as
though this happened all the time.

"Good night, my Chopinet," the woman said.

He said, "Good night, George," and so I knew her name was
definitely George.

Not long after Chopin retreated out of sight, Maurice yawned
and, kissing his mother, announced that he too was going to sleep.
George sent Solange off with him, and when the door closed on
their bedroom, I waited. I waited for George to stand up, to wash
her face, say her prayers, and follow Maurice and Solange to bed.
Funny to think, now, how little I understood her on that first
night. Certainly, I had no idea how long I would be waiting for
George to say her prayers.

Instead, she went to the desk she had positioned at the window, and lit a cigar. Everything was very still; the only movement
was smoke trailing upwards from her fingertips. It caught some of
the candlelight, orange and thick. There was coffee left over from
dinner, lukewarm and oversteeped, which she tipped out into her
cup. She used a sleeve to wipe away grainy brown drips from the
lip of the pot. Then she withdrew the papers from the leather en-

velope, dipped her pen, and started to write. Her hand made a whispering sound as it slid across the page, stopping only occasionally to dab wet words with blotting paper.

I listened to the hiss of her skin against the page and to the scratch of the nib. I murmured some of the words she was writing: I smelled the earthiness of her ink and the cigar smoke. Closer: her doughy, coffee-flavored breath. Closer still: the salty skin on the back of her neck. Surely she would sleep soon, I thought. But George stayed awake and continued to write as though sleep was just something that happened to other people. She burned through three candles in a row and however much, in those early hours, I circled and squirmed and pressed myself against her, I could only get inside her head for snippets, brief seconds before the shock of her alertness, the sharpness of her world and the brightness of the candle and the speed of her thoughts jolted me back out again. She stopped writing only to light cigars and sip cold coffee, and then she was at it again, her hand moving across the page so quickly it looked as though the pen was alive and all George was doing was trying to control it.

What are you doing here? I asked her. She did not look up.

What are you doing here? I wanted to scratch it into the walls, or the windowsill, or spell it out with pebbles in the garden. *What are you doing here?* written in ornate twists of orange peel.

What are you doing here and how can I persuade you to stay?

Her answer was to smoke and drink and write, as though the question had never been asked. I caught hold of: a tickle in her throat; a tightness at the base of her spine, as though she needed to click her hips into place; a glancing thought about a rabbit; the sensation of her blood moving through the veins and arteries around her throat.

She was writing about a monastery—not the Charterhouse but some other, imagined place that was similarly creaking, windswept, dark, and stony. She was writing about monks, which were, after all, my special subject, though these monks were like none I'd ever encountered: they spent their time worrying about their souls and their spirits and visiting each other's cells to talk about the *truth*, whatever that might be, and it seemed a strange contrast between the exterior of George, which was so certain and so solid, and this interior, which, though not yet easily accessible to me, was spilling out onto the page. I wanted to ask her about it. Or rather, I wanted her to ask me about it. I wanted to reach out and lay my hand on her hand and say, *You can ask me anything you want about the soul and the spirit and life and death. I have all the answers, if you want them.* But she continued to write, to move the monks around in their monastery through stormy nights and windswept days.

The sun rose around seven, but light wouldn't reach the Charterhouse until noon: the mountain it topped sat between two higher peaks, shading it from direct light for all but a few hours in the middle of the day. By three in the afternoon, everything would be shadow again. George didn't notice day had broken until near nine, when she looked up dimly, blinked, and pinched out her candle. She pushed back from the desk, which was littered with ash and ink splatters. The chair legs scraped the tiles. She stretched her arms above her head, yawned, flipped over the pages she had written so they were facedown, and went to bed. (This process took, at most, around forty seconds: kicking off her boots, shrugging off her jacket, unpinning her hair, and then, at once, catatonic on the mattress.)

At last she was asleep and I nuzzled her, tingling, waiting for the first dream, for a way in, a crack in the wall through which I could crawl and from which I would discover everything else I wanted to know: who she was, who she was going to be, who she had been before. This was a trick I had taught myself over the years. Once I'd found my way inside a person's head their pasts were right there, under the slop and tide of feelings on the surface, and I could see it all for myself, as though I was translating a language I didn't know I knew. I dove into George.

GEORGE REMEMBERS

Thirty girls are crammed into a dim, low-ceilinged room. There is a smell of damp throughout, and smoke from the stove. The walls are egg-yolk yellow, which makes the faces of the children look sallow and unwell. They fidget in their seats. They twist their sleeves into their palms and play with loose threads. At the front of the classroom a plaster crucifix is crumbling, flake by flake, onto the tiles below. Beside it is an English nun, mid-lecture, saying, *There is a place where languish the souls of the children that die unbaptized.*

At the back of the room there is George, thirteen years old, taking it all in and feeling a knot forming in her stomach: she doesn't like the shadows, the smell, the disintegrating cross, the sense that the room is not a room but the stomach of some dyspeptic creature that has swallowed them all. It is her first day of class at the Convent of the English Augustinians in Paris and she doesn't like the look of any of it.

What is the name of that place, asks the nun, *that place where the souls of babies languish for eternity? Tell me, Aurore Dupin, the name of that place.*

George, who at this point in her life is called Aurore Dupin, stiffens. She looks around for someone else whose name might be the same as hers. She sees: the yellowed faces of her peers and the back wall of the classroom.

Me?

She thinks of the sprawling grounds of her grandmother's house, where she was free to run and climb only days ago. There was so much time there, so much light. All the things that frustrated or upset her at the time—her grandmother's fastidiousness, her tutor's bad breath—seem tiny, forgettable, lovable even. If she could only go home now, she would lean in close to her tutor's face and when he coughed she would inhale, as though smelling fresh bread or some extravagant, blousy flower from the gardens.

The nun steps forward. *What is the name, Aurore Dupin, of the place where languish the souls—*

A hiss from somewhere behind George's head. Someone is giving her the answer. She waits, hoping they might say it again and more clearly but nothing more comes. The word she heard was something like *limpet*.

She takes a wild guess: *Olympus?* As soon as she speaks, the absurdity of it strikes her. She laughs a single, impulsive hoot, and claps her hand over her mouth.

Behind her, there is a snort. Everyone else is quiet.

The nun looks out of the small, grimy window as though distracted and then says, *You strike me, Aurore Dupin, as a very dissipated person.*

After class, George is approached by a girl with red hair. *I told you it was Limbo,* the girl says. *What did you say "Olympus" for?*

George knows the name of the redheaded girl. Or at least, she knows her nickname, which is "Boy." George has heard about her in whispers from other girls. It was practically the first thing anyone said when she arrived: how loud Boy is, how rebellious and terrifying, how boyish. They all professed to dislike Boy but they couldn't stop talking about her all the same.

George scrutinizes Boy, who looks not terrifying so much as unabashed. She is a year or so older than George, broad-hipped and beginning to look like a woman.

Without warning, Boy thumps George on the shoulder, hard enough to make her reel. George takes half a step back but holds her balance and absorbs the shock. She meets Boy's eye as she throws her strength into a reciprocal blow. Boy gasps and puts a hand to the spot George struck, stroking it with an expression of delight.

You can meet me tonight, if you want, Boy says, *in the cloisters.* She says it casually, pressing her lips together afterwards as though the words are sour. *If you're not scared to.*

George says she is not scared. Has never been scared in her life.

All day, she waits for the night. Moving between the yellow room where the lower class meets and the dining room and back again, through courtyards ringed with jasmine and grapevines, past plump statues of the Madonna and paintings of the English King Charles I, she thinks about Boy: Boy's red hair, Boy's punch, the spot on her own shoulder where a bruise is forming. She thinks about Boy's voice whispering, *Limbo.* She glimpses the heavy doors that lead to the cloisters. Still, that evening, she gets lost trying to find them. She turns corners to find herself exactly where she had started and starts to panic. Surely Boy will get bored of waiting and leave.

I'm never bored, says Boy, when George finally reaches her, and George feels something swelling in her chest.

They sit on the floor with their backs to the wall and Boy tells George about the imprisoned girl in the convent. Somewhere, Boy says, this girl has been shut up by the nuns in a deep, impenetrable hole: a cell dug inside the walls of the building, or a dungeon in the vaults, which stretch out beyond the convent walls for miles. If you find your way down there, you can walk right out of the convent into the catacombs, Boy says, or into the cellars of some of the great houses of Paris. Somewhere down there is the imprisoned girl and no matter how weak she is, how hungry and alone, no matter how far below ground she has been buried, Boy can hear her crying for help in the night. She will die soon if Boy doesn't find her and help her escape.

You can help me find her if you want, says Boy, and George, who knows that a thing can be both made up and urgent, follows Boy down dark stairwells into the lowest, blackest cellar rooms of the convent. They run their hands across the walls, hoping to find a catch or lever that might trigger an aperture. George kicks steps, seeking a trapdoor. She imagines the thrill of uncovering a doorway to a hidden room, the kind she has read about in novels, which would creak open and reveal secrets. Boy finds a hook in the wall, but when she tugs, it slides out in a small cloud of plaster dust and nothing happens.

They press their ears flat against the surface listening for the girl's cries. Boy says, *There! Did you hear that?* and George, who did not hear anything, says, *Yes.*

They set about demolishing the wall, throwing punches and kicks, hurling their weight against it. George imagines it giving way, the whole convent crumbling stone by stone, vine by vine, Madonna by Madonna on top of their heads. She imagines cowering under the rubble with Boy, their two warm bodies beneath all that cold weight. By the time they give up, sweaty and tired, they have not made a dent in the wall.

The next night, George and Boy return to the underground room, and the night after that, and the night after that. They stop kicking and try scrabbling with their fingernails instead, tearing away the plaster in dusty fragments. Scraped and dented, the wall starts to look like a musical score, crisscrossed with fine lines. Then they give up the scratching too and sit side by side making up stories about the captive—she is the illegitimate daughter of one of the nuns, she is George's long-lost sister, she is a foreign princess who has been abducted, she is the girl Boy was swapped with at birth—and sometimes George pretends that she and Boy are the imprisoned ones, that rather than a rescue mission they are attempting an escape.

What will you do when we find her? George asks, and Boy says, *I'll kiss her.*

And George does not believe in the girl, not really or even at all, but sometimes in the quiet moments between Boy's sentences, when she lets her head fall onto Boy's shoulder and feels the pent-up huffs of Boy's breath pushing against her cheek, she convinces herself she can hear someone crying, distant, intermittent, far below her and out of reach.

IN PERPETUUM

When I rummaged through people's memories, I looked for two things: formative experiences and rude bits. That is to say, I looked for those crystallizing events that shape a person into who they are and anything that had a hint of sex about it. The delightful thing I learned about George was that for her the formative experiences and the rude bits were often one and the same, and when I came across the convent and Boy, it seemed to me I had found a key to my own hopefulness. George was someone who confused the stagnant no-man's-land of Limbo with Olympus, home of the gods! She was someone whose first love, albeit tentative, unspoken, and unformed, was a girl called Boy! And not only that: she was someone who searched for lost girls in dark places. All of which, considering my circumstances, seemed like extraordinarily good luck.

As the air warmed towards midmorning, George slept on and the children began to stir. This was how it would be, I guessed, with this new family: an endless relay of wakefulness. First Solange, then Maurice. They opened their eyes and stared at the ceiling. It seemed to take them a moment to remember where they were. Then Solange leapt up, darted across to her brother's bed, and sat down heavily beside his head.

"I'm starving," she said. I tried to get under her skin to feel it myself—that gnawing, enlivening feeling, the sensation of the stomach yawning—but her wakefulness was a brittle shell around her and, like her mother's, was hard to penetrate. "Maurice, let's find some fruit."

Maurice wriggled upright and swung his legs off the mattress. I settled into his body and felt the cool tiles against his soles. There was a stinging pain under the little toe of his left foot, where the skin had hardened and split. He was looking at Solange and thinking, *She is being strangely sweet. Why is she being sweet? What does she want?* But he was also very full of love for her, and relief, and I caught a glimpse of a memory he was toying with, in which Solange was a very different child: petulant and stormy, a vicious little imp dressed up as a girl, stamping her foot and saying, "I won't, I won't, I hate you all." *Maybe Mallorca will be good for her,* he thought. *Maybe she threw up all her viciousness over the side of the boat.* And then he made a mental note to repeat that line to his mother, because he knew it would make her laugh. *Maybe all her viciousness came up when she was seasick,* he tried. *Maybe she puked all her viciousness into the sea.* He'd get it right before he said it aloud.

Rumpled, the children padded barefoot out into the central room, which still smelled of coffee and cigars—the smell made Maurice yearn for something vague and maternal; I felt him almost turn to go back to his mother—and from there into the garden. He looked at the trees and their offerings critically: not-yet-ripe pomegranates, the last quinces of the season, crisp medlars. He went, eventually, to the orange tree and shook loose some fruit, which was the very thing I'd been planning to do the day before when I had come across Chopin and George. He caught one in his open palm. Others hit the ground and rolled, and Solange fell over her own feet in her rush to gather them. When she plunged a thumb into the rind, a spritz of juice caught her in the eye. She twisted a round cheek up into a squint. Maurice watched her and ate. His mouth was awash with juice. He remembered his mother telling him about Mallorca: "For how long?" he had asked, and she said, airily, "For as long as we like. Maybe forever." I thrilled to hear it.

He tongued a membrane and silently conjugated the Latin verb "to eat": *edo, edis, edit, edimus, editis, edunt.* The rhythm lulled him. *In aeternum,* he thought. *Forever. In perpetuum. Also forever.*

There was a rattling noise. Maurice looked up to see the shutters of Chopin's bedroom opening and clattering against the outer wall of the cell. Chopin's face: framed in the window. His hands: retreating into the dark room. He looked as though someone had said, "Curtain up!" before he was ready, a little stage-frightened.

"He's up!" said Solange, and it was as though she was saying the sun was up, as though the day had only just started. She wiped her mouth with her sleeve.

Maurice's heart sank. I rummaged through his mind to find out why. He wasn't thinking clearly, was just feeling glummer at the sight of the opened window, the parted shutters. He thumbed a sliver of pulp out from between his teeth and said, "Where are you going?"

Solange was halfway across the garden.

"To see him, obviously," she said. "To say good morning!"

Maurice put an end to my confusion with a clear, sullen thought: *Why did he have to come?* Through the window I heard Solange's voice cooing, "Good morning, Chip-Chip! Did you sleep well?" Maurice scowled, peeled another orange, and then, realizing he was full, dropped it and flattened it underfoot. He listened dully to the sound of Chopin and Solange talking, trying instead to focus on birdsong, the goats' bells clanging below the Charterhouse on the hillside, the occasional hiss of breeze. A cluster of ants had already discovered his discarded orange and were busying around it. Maurice took a deep breath and tried to return to the equilibrium he'd felt earlier. They were still in Mallorca after all; it was all very pretty; at some point his mother would wake up and something good would happen.

"Let's go for a walk."

George took us both by surprise, standing, fully dressed, in the doorway. She couldn't have slept more than a couple of hours. Maurice spun around to see her.

"Come on," she said. "Let's go." And almost at once Maurice was at her side, and they were making a plan to walk together through the village, and I was beginning to worry, was trying to explain why they should rethink, saying, *No, no, no, don't go out like that.* Was saying, *You surely don't mean to go out like that!*

Dark slacks. Big, heavy men's boots. A stiff shirt. George's outfit was the one she had worn the previous day but it shocked me all over again that she was planning to wear it beyond the Charterhouse walls. I had imagined, I suppose, that it was some private fetish of hers, to strut around her own territory in costume. There was no shame, I felt, in playing at being a man—in imagining it. I had certainly imagined wilder things myself, in private. But I had not supposed that she would parade like that through a village of farmers and peasants, who still, in the mid-nineteenth century, considered a woman lifting her mantilla on Sunday somewhat risqué.

An example of what we were working with at this point in time: around the turn of the century, the local butcher had been visited by his cousin's daughter from Barcelona, and she had ridden a mule with her legs on either side of the saddle, and forty years later, people were still talking about it. (The girl in question did far more interesting things while resident in Valldemossa—most memorably, to me at least, she stole her uncle's wine and got so drunk, hiding alone in the bushes behind his house, that she whispered a tender and intimate love song to a cactus—but the only one observed by the locals, and thus the only one that mattered, was the mule riding.) So I knew what I was talking about when I told George, in no uncertain terms, that she should not go out like that.

Solange, who had been flitting between the three rooms, fussing over Chopin and getting underfoot, reappeared wearing boys' overalls. Her hair was pulled up inside a cap, and at first the effect was convincing enough that I thought she might get away with it. But a curl fell down around her face, and then another, and it was clear that while the getup might be a costume to her, it was not a disguise. She was undeniably what she was: a little girl in boy's clothing.

Absolutely not, I said. *Go back in and change, the pair of you.*

Maurice joined them in long trousers, the only sane one of the three, and George took her children's hands. They walked together down the corridor to the Charterhouse door, which George hauled open. Outside in the bright square, they squinted and shaded their eyes, and it was only then that I realized they had left Chopin behind without a word. We had all forgotten him.

"Which way?" said Maurice.

"I don't know," said George.

This way, I said. *This route takes you out of the village, down through the fields of almond trees, and then, further down still, to the house where I used to live when I was a child and alive.* That way they would avoid being seen by anyone, crucially, and in any case I wanted them to see my old house—as though, in seeing those decrepit old walls, and the decrepit old lady who lived there alone, with her cataracts and tremors (my multiple-times-great-granddaughter) they might, in a way, see me. *Go on,* I urged. *Take this route.*

Of course, they went the other way, out through the square and down towards the center of the village. It looked more inviting; the track was better worn across the stones. Solange held Maurice's hand. I felt the slick of sweat between their palms.

The housefronts eyeballed each other across the narrow path, and even though everything was noisier here—voices inside cottages and cartwheels on cobbles—it seemed oddly hushed as the family arrived. It was late morning and people were cooking lunch: everything smelled of garlic and bad olive oil. The harvest had been spoiled that year by unexpected rains and the oil had turned rancid, but nobody had any choice but to use it.

Solange pinched her nose as we passed open windows. "What *is* that smell?"

"It's what they eat here," George said.

"I hate it," said Solange.

The woman who lived in the old bakery stood with a broom in her doorway, wide-eyed, and said nothing as the party approached. As we brushed past, I expected to feel hostility, but instead it was fear, spluttering off her like a dying flame. *What do you want?* she was thinking. *What do you want from us?*

An elderly man selling wilting bouquets from a tray saw a man and two boys approaching, and simply nodded and smiled and proffered the flowers, saying, "Gentlemen. Flowers. Young gentlemen. Flowers."

Then there was Fidelia, a girl a little older than Maurice, who looked him up and down appreciatively and liked the way his hair fell across his forehead, the way his hands swung from his wrists. She felt a flicker of excitement. *Who is he?* She didn't even notice George and Solange. She had eyes only for the boy.

I told myself to relax. Hadn't I thought, as soon as she arrived, that I didn't need to worry about George? George was fine. She could take care of herself. Even then, as she strolled through the village with her children, she was taking care. She was nodding in greeting to the suspicious faces we passed, the housewives and traders and workmen and farmers of Valldemossa, even if they did nothing in return except forget to blink. And nothing bad was happening. Nobody was attacking them or wishing them harm. *Really, Blanca,* I told myself. *You're getting to be so neurotic.*

Still, I wished they weren't behaving like crazy people, which, unfortunately, they were. It wasn't just the clothes. They seemed drunk, the three of them, exclaiming at every small mundane thing we passed. The pebbles! The aloe plants! The moss! The brambles! Flowers, bushes, trees, even the flies that followed them and tried to rest on their skin. Solange and Maurice were constantly picking things up off the ground: small rocks, mostly, which they held out to George in their palms, and which she would marvel at, saying, "Look at that! Look at the colors! How lovely!"

Solange darted forwards and crouched to scoop up something from the path. She turned, cupping a dead lizard in her hands, and they all exclaimed over even that, even a dried-up dead little lizard on the lane.

So who could blame all the eyes that were turned on them? Eyes through windows. Eyes in doorways. Eyes passing them by on the lane. And wasn't I just like everyone else? I was staring at these foreigners, curious and astonished. I couldn't leave them alone.

And then it came, sharp and precise: a stone hit Solange in the back of the head. She cried out and spun around, but there was nobody in sight.

"Mama!" she said. "A stone just hit me!" As though it was the stone's own doing. She picked it up and fingered its sharp edges for a second before remembering to cry.

"Who threw it?" said George, wheeling around to survey the street.

Even I couldn't see who had done it.

"He that is without sin?" offered Maurice, which Solange did not understand and George did not acknowledge, but which I thought was quite a good joke.

They stood looking back at the road. The windows and doorways were empty. The shadows belonged to plants and walls. I could see in their faces that their giddiness had subsided, that the shine had been rubbed away from the day. The children stopped exclaiming at pebbles. George walked a little more stiffly and smiled less warmly at passersby. When, eventually, they turned and began the ascent to the Charterhouse, I raced ahead of them feeling spooked and uneasy, as anxious as they were—or perhaps even more—to get home.

Which meant that I was alone and completely unprepared when I burst into Cell Three to find Chopin at his piano and the rooms full of a sound that, in all my hundreds of years, I had never heard.

PRELUDE NO. 11
IN B MAJOR, VIVACE

Imagine you are about to bite into an apple. Imagine never having bitten an apple before. The fruit at your lips is an unknown thing. It might burst like a tomato! Yield like a peach! Snap like a carrot! You have no idea about its insides: what color or texture. You have no reason to suspect it will be cloud-white, bloodless, foamy, crisp. An apple could be like an orange: segmented, oozy. An apple could be salty and jaw-breaking like a rock.

This is what it was like for me, the first time I heard Chopin play the piano.

Your head is full of apple. Your head is an apple. The flavor of it is indescribable, really, except to say: *appley*.

The piece he played took half a minute, start to finish. A sudden off-loading of skittish joy. Fingers over the keys like wings. An *I-just-couldn't-hold-it-in-any-longer*, as though it had burst out before it had been entirely thought through, a little garbled and then cohering around the thing that, at the heart of it all, was what was really being said. With each repetition, the melody sounded more and more like itself, and Chopin stopped and started the

though they were the unruly fronds of a plant. Nothing worked. Sometimes his fingers wouldn't do what he wanted on the keys; they were sluggish and slow, and those were the worst days. Even the air felt abrasive.

I came to understand two important things: the first was that Chopin was very ill, and the second was that, if the illness didn't kill him, that piano surely would.

I took the opportunity to root around in Chopin's past when I could, and found that it was lovely: a real masterpiece. I scanned it, out of habit, for sex, flirtation, intrigue, and was not disappointed: a girl at the school near where he lived, just out of reach but the subject of many lewd fantasies; frustrated trysts between schoolboys and scrawled love notes: *Titus, tonight you shall dream you are kissing me!, I want you and I expect you clean-shaven,* thrilling! Then there was a pretty sixteen-year-old girl who sat beside him on the piano stool, ostensibly learning to play, the bare curve of her neck distracting him from her hands on the keys. His taste was eclectic; there was no ostensible pattern. Titus was a broad, rosy-faced young man; the girl at the piano was willowy and pale.

Alongside the lovers, I found the enveloping misery of his ill health. It was tidal, shrinking and spreading over his body by turn. Colds that lingered and took hold. Headaches that felt as though his skull was disintegrating. Food that made his stomach twist, and resulted in days of watery diarrhea and shooting pains. Coughing, so much coughing, which made his organs feel rearranged, strong enough to bring up spots of blood like a scattering of musical notes across his handkerchief. There were moments of respite, when he would wake up feeling neither sick nor sore nor sorry for himself, when it felt as though he was hearing music clearly for the first time, had never heard anything so clearly before. He would promise never to take for granted the sensation of not-being-in-pain. But just as he began to forget what it was like to be ill, when normality began to feel normal, the cough would come back.

And then there was George. I'd anticipated that the George of Chopin's early memories would be young, girlish, a few years out of the convent I had seen in her memories. But instead, Chopin's first sighting of George had taken place only two years previously. Only two years! I reconfigured my understanding of the family: the children were not his, were nothing to do with him, and he and George were still new to each other. In his first sighting of her, she was on the other side of a room full of people, wearing a dagger around her neck and looking horrifyingly, depressingly, revoltingly ugly. She looked as though she smelled bad. Her smile was lecherous and untrustworthy; it made his insides tighten and recoil. All the interest and joy and hope he felt when he saw her now, and when I myself saw her, was missing. She was standing half a step back from a group of people, and looked as though she would rather be elsewhere.

"Is that really a woman?" he said to his friend. "I don't believe that is really a woman."

They kept running into each other at parties—Chopin surprised every time and George less so, which made me suspect it wasn't an accident on her part. She sent messages via mutual friends, telling him about gatherings she was organizing, which at first he treated as a helpful list of places not to go. But over time, Chopin's view of George softened and improved: the bad-smell look evaporated, and the smile became less distant and therefore less threatening. She was always staring at him, even when in conversation with someone else, and Chopin stopped disliking that about her. She left the dagger necklace at home. When she thrust her hands into her pockets and rocked from the balls of her feet to her heels, she looked as though she was holding back a secret.

Eventually, she was irresistible, prettier even than she was in Mallorca: dark eyes taking up all the space in the room. They sat together in chairs that felt, to Chopin, irritatingly far apart. He did not know what to do with his hands; he fiddled with his gloves, and then with his topmost coat button. She did not seem interested in any of the things he knew how to talk about—fashion, music, interior design—except for gossip. She loved when he told her gossip. "And what did Liszt do *then*?" she would ask. "*Surely* the Countess wouldn't allow such a thing?" Despite her interest, he had the impression she knew everything already and was humoring him.

To other people he called her "La Sand" in that familiar, faintly derisive way that all his friends had when they wanted it known that they knew her. He never called her "La Sand" to her face. He called her George, which he only occasionally remembered was not her real name. He kept forgetting her real name.

He found himself thinking about her shoulders. He found himself thinking about the dark triangle at the corner of her mouth when she was holding a cigar between her teeth. He found himself thinking about sex a lot: what it would be like with her. He couldn't imagine it. When she kissed him it was a surprise. She tasted of tobacco. It was like kissing a man.

And then she told him she was going to Mallorca. "I want to take my children to a healthier climate," she said. "The doctor says it will do us all good, and in any case, the further we can get from my husband the better."

Chopin took this news in, and found himself blurting out, "I expect I shall die very young."

He found himself saying, "I wish *I* had someone who loved me enough to take me to Mallorca."

He said, "If *I* were to go to Mallorca in Maurice's place, I know I would be cured at once."

She was quick to say yes, he could come, not in place of Maurice but alongside him. In fact, he absolutely should come. It was a wonderful idea.

At which point he panicked and regretted having said anything. He knew nothing about Mallorca, and while he was fairly sure he was in love with George, he knew nothing much about her either. Why would he ever leave Paris? Why would anyone ever leave Paris? He looked around at the rooms he'd had decorated, to his exact taste, in what he called "pearl colors": pale yellows and pinks and blues, like a wintery dawn. He had a good servant and he liked most of his friends and any time he needed money he could simply announce he was giving a concert and then he'd be rich again. There was champagne in Paris. There were truffles in Paris. Were there truffles in Mallorca?

But he couldn't back out now. George was excited. The climate! The sunlight! The health-giving properties of the Mediterranean air! And where better to spend the winter entwined, where better to forge a life together as artists and perhaps as a kind of new family, than in Mallorca, where living would surely be easy and cheap and her children would thrive and Chopin himself had said he would be cured?

"What about my piano?" he said. *What a shame. Would have loved to. But, oh look, I can't leave my piano.* It was a beautiful, irreplaceable instrument, made by Pleyel; the only piano he could possibly work with.

George said it would be no problem at all. They would have the piano shipped. It would be waiting for them when they arrived.

But this, like all of George's predictions, turned out to be inaccurate. When they arrived at Palma they were informed that the Pleyel piano had yet to leave France and required various duties to be paid before it could even be loaded onto a ship. George, determinedly optimistic despite that setback and several others (there were no hotels in Palma, and nobody willing to give lodging to five foreigners who didn't speak Spanish and did not seem entirely healthy; the journey had been terrible and Chopin was coughing up blood; whenever locals noticed his illness they backed away as though he could infect them on sight) said they would find him another piano. She would get him a Mallorcan piano.

Lodgings were sourced, first in noisy rooms by the docks, then in a nice but leaky house on the outskirts of town, and then at the Charterhouse in Valldemossa. Doctors had been inquired after, and an acquaintance of George's at the French consulate had given them some names. And, finally, the substitute piano had been delivered to the Charterhouse on the day of their arrival, jangling and inadequate.

Such challenges, Chopin knew, were sent to try us, and the piano had been sent to try him very much indeed. But still, when he sat down to play there were those dreamy moments of disembodiedness when he became ghostlike, relieved. When George stuck her head around the door and watched him work, his stomach clenched and his skin tingled. The feeling was like a phrase ending on a deceptive cadence, hovering, deliciously unresolved. There was something unsettling and adolescent about it, as though they were both teenagers and falling in love for the first time.

I REMEMBER

It is a feast day and the brothers from the Charterhouse are processing through the village. I am thirteen years old and slack-jawed at the sight of them. Impossible not to be. To think of them living above us at the Charterhouse all this time, all these bodies, hidden away in that dim old building. So much muscle and heft and fat and their lovely broad shoulders under their habits! So many feet, dusty and heavy and suddenly here. Rosaries dripping from their fingertips that make you think, really think, about the way they use their hands or could, about what my sister María tells me she does with our neighbor Felix, or rather, what he does to her, and how when she whispers about it at night, her voice gets tighter. Hard to get it out of my head when I'm trying to fall asleep, or now.

The brothers never leave the Charterhouse like this—it's a special occasion the reason for which hasn't really been communicated to us, but everyone is happy to see them. Now is our one chance to gawp, to really take a gulp of them, and everyone is hovering in their doorways, staring. They have nearly passed us now, we are at the tail end of the procession, just the smaller ones, novices, left. My mother puts a hand on my arm and says, *Blanca, we live amongst beautiful men.*

Where are they going? I ask, but she doesn't know.

I think: *I could follow and find out.* I am supposed to be watching the pigs, but that seems to have been forgotten in any case.

I turn to my mother. *Can I follow them?*

Her eyes widen. *Go, go,* she says. *Don't lose them. I want to know exactly where they go. Tell me what they look like when they're sweaty from the sun.* My mother is always appreciative of sweat on a man. She recounts the sweatiness of my father, in his life and on his deathbed, with great fondness. I watch her surveying the damp crowns of the brothers as they approach the bend in the path; she will want to know every detail, every rivulet, every last bead.

I hurry away from the house towards the novices at the back. A glance over my shoulder: my mother shuffling to our neighbor's house and saying the thing about living amongst beautiful men again. I fix my eyes forward on their beautiful spines and hurry after them, kicking up dirt.

The brothers are moving away from the village, beyond the houses now and into farmland, where gawping women are replaced by goats and olive trees and occasional farmers, who look up at the disturbance, and then at me, as though we are no more or less interesting than livestock.

Wherever we're going, it's a long way in the heat and I'm thirsty. To distract myself, I focus on the man, more like a boy, at the back of the procession. I like the pink curve of his ear, poking through his hair like a newborn mouse in a nest. I like the way his novice's cloak flaps around his hips, too heavy for processing on a hot day, too big for his narrow shoulders. He is probably my age, perhaps a year or two older: fourteen, fifteen. As he walks, he glances from side to side at the farm huts and the animals as though he's about to make a break for it.

And then that is exactly what he does. He veers left, away from the procession, down a track between two large trees. I stand at the fork, watching the brothers continue straight, and this boy scurrying away from them. He's scrambling down the slope, lower legs already out of view. I take a step in the direction of the brothers and then—as though my feet know my mind before I do, I find myself in hot pursuit of the novice.

Harder to chase a single person without being noticed. I cling to shadows and move forwards in little bursts, cat after a bird. He is making quick progress along the path as it tilts towards the coast, over boulders and across small corners of farmland. I am short of breath and sweaty now; from behind he looks unflappable in his billowing cloak, nimble and quick. The horizon flattens out, and he picks up his pace. He is going to the sea.

The final descent to the water, when taken at this speed, is more of a slide than a climb. He sends up plumes of dust as he skids and scrambles, grabbing at rocks and bushes to steady himself. I slow down now: there is only one place he can be going, after all; I'm not going to lose him. I take a breath. The air coming off the water is soft with salt. A spear of aloe catches my ankle and draws a line of red across the skin. I proceed in cautious, shuffling steps until the beach comes into view, really just some pebbles ringed with rocks, the novice's clothes in a heap at one side, as though he has evaporated.

Are you coming?

The voice almost makes me lose my footing. The novice is up to his neck in the water, just a floating head, bobbing like a duck or a piece of driftwood.

Aren't you coming? he calls.

I scramble down over the last few rocks and land with a crunch on the pebbles.

Come! calls the novice, even further out now, hair wet and black.

I slip off my shoes. Pause. And then, because I have come this far and it's hot and I am already wet with sweat, and because the water is clear and bright and inviting and the novice, now his face is turned towards me, is also clear and bright and inviting, I follow him into the ocean.

The swim is brief and mostly silent. We splash about and stare at the horizon. His foot kicks against my leg and I feel the ripple of his toes brush my shin. Then, without saying a word, he starts for the beach. He is entirely naked, and when he emerges from the ocean I stare at his buttocks, hollow-looking and small, and the wet hair flattened against the backs of his legs that makes the skin look gray. He dresses with some difficulty, turned away from me. *I'll be back here next week,* he says. None of his clothes are on straight. Everything at an angle, ruched and crumpled. *Do you want to swim again next week?*

I crouch in the shallows, silent, then watch as he scrambles up the cliffs and out of sight. But I think of nothing else all week. Breaking eggs into a bowl, I think: *Should I go swimming with the novice again?* Sweeping floors, washing dishes, brushing a spider's web complete with spider away from the window frame into the street: *Why wouldn't I go swimming with the novice again?*

And so I do.

I could meet you here anytime, says the novice. *We could make it a regular thing.*

We are treading water out in the deep, past the cloud of seaweed. The bottom, unreachable, is dark, the water almost green; it seems thicker out here than the turquoise of the shallows. It feels harder to stay afloat. Colder.

Why? I say.

Why wouldn't we? he says. *We're friends now, aren't we?*

A wave rolls in. Our heads rise over the swell of the water. I tilt back so I'm almost horizontal. A splash of salt gets up my nose. It makes me feel very wide awake.

What's your name? I say.

He responds just as a seagull screeches overhead. What I hear is the word meaning "ham."

Ham? I say and he just says, *Yes.*

My name's Blanca, I say, though he hasn't asked, and he just says, *Yes*, again.

It's just that the brothers don't really swim, I say. *The brothers never leave the Charterhouse. We never see them.*

He flips onto his back, chest protruding above the water, nipples pinched and pale. *I'm not a brother yet. I'm just a novice.*

Aren't you going to be a brother?

He flaps his hands by his waist and maneuvers himself closer to me. His hair in the water: a brown blur fading out from his skull, as though his head is melting. He is now close enough that the water feels warmer.

I don't know, he says. *Do you want to kiss?*

I consider it.

Kissing Ham, when it happens, is mostly seawater. We struggle to stay afloat together, lips pressed wetly to lips. His hands on my upper arms make it harder to circle them downwards, harder to propel myself up. I get great gulps of the ocean in between the hot inside of his mouth, his tongue flopping like a fish. Occasional sensation of teeth, grit, sand. When I pull back to breathe, the wind blows right into my cheeks, and I puff them out like sails.

Do you want to kiss again? Ham says, at once, looking as though breathing has come easily to him all along, and I don't, not really, at least not without the support of dry land, so I start swimming away from him towards the shore. I twist my head back over my shoulder but he's not following me, he's still all the way out in the dark green water, just a head and occasional ripples where his arms are waving below the surface.

I sit on the rocks, clothes clinging to me, and wait for Ham to follow. Instead, he swims towards the horizon, so far off the sun gets in my eyes when I try to make him out. I wonder what I would do if he just never came back, if this was the last I or anyone ever saw of him, and whether in weeks' or months' time a rumor would reach us in the village about the novice who vanished, and I would be the only one who knew the truth: he drowned himself because I wouldn't kiss him anymore. All the more frustrating to find that now, with the sharp peaks of the rocks digging into my hands and backside and my clothes starting to dry in the heat, the idea of kissing him seems more appealing, urgent even, and I start to feel panicked by the blankness of the water, the undisturbed waves, the lack of Ham.

When he finally emerges, red-cheeked and panting, he acts casual, reclining in the shallows for a while before standing up. I can see everything now: he's facing me and naked as ever, the first penis I've ever seen. I stare because he doesn't seem to mind.

You're probably not going to become a brother, I say. A question really.

He laughs. *Probably not.* Then he says, *Free food though.*

I nod. *Free everything.*

What are you probably not going to become?

I ponder it. My future as blocked doorways. *A brother,* I say, *probably.*

He nods. I nod.

I'll swim with you next week, and I'll kiss you again now, I say.

I shuffle off the rocks to where he is standing, still naked, feet still submerged. When we kiss for the second time, it is less oceanic. His tongue firmer, teeth smoother. Now it is all air and skin smells, wind and hands, his penis alert and pressing against my leg like something strange washed up on the beach.

WHAT ARE YOU DOING HERE?

I made a habit of sitting up with George through the nighttimes, nestling into her thoughts, settling alongside her as she wrote her book about the monastery. She was so clear, so straightforward in those early days. It got easier and easier to be with her, as though her mind was meeting mine without her knowledge. As though she almost, sort of, maybe knew I was there and was untroubled by me. Or at least, that's the sort of thing I told myself at the time. She was bright in the dark cell. She was very open, very alert. There was an answer to almost every question I had.

Question: *Who are you? Who are you really, George?*

Answer: George would listen out for signs that her children were still sleeping, that Chopin was safely resting in his room. Sometimes a cough or a creak would make her heart race, would spark immediate panic, fear that any one of them might be unwell. The thought of Chopin being in pain tore something in her chest. Her children being ill: unbearable to imagine, though she did imagine it, frequently, a kind of scab-picking compulsion. They were all so beloved, she thought. They were all so extraordinarily lovely and precious. And yet, when she heard them stirring in the night, her fear for them combined with a secondary horror: that the time she had to herself might be coming to an end. If they were to wake up, if they were to cut short her nightly aloneness, if they were to wander into her space in the early hours wanting something—because, God, they were always wanting things, all of them, all the time—she thought she might punch them. All she asked from them was these empty, dark hours alone with her candle and her writing and her cigar.

George thought: *I have to finish this novel.* She thought about her publisher, who was waiting for the manuscript, about her readers, about the words on the page, some of which she liked, some of which she struck through as though they had been written by someone she hated, as though they were personally offensive to her. She moved the characters around like a hostess laying a table, arranging place settings and name cards and then changing her mind, reordering everything from scratch. Some nights she did nothing but write, and others, she did nothing but cross out what she had written the night before. Several times she fed pages to her candle as carefully as though she was spooning porridge to an infant.

She spent so much time at her desk, working and smoking and staring at the garden through the window, that she looked out of place sitting anywhere else. The chair seemed forlorn and awkward when she was not in it, the pages of her writing carefully placed facedown. Sometimes when George was called away from her work to deal with something else, I noticed her right hand twitching against her thigh, fingers bunched against the tip of her thumb, as though she were still at work.

I had never seen anyone like her. That was the thing. No woman had ever been as definite, as robust. No woman, no man, nobody had ever been so much like themselves as she was.

As soon as she woke each day, after her few hours of sleep, she began, piece by piece, to collect herself, to put herself back together in the shape of a mother, and, at the same time, to recede. It seemed that everyone forgot who she really was until after dinner. There were endless demands on her time and focus. Solange wanted help with her lessons, and then an audience for a one-child play she had written, and then assistance untangling her hair. Maurice wanted to show her everything he did, every note taken from his philosophy books, every little choice made in his translations and grammar exercises. Amélie wanted to know whether there should be food prepared for Chopin, and if so what, and if so when, and if not whether the doctor was required. It was unrelenting. It was, she sometimes thought, what constituted her "real life." But I knew—and she knew, really, she did know—that her real life happened briefly and darkly in those snatched nighttime hours.

Question: *What are you doing here, George? Why have you come to Mallorca? What do you want here?*

George thought, again: *I have to finish this novel.* She thought about Chopin's preludes, too. She imagined that maybe he would die, and the thought made her sweat, even though cold was creeping into the cell, through cracks around the windows, through the stone walls. She thought: *It's colder than I thought it would be here.* They had come here for the climate, after all, for the warmth of a Mediterranean winter, which would make the children strong and keep Chopin alive. George had had visions of blue: sky, water. She had imagined fresh, wholesome food; less cream than they ate in France, less sugar, more fish. She had imagined that their bodies would strengthen and unfurl like shoots towards the sun, and that everything would be easy: her writing, her children, being in love with Chopin.

Question: *Could you ever love me, George? Could you love me more than anything, more than you love the others? Could you love me so much that you wouldn't even mind if you found out I was here in the nighttimes, encroaching on your solitary hours, if you found out you weren't alone after all?*

To this I found no answer, not really, though I ransacked her memories for clues and continued to buzz around her, enrapt, marveling at the single white eyelash nestled amongst the black, at the pink nub of cartilage in her inner ear, at the hangnail on her ring finger. George, I came to see, was a person who fell in love easily, and people who fall in love easily are easy to fall in love with. What a thing it is, to fall in love, to want to know everything there is to know about a person and yet, at the same time, to find the smallest detail—a blade of loose skin peeling from the lower corner of the fingernail—entirely overwhelming, too lovely to bear.

GEORGE REMEMBERS

George is getting married. She sits at her desk and repeats this to herself: *I am getting married. I am going to be Madame Dudevant. Good morning! I am Madame Dudevant. And this is my husband, Casimir Dudevant. My husband! I am going to have a husband.* She is eighteen years old and she is going to be married. She imagines how serious she will feel, how significant. Then she picks up her pen—she is midway through a letter, her mind has wandered—and cannot think of a single thing to write.

She thinks: *I am going to be a wife.*

It is as though, already, her wifeness has become the most important thing about her. She imagines it squatting somewhere inside her head, crowding everything else out. For some reason, she pictures wifeness as a kind of toad, bulky, warty, its throat undulating over its breath. Obliterated underneath it: whatever it was she was in the middle of writing; who she used to be before she fell in love; all the people, old and young, men and women, with whom she had thought herself in love before this. She does not exactly know how to feel about the toad.

She first met her fiancé in Paris, at Tortoni's, where she was eating apricot ice cream after the theater. She was sitting in the window looking out at the street, which was dark, drizzly, horses kicking up mud towards the café, when one of the friends she was with said, *Look, there's Casimir!* and tapped on the glass. George was in a bad mood; the play had been boring, which was worse than if it had just been bad, and her brain had felt dampened as a result. She had been ignoring her friends' conversation, focusing instead on taking bites of ice cream that made her lower teeth throb. But then there he was, a man called Casimir, attractive and tall, crossing the street towards her. He shouldered the café door and looked her up and down. In a whisper loud enough for George to hear every word, he asked the friends who she was.

Well I accept, he said, *if you wish to give her to me.*

She's not ours to give, said her friend.

But George, relieved not to be bored and thrilled by the thought of being carried away into the rain, said, *Well I accept too.*

It was a joke from that very first moment that they would get married—a joke until suddenly it wasn't.

Why did she like him? He never seemed to pursue her, in the early days of their acquaintance. Rather he teased her and treated her like one of his school friends. He referred to her as a *good fellow*. She felt a little wild in his company, as though his mannishness brushed off on her, as though his confidence and the ease with which he moved through the world were becoming hers. They played children's games in the garden of their friends' country house—races, stuck in the mud, tag—and as she ran after him, their friends would shout from the window, *Go on, Aurore, catch your husband!* And now here she is, having caught him: in love and getting married.

She has been in love before. She has felt flutterings and stir- rings, has been unable to concentrate on anything but reconstructing in her mind's eye a particular wrist or neck or walk. The objects of her affection have been classmates, teachers, people in the street. But it has never felt the way it does with Casimir, because with Casimir it is overt and on purpose. There is nothing surreptitious about it, nothing covert or clandestine. In fact, it is encouraged by their friends and families. This romance with Casimir is like being onstage, everybody applauding night after night, demanding encores.

So, she is getting married. The whole affair seems at once implausible and inevitable. Implausible that she, who feels herself to be a strange and inconsistent person, would find a man she wants to marry, who wants to marry her. (And she is aware too how very convenient it is to have found someone she wants to marry just at the moment in her life when getting married is expected of her. It is a relief not to have to marry someone for the sake of it, or to have to make a stand and marry nobody at all.) And then, at the same time: inevitable. What were the chances that, aged eighteen and eating apricot ice cream on a drizzly evening in Paris, she would look up and see the man she was going to marry? One hundred percent, she thinks. It seemed to her that she and Casimir had known each other all along, that the time she spent yearning and lusting after other people was simply rehearsal. She thinks of herself as an animal following a desire line through a meadow, unwittingly guided forwards.

It is all in motion now, in any case. The wedding, where they will go, where they will live (in her childhood home, which is still her home; she practices thinking *our home, our home, our home*). Her life, so to speak, is now arranged. To be a wife, a mother, one baby after another, to keep house and have interesting conversations with her husband until they die. The sharp edges of her personality will be smoothed over. The burden of being difficult, headstrong, and impulsive will gradually lighten. She will become poised, calmer. And yes, the idea of wifeness, this toady disturbance in her mind, distracts her when she wants to get on with writing and thinking and reading. It leaves so little room for the rest of her. But surely this, like everything else, will ease over time. She pictures reading with Casimir, the two of them side by side with books and wine and a sleeping dog sprawled between their laps. It is as simple and pleasing and reassuring as the taste of apricot ice cream on the tip of her tongue, the clatter of the café counter behind her, through the steamed-up window the Paris street speckled with rain, and everything happening exactly as it should.

KNOCK KNOCK

The three doctors came on three consecutive days, like a joke. *Patient: Doctor, Doctor, I'm addicted to getting medical advice. Doctor: You've called just the right men.*

Here was a real-live setup, knocking on the Charterhouse door and being ushered into Cell Three by María Antonia: Doctors Vilar, Grec, and Porras.

Q: What did the terminal consumptive say to the doctor?
A: I can't stop coffin.

The family had been at the Charterhouse for four days by then, during which time Chopin's health had not improved from its low point during the sea journey. When the Sacristan came by to introduce himself, having recovered from what he described as "a debilitating ailment" (there had been a lot of bread in his soup), Chopin was barely able to get through the required pleasantries before retreating to his room. In the evenings, when the temperature dropped, Chopin's bones throbbed and he felt as though he couldn't breathe. He'd sit helplessly at the piano until Amélie brought him a drink. Seeing him struggling, she would back out like a cat that had seen a dog and then tell George that her "friend" was having difficulties.

"He needs a doctor," said George. A sort of thunder was brewing in her chest, dark. She resented the situation: a problem, an obstruction, things not going to plan.

"He needs a hundred doctors," muttered Amélie, which I admired because it was a joke for her benefit alone, neither funny nor helpful; as though the effectiveness of doctors might be cumulative. At that time, there were only seven doctors in all of Mallorca, and even fewer who could be persuaded to treat a spluttering, germ-ridden foreigner in a remote charterhouse on a mountaintop.

The first to arrive, Doctor Vilar, tall and plum-cheeked, was a stranger to me. His was one of the names given to George by the wife of the French consul in Palma: a favor of questionable value, it had to be said, since Doctor Vilar was an anxious traveler and had calmed his nerves on the narrow mountain roads with wine. His breath smelled of damp and alcohol.

He did, at least, speak French, so the what-seems-to-be-the-problems were relatively easily covered. What seemed to be the problem, George explained, was that Chopin seemed to be dying.

Doctor Vilar swayed and said, "Oh surely not, surely not, madam." People were often thought to be dying, he explained, but they so rarely actually died.

If I could just— I said. *If I might perhaps offer some anecdotal evidence to the contrary?* But no. Nobody was listening to the one person in the room who knew anything whatsoever about death.

George explained that Chopin had traveled all the way to Mallorca from Paris for the express purpose of improving his health, but despite their initial optimism, he seemed to have made little progress; each day he played the piano less and complained about it more, and in between his grumbling, he coughed up blood across its keys.

Doctor Vilar frowned. "But why, if I might ask, would you come to an elevated position such as Valldemossa, so poorly served by such terrible roads, especially in the winter months, when the storms can be very severe, and the temperature far from warm?"

That is a very good question, I said.

George laughed and gestured at the sunshine in the garden. "The weather is delightful, Doctor Vilar." She thought, briefly, of the cold creeping into the cell in the nights.

Doctor Vilar and I both responded with variations on "That is likely to change."

Chopin received the first doctor wearily, a little irritably, but perked up on hearing his French. He described symptoms I knew to be true: the coughing, exhaustion, night sweats, aching bones, and bloody phlegm, a sense that under his skin everything was made of the same bubbling, toxic mucus, and that at some inevitable point it would take him over entirely. For greater impact, he added some symptoms that were, he knew as well as I did, nothing to do with his illness and everything to do with the piano: terrible headaches, an inability to concentrate, depressed mood.

Doctor Vilar listened to Chopin's description of his bad sleep and feverishness with the expression of a man pretending to pay close attention, perking up only at the mention of the phlegm. He produced a handkerchief from his coat pocket, not entirely clean, and requested Chopin cough into it. Chopin, who already thought everything in Mallorca was untouchably dirty, including himself, pinched it in a gloved hand and held it ambitiously far from his mouth. It took him several attempts, with George, Solange, Maurice, Amélie, Doctor Vilar, and I all clustered around in awkward silence, to produce the requisite spatter. When he finally did, Maurice and Solange applauded.

"Congratulations," said Maurice. "Your greatest show ever." Immediately, Maurice began to ruminate on how he might better have expressed this. *Your greatest composition? A legendary performance?* He was full of sour feelings and doubt. *A marvelous production?* That would have been better.

George did not seem to notice her children. "What do you think, Doctor?"

Doctor Vilar put his nose upsettingly close to the contents of the handkerchief. He sniffed, peered, and prodded at it. We all watched in horrified silence as he folded it up and replaced it in his pocket. Nobody said a word. There was a long silence, and then Chopin coughed.

"Madam," Doctor Vilar said to George. "A word in the other room?"

The word he said in the other room was "dead." "The patient, madam, is dead."

George suspected his French was failing him and asked that he repeat himself. He did so in exactly the same terms. It was one of those rare occasions, apparently, when a person actually did die.

George thanked him for his opinion, and wished him luck with the roads on the way back to Palma. It had started to rain— a very light drizzle—and Doctor Vilar's heart was pounding at the thought of the mud and the swaying of the carriage. He patted the pocket where he kept his flask, which was also the pocket into which he had deposited the handkerchief.

"Safe travels," said George, smiling, and when the door had closed behind him called out, "Did you hear that, Chopinet? You're dead, my darling."

"I thought so," he said. "I knew it."

This is what Chopin told Doctor Grec, who came the next

day. "Doctor Vilar pronounced me, essentially, dead. Or literally. Or perhaps metaphorically. He was an unclear person."

Doctor Grec, very jocular and no taller than Maurice, beamed and said, "My immediate clinical impression of the patient is that he is still of this world." Doctor Grec was not a speaker of French. The family understood about a tenth of the words he used, but most of his gist. There was a lot of mime during his visit. Doctor Grec patted his own cheeks. "He is very much still with us."

"Well," said George. "Who'd have thought?"

Doctor Grec maneuvered Chopin as though he were a manikin, bending him forwards and then pressing an ear to Chopin's back. He listened to Chopin's breathing, his coughing, and the sound of him holding his breath. I pressed myself alongside him, feeling the lumps of Chopin's ribs and spine, hearing the rattles and creaks and gurgles beneath them.

"Do you want me to spit in your handkerchief?" Chopin offered.

Doctor Grec looked horrified. "No," he said. "Goodness, no. I want you to spit in your own handkerchief."

At the end of the visit Doctor Grec summoned George into the other room.

"How old is your husband, madam?"

"He's not my husband," she said.

Doctor Grec shook his head and repeated his question, slowly and more loudly. "No, no, how *old* is your *husband*?"

"He's not my husband, he's my good friend," she said. This was not news to me, of course, by that point, but I was still shocked that she thought it was the sort of thing you could just mention in passing.

"*How old* is your *husband*?" Doctor Grec had no mime for *old* but he kept pointing at Chopin's room for *husband*.

"He's twenty-eight."

I could have figured that out for myself from digging around in Chopin's past, but I hadn't. I had experienced his body as he himself did, and felt in his bones the aches and pains of an older man. I would have guessed he was approaching his forties at least.

"Twenty-eight," George said again, holding up fingers.

Doctor Grec nodded, still smiling but awkwardly now, and said, "What a shame. A man so young. He is dying."

And so when the third doctor arrived, uncalled for, George was willing to let him in. I knew Doctor Porras well, since he was the doctor local to Valldemossa, and lived in a large house on the outskirts of the village with a very beautiful wife. He was from a long line of medical men, though not as long as he claimed. "There have been doctors in my family going back six centuries," he liked to say, which I personally knew to be an absolute lie, because if there had been such a thing as a real doctor in Valldemossa in the fifteenth century, perhaps I would have lived past the age of fourteen. Whenever he said this sort of thing, I liked to swat him in the jowls, which he experienced as a breeze or a draft and which never seemed to deter him.

He had heard that there was an invalid at the Charterhouse, he told George, and that the family had been seeking medical attention. He worried that, being foreign to Mallorca, they might accept the advice of a charlatan, not knowing who to call, and he wanted to make his services available to them that they might benefit from expert, trustworthy, and very reasonably priced advice.

Chopin was bored of doctors by that point and responded to being bent over and listened to and twisted and tapped with a blank face and occasional eye rolls. He answered Doctor Porras's questions in monosyllables and, since Doctor Porras insisted on speaking in terribly accented French and Chopin's mind was elsewhere, often misunderstood what was being asked.

"Do you suffer from high fevers?"

"Five foot seven," Chopin replied.

"How is your appetite?"

"Yes," said Chopin.

Based on this information, Doctor Porras recommended bedrest and a diet consisting of milk, raw eggs, a little bread, and some concentrated beef juice. "Mostly milk," he said.

"How will we get milk?" asked George. "I don't know where to buy milk."

"I will tell the boys to bring you some daily," said Doctor Porras.

He did not say which boys. I was curious about that and suspicious that he might not keep his word. At the end of the visit ("He is not exactly dying," he told George, "but it may well be consumption, which means that he is certainly *going* to die," to which George thrust her hands into her pockets and said, "Well, aren't we all?" though the thunder in her chest got louder, pressed harder against her ribs), I followed him down the hillside from the Charterhouse. He pottered through the village, pausing to exchange very dull pleasantries with almost everybody he met, and then stopped by the house of a friend to invite him to come for dinner. They walked through the valley to Doctor Porras's house together, surprising Señora Porras, who had only prepared enough food for two. Stone-faced, she served her husband's friend her own portion. The men's conversation was chillingly boring at first, as they asked after each other's wives. *Your own wife is right there,* I told Doctor Porras, and I pointed her out in case he could not spot her. She was hovering in the doorway of the kitchen, trying to get a word in so she could ask what they wanted to drink. *She could tell him how she is for herself.*

"What brought you into the village?" the friend asked, and when

Doctor Porras explained that he had been offering his professional services to the newcomers, the friend said, "The foreigners in the Charterhouse?" and was full of curiosity and questions about them.

Doctor Porras began to speak his mind. The Charterhouse resembled an insane asylum, he said. There was a woman there who dressed as a man. There was a little female child who was emulating the mother in all of her worst traits, and a young man who was, apparently, an idiot, murmuring things to himself and looking constantly distracted. And then there was an invalid who should never have traveled from his homeland, who minced and spat up blood and wouldn't take his gloves off.

"This is extraordinary," said the friend, thoroughly entertained. "Everybody has been dying to know."

Doctor Porras frowned. He considered a joke along the lines of *They'll be dying soon enough, once that consumptive up at the Charterhouse infects us all.* It was low-hanging fruit. But he cleared his throat and said, instead, "The man himself may well die. He's not well at all, not at all well, not at all."

Doctor Porras's friend gave a single, mirthless laugh and said what lunatics foreigners were. But Señora Porras was still in the doorway, and her eyes had widened at the mention of the blood spitting. She knew the symptoms of consumption, knew what that meant for the patient and the family and anyone near him. Her pulse quickened, resolve heightened. These people were dangerous, she thought, and reckless. They could get everyone sick, and then people would die, and it would all be their fault. And it would be her fault too if knowing all this, she did nothing.

She decided she should mention it, discreetly, to a select few of her friends, naming no names and no exact diseases.

THINGS THAT WERE
GOING TO HAPPEN

When I was alive, I had a habit of letting my thoughts race forward. I imagined catastrophes. I fantasized about dazzling possibilities. I was no good at living in the present, and in death I am even less so: once I'd mastered the art of seeing into people's pasts, I discovered it was possible to see their futures too, though this was a trickier, riskier undertaking. Still, in those early days of George's time at the Charterhouse, I did my best to stay in the moment, the here and now; to resist the temptation to get ahead of myself.

George's vision for their stay—the pursuit of wellness, the postponement of death—was for obvious reasons close to my heart. I wished them healthy! I wished them well! I wished them to stay with me *in perpetuum*! But I had serious reservations about their plan. It was an odd choice to come to Valldemossa in November.

The village, in the week of their arrival, was clinging to the tail end of the year's warmth. There were still heat-soaked afternoons and the low sun made everything look golden and warmer than it actually was. The trees were messy with fruit. Goats wandered up and down the hillside, the bells around their necks clanging faintly. Lizards darted in and out of crannies, licking the air. The whole place seemed alive in a way that people who knew no better associated with summer. It certainly did not look how November looked in Paris, or in Warsaw: there was no snow, no ice. So I could see why, at first glance, they might think they had landed on their feet. Their stupid delight in normal things, exclamations of joy at the sight of drystone walls or perfectly ordinary insects was the stupid delight of people who had no idea what was coming.

I, on the other hand, did know. Both in the sense that I had occupied that spot at the top of Valldemossa for centuries and understood its climate better than anyone, but also because of the thing I had taught myself to do—the thing where I could see into the future of the people I was with. For such a complex skill, which even I didn't truly understand, the reality was simple: their future was just there, beneath the surface of the people whose minds I got inside. All of their life was inside their heads. There was their past, which I allowed myself to access fully, because it didn't feel like cheating to know as much about them as they did themselves. But there was also everything else: their tomorrow and their next month and their years right the way up to their deaths, all this time inside them that they were set to fill in some specific way or another. I could see it all. People were like the little mechanical toys that were all the rage amongst the rich children of Valldemossa at that time in the early nineteenth century. Once they were wound up they just kept doing whatever movement they were made to do, until they ran out of energy and stopped. They never did anything else.

In the case of George and her family, it's not accurate to say that I *did* know what was coming, specifically, but rather that I *could* know. And the option of knowing, the temptation of knowing, of getting ahead of myself again, was what I was grappling with. I felt about it the way an alcoholic monk thought about wine: *I mustn't I mustn't I mustn't.* Those monks always did end up drinking again.

The first future I saw did not belong to a monk, or to one of the other inhabitants of the Charterhouse. It was the future of my great-great-granddaughter, and I saw it on the day before her fourteenth birthday. I spent a great deal of time with my family after my death; being around them was an antidote to my time spent with the monks. They helped me remember who I used to be. I understood the little in-jokes, their grudges and patterns, the easy, careless way they loved each other. I didn't have to be angry about anything.

My great-great-granddaughter was named after me and I loved her more than I knew what to do with. It was late afternoon, and in the morning Blanca would turn the age I had been when I died. I wanted to be cheerful for her, to relax, but found that I was filled with dread. I had a sense that this girl, my best friend in the world who never knew I was there, was about to experience something terrible. Her mother, my great-granddaughter, seemed oblivious, humming to herself and eating little pieces of cheese.

Perhaps it is not a coincidence that this happened around the time that I was teaching myself to read. I couldn't say why or how those two things might be linked, but when I think about this period, the whole memory is infused with the texture of paper and of leather binding, and of the full-bodied (disembodied) rage I felt when I learned to decipher words that, when I was alive, had either been read *to* me or simply not mentioned at all.

I started with the letters the monks wrote to each other. There were a lot of them, because a lot of the time the brothers were not supposed to speak. I wriggled into the head of whichever brother had received the note, and as he read, I would follow along, matching the words he was thinking and the feelings he was feeling to the shapes on the page. *My brother, my love* (this was how my favorite one went, and I read and reread it all the time), *I can hear you breathing even when you are not near.* This sort of thing delighted me. I thought it was wildly romantic. The first word I learned to read was *when. When* will you come to me? *When* will I see you? They were always in such a hurry to be near each other.

Next I read the Bible and was irritated. I was irritated by all the things that the priests must have known were irritating, because they had decided not to mention them to the congregation. Let's just say I read about what happened to Tamar—"he would not listen to her voice, but, being stronger than she, forced her"— and decided to call it a day with that book. In any case, since I had personal evidence that undermined the premise, the whole project had credibility issues with me.

But what made me angry, truly, wantonly, beyond-control angry, was poetry. That was when I really hit the roof.

> *Our lives are rivers*
> *Running into the sea*
> *Of death.*

How was it that the poet knew this—that life and death were made of the same stuff, that life was very little and death was very large—and could write it down as though it took no effort at all to do it, and nobody had ever told me, or shown it to me, or bothered to teach me how to read it for myself? How was it that I had never known? Poetry made me incandescent with indignation and sorrow, and I spent the next week knocking everything over and throwing Bibles out of windows, terrifying the brothers into thinking they should perform an exorcism. *Ha!* I laughed in their faces and, briefly empowered by rage, twisted a candlestick into a loop. *Exorcise this.*

All of which is only worth mentioning because it was what had been going on for me in the run-up to Blanca's fourteenth birthday. That afternoon she was sitting in the window of the house, looking out at the street. She was thinking about turning a year older, about how old fourteen-year-olds had seemed when she was younger. About whether her best friend would remember her birthday.

And then I just found myself turning the page, so to speak, and reading ahead. It was the easiest thing. I barely noticed I was doing it. Overleaf, I saw Blanca waking up the next morning, and running at once to announce that she was fourteen to her mother and father. I saw that her best friend would not forget her birthday, and would come by the house with a flower picked from a roadside tree, which seemed to me like minimal effort but which would thrill Blanca beyond words.

I saw that Blanca would get her first period three days later, and that this would appall her. It would make her feel like she couldn't walk properly. She would waddle like a duckling with rags stuffed between her legs, and cry with frustration when she was alone. She felt filthy. Sticky. Abominable. In pain. She could not believe, it seemed impossible, that this was going to happen to her every month for years and years and years. "How can I make it stop?" she'd asked her mother, who had smiled in an infuriating way that I remembered from older women when I had been alive, and said, "Oh, there's a way, but you won't know about it until you're married."

For Blanca then: a bad choice. She would either have to suffer the misery—indignity, inhibition, bad odor, discomfort—of having periods, or she would have to get married and get pregnant, which was not at all part of her plan at that point. So she devised another way, which involved giving up food, growing thinner and thinner until she was smaller than she had been when she was six years old. Her body became brittle and grew vole-like hair all over. Her eyes receded in their sockets and the skin stretched back around them so that she looked wide awake all the time, even when she was so tired she could barely lift her head. Her periods stopped. But still she could not bring herself to eat, in case that one piece of bread, that drop of oil, that scrap of chicken, would be the bite to bring the blood back.

I saw that all of this would happen and that she would be dead before she turned sixteen.

And having seen that, I had to go back to the day in question, the last afternoon of her thirteenth year, when she was as innocent of her future as I had been moments before, and then I had to celebrate her birthday with her.

From that first time, I learned the dangers of looking at the future. I learned how deadening it was to know what was about to happen, how it turned everything sour. I learned that the worst feeling in the world is the happiness of receiving a sprig of almond blossom from your best friend on your birthday when you are about to starve yourself to death.

I was careful, after that, to only look into the futures of people

I didn't care much about. But even then, it made things worse. Knowing what was about to happen dulled the interludes between now and whatever was to come. It made time pass slowly, a sickening drip-drip-drip of action after the flood of knowing everything in one go. How boring everything was! How long it seemed to take for people to get where I knew they were going! I tried to swear off it altogether.

With George and her family, I resisted and resisted and resisted. Whenever I felt my mind, inside theirs, drifting in the direction of *what's next?* I shut it down, closed the book, became blank. I put my fingers in my ears, so to speak, and sang *la la la* until I was sure the impulse had passed.

This is not to say that I did not know with absolute certainty some of the things that were going to happen. I knew without having to look, for example, that María Antonia was going to steal their money and their food and a few of their possessions. I knew that there would be Mass every Sunday. And I knew that within a week or so of their arrival, the first of Valldemossa's winter storms would roll over the mountain and turn everything black.

I REMEMBER

My sister María is going to marry Felix who lives next door, and I am going to marry Ham. Only one of these things is definite, but I remain convinced of both; there seems no other possibility. María has a date set, and our mother is making her new clothes, and when I look forwards into my own life there is only one vision: I am Ham's wife. It has been five days since we swam together for the second time and kissed for the first time.

I will be Ham's wife. Ham will leave the Charterhouse and find work in the village. He will bring home food and we'll have babies, which I will love a little, but not as much as I love him. Of course he will leave the Charterhouse; he will give up the idea of monkhood entirely. In its place there will be him and me: my life, transplanted from my mother's care to Ham's, suddenly elevated, suddenly important.

When I walk through the village, I walk with the assurance of a woman who has been picked by someone.

When María talks about Felix, about their future life and what it will entail, I am impatient, wanting to say, *Yes, yes, I know, I actually do know.* I have not told her about Ham, yet. I haven't told anybody. But still the urge to shake my head and blurt it all out is strong when María and I lie side by side in the dark, and she starts telling her Felix stories again. *First he did this, and then he said this, and then I felt this* . . . She only lets him use his hands and mouth, she says. The rest is for after they are married.

When I am alone I think about Ham, a person I don't know at all, and imagine all the things I might discover about him: that he is funny (probable), that he is very clever (almost certain), that when I am uncertain or worried or confused by myself or my life, he will stroke my hair and cheek and trail his fingers over my lips and explain it all, and tell me everything will be good (surely). I have surveyed the husbands of the village in search of a model on which to base this fantasy and found them all wanting. So I have patchworked together some memories of my father with the more fantastical things María says about Felix with some general impressions of good husbandly behavior gleaned from what my mother's friends say when they complain about their marriages. I add to the list: Ham will be clean, he will not be drunk, he will come home when he says he will, he will wipe his feet before entering the house, he will not forget the names of his own children.

The day before my third swimming rendezvous with Ham, I ask María what I look like.

Short, she says. *Why?*

What else?

Dirty, she says. *Smelly.*

You can't look smelly, I say. *What else?*

She relents. *Cute,* she says. *Sweet. Pretty smile. You're growing up.*

I think to myself: *Cute. Sweet. Pretty smile. Growing up.*

That night, as though my body was listening to María and realized some catching up was in order, I get my period for the first time: a clenching in my lower stomach and then the hot, worrying sensation of having wet myself. The flow is heavy and unrelenting. In the morning, the sheets look as though something has been sacrificed. The mattress is ruined and my mother screeches and mutters about having to burn the whole thing and do I want to ruin us all. She is still annoyed after breakfast, barking orders at me to clean and wash and feed the pigs, and I worry I won't be able to get away. Hot-faced, panic rising, the thought of Ham waiting alone in the water, bobbing and drifting and forgetting all about me. María, in a moment of surprising empathy, catches my eye. *Go lie down*, she says. *I hated mine too at first. If the cramps are bad, drink hot water.* And so I make as though to sleep, then slip out and waddle as fast as I can towards the coast. The rags wedged between my legs shift and slide out of place and require constant readjustment. I shelter between trees to shove my hand down and rearrange them; when I withdraw it my fingers are sticky and red. I wipe them on grass and bark.

Ham is waiting for me on the rocks, still clothed, and I slither down towards him aware that there is something about me today that smells metallic and meaty. I want to keep my distance from him, or at the very least dive straight into the water to rinse off.

You're here, he says. *You look nice.*

You look nice too, I say, surprised somehow by the sight of his face, which in the week since I last saw it had morphed in my imagination into something somewhat different. He looks rounder than I thought he did, his cheeks puffy and young, his chin gently cupped by another, lower chin.

Do you want to swim? he says.

Yes.

Take your clothes off, he says. *It's easier. The water won't try to drag you if you're naked.*

Take my clothes off! I say, to buy time. I hadn't anticipated this, and now can't think what to do. If I swim in my clothes the chance of the period rags drying afterwards are slim, and I will have to walk the whole way home with a squelching mess between my legs, or else I'll have to carry them while bleeding into my skirts, and walk through the village like that. If I swim naked, though, I imagine the whole sea will turn red, and Ham and I will both be covered in it.

Take your clothes off, he says. He starts undressing himself. *What's wrong? Why won't you take your clothes off?*

I'm bleeding, I say, and he says, *So?*

So I do what he says. Feeling of air on my skin—stomach, thighs—bright and forbidden, thrilling. I scurry from the shore into the water, anxious to hide myself as soon as possible. It's warm and dappled in the shadows, and Ham's hand is reaching for my shoulders, my neck, my breasts. When I look down, a small, pink cloud is floating around my crotch, hazy, the way the water looks around a fish that has been hooked and thrown back. Ham notices it too, but doesn't stop fondling, stroking, and this reaction feels correct, pleasant even, in the man who will be my husband.

His penis is hard again, distorted slightly in the water so that it looks rippled. He's close now, pushing, bobbing slightly, between my legs.

Do you want to do this? he asks, gesturing oddly with his hips towards mine.

I'm bleeding, I say.

I know. That's good. That means you won't get pregnant.

I don't know how he knows this, or why he thinks this would be true, but I say, *All right,* and he moves my legs around his waist, my arms around his neck, his hands fiddling at my groin, search-ing for something.

What is it? I ask.

He grimaces, concentrating, and we stay like that for several minutes as he attempts to get the right angle, the right point of entry. I bob up and down, clinging to him while he prods and grapples. At one point it almost seems as though he's got it in— a strange, burning bulk—but in the next moment it's gone and he's grunting and fumbling again.

Maybe it doesn't work in the water, I say.

He frowns. *I didn't think of that. Maybe it doesn't.*

Do you want to try by the rocks?

But he's soft now, and his cheeks are pink, and he says, *I have to go back to the Charterhouse actually.*

Do you want to swim again next week? I ask.

He's already clambering out of the water.

Maybe, he says.

I flip onto my back and stare at the sky, so bright I have to squint, and try to think of things that aren't Ham. When I close my eyes I see myself floating, exactly as I am, except I am drenched in blood and the water is blood and for a moment the image is oddly calming: the end of the world and me drifting atop it. When I look back at the shore, Ham is gone.

PRELUDE NO. 4
IN E MINOR, LARGO

At first there was only a patter of rain, turning the flagstones around the courtyard dark gray. There had been occasional drizzle since the family arrived, but this was the first to become a real downpour: fat drops spattering when they hit the ground, a crackling sound from all sides. The garden was suddenly thick with the smell of wet leaves and wet earth. Amélie, who had strung out laundry between the trees to dry, sheets and shirts and Chopin's little handkerchiefs, dashed out and began to gather them. A bird, moving so quickly I couldn't see what it was (yellow wings?), took off at speed from the bushes, water spritzing around its tail feathers.

From his seat at the piano, Chopin looked up. With one gloved hand, he played a single note to the rhythm of the drip-drip-drip of water sliding off the leaves of the pomegranate tree, and with the other he reached for his milk.

That morning, two little boys had arrived at the Charterhouse, swinging between them a pail of white liquid. It had been milk when they left the farm with it, fresh from their family's goats, but by the time they reached the top of the hill, they had drunk and replaced so much of it with water that it was not really milk anymore.

"What is this?" María Antonia asked. "Who sent you?"

"Doctor Porras did," they said. "It's milk."

María Antonia smirked and sent Amélie to rouse George, who had only just gone to bed. "Tell her she needs to pay for the milk."

María Antonia dipped a cup into the bucket and sipped. A pursed smile formed when she swallowed, and when Amélie returned with the money, María Antonia gave only half of it to the boys and put the other half in her own pocket, saying, "That is only half milk, at best, young men. You'll not get full payment from us!"

In the privacy of her own rooms, she skimmed off several cups and topped the pail up with water. When she shuffled into Cell Three, she set it down so heavily it sloshed onto the floor. She said, "Look! Milk!" which was paradoxically both obvious and by that point not at all true.

For the rest of the day, Chopin followed the advice of Doctor Porras and drank as much of it as he could. He found it a challenge. The goat's milk, weak but pungent, swilled around in his stomach. He could feel it churning like an ocean inside him when he turned between his paper and the piano keys. His compositions were interrupted by sporadic gurgles and waves of nausea.

Then the rain started and the air suddenly cooled. He was relieved to be distracted from his body and his work and from the piano, which was driving him crazy. Moments later the damp made him cough. Within an hour, the rain was heavier and relentless and Chopin's limbs ached. His skin felt too tight. Two hours later he was crouching in the corner of his room, throwing up all the watery milk into his hat.

At the first thunderclap, Solange darted out into the garden as though it had called her name. She stared up at the sky expectantly, and when lightning struck between the clouds, she screamed. The sound went right through me. It sent me into a panic. I thought something terrible had happened, that I had failed to keep her safe, that while I'd been distracted by Chopin's battle with the milk, some predator had attacked Solange. But then she screamed again, and I saw that her eyes were bright and her mouth was cracked open in a smile. She began to twirl. She was having the time of her life.

"Mama!" she shouted. "Mama!" When another clap of thunder hit, she hallooed across the mountain, wild and odd, a little storm inside the big storm.

George appeared in the bedroom window, the skin of her cheek imprinted with the creases of her pillow. She leant out so that the rain hit her face. "What's this?" she called to her daughter. "A party?" She minded her sleep being disrupted less than her writing. Sleep was a boring necessity, like going to the toilet. She would much rather watch her daughter howling and prancing in the rain than close her eyes again.

"Yes!" said Solange. Her trousers were clinging to her spindly little legs; her shirt, soaked to translucence, showed the dark grooves between her ribs and the shadow of her navel. She shook herself like a dog.

The rain on the roof and the ground and the leaves of the plants sounded like raucous applause. Everything was a din: the thunder and Solange's footsteps as she chased through torrents and puddles. Further off, suddenly audible, or at least easier to imagine, the sea was wild and crashing and roaring at the shore.

"What was that?" cried George. "What did you say?"

"Yes!" Solange shouted back. "A party! Yes!"

Above her, a seagull shrieked.

The storm party lasted all afternoon and into the evening. George came out to the garden with Maurice in tow for the sole purpose of being drenched together. Whenever they opened their mouths to speak or laugh, they swallowed gulps of water. They ran through the cloisters, weaving in and out of wet air and dry air the way birds dart under the canopies of trees, and when the wind picked up and howled they howled back at it. Gusts blew through the arches, making fronds of ivy wave, blowing loose stones out of walls. They found parts of the monastery that had been ignored for generations, and which even I barely visited. When they shouldered open the door of a dingy old chapel, unused for a hundred years or so, a flurry of leaves and debris blew in and landed at the feet of a dusty-eyed Madonna. The face of the statue looked mild, exhausted, unsurprised at their intrusion. Wind stirred up a lingering smell of incense.

It did not occur to any of them to check on Amélie, who was cowering in her cot in María Antonia's cell, terrified of the storm and flinching with every thunderclap. Her heart hammered against the inside of her rib cage: *let me out, let me out, let me out.* When the wind briefly dropped she would calm a little, and then the sound of the rain would start up again, the gale twisting around loose bricks, finding its way into the cell and chilling everything.

Amélie thought about how, in Paris in the rain, the bright lamps in the shop windows made the wet roads glow, but the memory of home made her loneliness more acute. *What the fuck,* she thought. *What the fucking fucking fuck.* This country. This weather. The chill in the air and the cabbage-smell that followed María Antonia around and the way the wind sounded like screaming and nobody seemed to care about or notice her. *Why the fuck am I here?* she was thinking. *I want to go home.*

The rain finally abated. Overhead, the pattern of black clouds and gray clouds and deep shadow and deeper shadow began to lighten and thicken as nightfall approached. A large, brazen moon flashed through occasional breaks. Its light curdled the clouds into fog, which seeped down the hills, milky and opaque, pooling in the courtyards of the Charterhouse and threading through its archways.

George and the children lit lamps in the new darkness, teeth chattering, giggling, wringing water out of their clothes. Maurice was first to drift off into the mist, and then the other two went too; I followed first one flame and then another as they wound between pillars, casting shadows. Solange breathed hot steamy breaths in front of her face, rippling her fingers through the brief heat. Maurice angled his lamp to cut through the white curls and twists in the air, finding the Latin names for everything he saw: *caligo, lux, soror. My "soror" is a horror,* he tried, then shook his head. George watched her children for a while, then wandered further off to gaze out at the hillside and the clear sky emerging beyond the mountains, dark blue.

In his room, alone, Chopin had no more watery milk to throw up and no more energy to stay upright. He crawled to his cot, and rolled onto it, panting and balanced on his side, ready to retch. *Are you all right?* I asked. *Can I get you anything?* In response: a fluttery heartbeat.

Under his skin there was fatigue, a pounding headache, a sore throat, and beneath all of that, rage. He wanted George to come to him. He wanted George to notice he was sick. He wanted George to be at his bedside, soft-voiced and consoling. He could hear the shouts of her children outside, but from his cot in the cool, high-ceilinged room, they sounded far away. He had a looping melody stuck in his head he was trying hard not to forget. Once I'd got the hang of it I sang it back to him as loudly as I could, hoping to lodge it in his mind. He panted and waited and wanted George, and when still she did not come, his mind returned to the piano, imagining heaving himself upright and towards it, feeling for the keys as though reaching out for another person's hands.

He could hear every detail of the new piece. The melody would be clear and sustained, glassy like the surface of a lake. The left hand would play restless churning chords that pulsed faster and then slower, lower and lower, stirring in the depths. There would be a knowing air to the music, world-weary, as though it was expressing something that should have been already clear. But it was doubtful, too: reassuring words spoken by someone whose heart is sinking. Halfway through it would almost lose its nerve: the left hand would stop and the right would dip towards the deeper, unsettled register. Teetering. A brink. And then there would be a breath, a climb, the pulsing chords would resume and the piece would go on as seemingly calm as—calmer even than—before. The overall effect was of doubt in the left hand and love in the right: the two sides competing, ignoring and consulting one another by turn. There was a sort of dread in it. While he lay prone, eyes closed, Chopin's fingers twitched as he thought his way through the whole thing.

In the cloisters, neither George nor the children seemed to notice that even without the thunder and the clapping rain, they could not hear the stop-and-start jangling of Chopin's piano. But I had grown so used to the sound of his working, the phrases repeated over and over, the trills and thumping chords, that the silence jarred. As I left Chopin's room and drifted through the corridors, under dripping archways and out into gardens awash with surface water and moonlight, the absence of music made everything feel off-key.

DECEMBER

MASS

When the sun came up the morning after the storm, the old stones of the Charterhouse looked dark. The whole village seemed dampened, browbeaten. Grasses and shrubs that had been yellowing were suddenly dark brown; tree branches had been blown bare; and on the hillside, the goats seemed gloomy as they clanged about beneath the olive trees. It was Sunday, the family's first in the village, and the church bells were ringing for Mass.

Before Chopin fell asleep the previous night, George had poked her head into his room. Her cheeks were pink and her hair hung wet on either side of her face. "How's my Chopinet?"

"Dead," Chopin said, still full of moroseness and indignation at having been forgotten. But if George noticed his mood, she didn't acknowledge it. She crossed to the piano, where his unfinished cup of milk sat.

She sniffed it. "What's this?"

Chopin said, "Milk."

George put her lips to it and then coughed. "It's definitely not."

"The doctor said to drink it."

"The doctor said to drink milk. That is not milk."

She coaxed him out of bed, and threading one of his arms over her shoulders, taking firm hold of his waist, led him into the central room, where Solange and Maurice were eating bread in great chunks, torn from a damp loaf. Chopin let himself be guided, coddled, petted. The little travel clock George had brought with them began to chime. It was midnight but nobody moved to go to sleep. They sat up into the early hours, eating and occasionally talking, and when they went to bed, for the first time since their arrival, George followed suit. Instead of sitting at her desk with her papers and tobacco and coffee and candle, she curled up next to Chopin in his too-small bed, hooking her chin over his shoulder and her arms around his middle. They slept that way all night and when the sun came up and the church bells began to ring, they slept on, unmoved.

I crept up on the starlings in the trees nearest the windows of the cell and shook the branches so that the birds rose up with a swoosh, chattering loudly and indignantly, which woke Solange and Maurice but not George and Chopin. George was not quite snoring but making little "humph" sounds on each exhale, dreaming something fitful about horses. I shoved the bed as hard as I could and she stirred, then opened her eyes.

I was pleased, relieved, excited, and as the family stretched and yawned and wanted coffee, I set off ahead of them for church. I wanted to see the lay of the land, to check what they would be faced with. I wanted their first Mass in Valldemossa to be seamless.

Almost everyone was already there when I arrived. María Antonia was present and beside her was Amélie, looking puffy-eyed and sallow. The residents of Valldemossa had made a particular effort to look nice: little girls like hillocks of lace, Fidelia fiddling with her veil, expectantly biting her lips to keep them red. Doctor and Señora Porras were in the front row. He looked hungover. She was twisting in her seat to catch the eye of a friend, surreptitiously waving. And there was my oh-so-great-granddaughter, Bernadita, doddery and lost-looking, sitting arm in arm with her closest friend. They patted each other's bony hands, as though to check they were still there and still together. (Bernadita had no children. She was the last of my direct line. After her I would have no more relations in Valldemossa, which was a tremendous relief to me, and a source of vertiginous fear.) I went to her and kissed her lumpen knuckles and her forehead. Her skin was slack around her skull, and papery. It wrinkled when I kissed it, though she didn't notice.

There was a conspicuous gap at the right-hand side of the church, near one of the more gruesome statues of Christ. There was not only room for a family of four but plenty of space all around, so that nobody would be directly next to them. People kept staring nervously across at the empty seats, as though George and her family might appear in it at any moment.

I was excited. This was a chance to start afresh, since things between George and the locals had got off to a rocky start. There had been the rock incident with Solange, of course—more like a pebble in reality, but in her retellings it had been magnified into a boulder—and then the worrisome diagnoses of the doctors. It was a good sign, I thought, that everybody had shown up so promptly and so nicely dressed. (Just as I was thinking this, the Sacristan shuffled in with his sister beside him and darkened my mood immeasurably.) It was a good sign, I reiterated. Everybody wanted to make it work. (The Sacristan coughed, then coughed again, and seemed generally under the weather; I cheered up a bit.)

We waited. People twisted around to look at the door, as though that would force George and the family to appear through it. There was a little murmuring. In the vestry, Father Guillem was on edge, occasionally peering out to see whether the foreigners had arrived. It would be awkward to begin without them, he was thinking. But it was awkward to start late, and they were making him late. His stomach was rumbling and gurgling; he was hungry and keen to get things underway.

His congregation was growing restive. He made to head out into the church, then second-guessed himself and sat down, fingering the square edge of the bottom of his crucifix. *Damn,* he was thinking. *Damn, damn, damnation.*

There was nothing for it: I went back to see what was holding George up. I imagined various glitches—Solange reluctant to wear a dress after the freedom of her slacks, Chopin not feeling well—as I made my way to the cell. None of the imagined scenarios could possibly have prepared me for what I was to find.

Solange: lying on her front beneath the trees, drawing ghoulish faces with her forefinger in the damp earth.

Maurice: straddling the wall at the back of the garden with sketch pad and charcoal, drawing his sister drawing faces.

Chopin: motionless at the piano, staring in apparent horror at the ceiling. I was about to work my way inside his head to figure out why when—

George: strolling into Chopin's room saying, "Chopin, what is this?"

She had her hands behind her head, lifting her hair off the back of her neck. (Her neck! Displayed like that: long, taut; I rushed to be near to it.) Chopin had not been working, but instinctively arranged himself as though he had been. He looked up at George from a blank score and said, "Hm?" as though she had distracted him from something more important.

She patted the nape of her neck, turning her back on him to show it, and said, "What's this?"

There was a mosquito bite, large and red, nestled amongst the fine hairs.

He reached out and pressed it with a single finger. The skin, where he touched it, turned white before the blood returned.

"An insect bite," he said. "Is it itchy?"

It crossed my mind, then, that perhaps they had just forgotten the day. Perhaps in all the commotion of their first week, they had lost track of time. Chopin had been ill. The storm had been disruptive. It was normal, wasn't it, to become confused in moments of stress and change?

I wondered if there was some way I could intervene and remind them: *It's Sunday!* I shouted. *It's Sunday! You're late! Have you forgotten it's Sunday?*

George looked up and over her shoulder towards the other room, as though—it really was almost as though—she was wondering where the voice she'd heard was coming from.

Yes! I yelled. *Sunday! Remember?*

She crossed to the door and pressed it shut, firmly, before returning to Chopin. She ran a finger down the side of his face. The skin felt hot, surprisingly rough. And almost at once, then, she was astride him on the piano stool, facing him. They were kissing, and his hands were on her chest, unbuttoning her shirt. I continued to shout, pointlessly, frantically, getting right up inside George's ears: *Sunday! Sunday!* as she put her face into the crook of Chopin's neck and said, "Shall we go back to bed?"

George lifted Chopin's fingertips to her mouth and bit the tips of his gloves. He slid his hands out; they suddenly looked naked, very pale, newborn, odd. As George and Chopin tumbled onto Chopin's mattress, Chopin on his back and George atop him shrugging her shirt off, I realized the obvious truth. They knew it was Sunday. They knew that they were missing Mass. They just didn't care.

They had sex the way two women do. Chopin slid a hand underneath George and she moved up and down onto his fingers. He held her right breast with his other hand and she pressed both palms down over his grip as though she was worried he might let go. He never looked away from her. She closed her eyes. They stayed like that for a long time.

I waited, half watching them, half-distracted by my own anxieties. I knew I shouldn't be there, should leave them to it, should be nowhere near their thoughts or bodies when they were doing this, but I was worried, fascinated, distracted, enthralled all at once. I found that I was just standing there, gawping, not as close as I could be, but not nearly far enough away.

I was trying to figure out what to do. The people of Valldemossa, my friends and family, might have been suspicious of the newcomers, instinctively hostile, but they had never—*I* had never!—suspected this. The community had been willing to tolerate their presence, had been curious, and some of them (I thought of the way Fidelia had looked at Maurice) had been willing to more than tolerate them. But now? Now that the family had announced in absentia that they were not only foreign odd consumptive cross-dressers, but Godless foreign odd consumptive cross-dressers? Now things would be much, much worse.

As George and Chopin lay cuddled up together on his bed, disheveled, I returned to the church. The service was wrapping up. The empty space near the statue of Christ seemed even bigger, even more disruptive. The people nearest to it edged further away, as though it might swallow them up. Father Guillem swung his incense dolefully.

Outside, afterwards, Amélie rushed away. She kept her head

bowed, but still she could feel eyes on her, could sense the whispering following her back to the Charterhouse. Señora Porras was muttering urgently about certain strangers bringing certain strange diseases into the community, and the risks such people posed to their children, their babies, their elderly parents. Her friends were nodding seriously and shaking their heads occasionally, lace fluttering like insect wings, agreeing that the only way to contain consumption was to burn everything the patient had touched. The Sacristan and his sister tried to distance themselves from the situation: they had not been given any sense of the type of people who were coming; it had all been arranged by letter; they could not possibly be to blame for bringing these foreigners into the village; no, no, there was nothing to be done about it now.

María Antonia found herself the center of attention. A little cluster of people formed around her asking questions. Yes, it was true that they were staying in the cell next to hers, and that they trusted her with all their secrets. The gentleman had been very unwell, she explained, and was unlikely to live long. There had been countless doctors visiting. Surely he would die right there in Valldemossa! But no, the children and the lady were all in perfect health. Yes, she had seen them just the night before; she had brought in coffee as she always did in the evening. Yes! Coffee in the evening, despite the storm! Because the lady stays up all night writing, and drinking coffee, and smoking. Yes! Smoking!

And so on, peeling back layer from layer of scandal, until they reached the central, scandalous heart of the matter.

"Oh," said María Antonia, "but you know, he's not her husband. She said as much to the doctor. They are—I expect the French have a word for it—friends who keep each other company. He's not her husband at all."

GEORGE REMEMBERS

George no longer feels like a wife, though she remembers feeling like one in the early days of her marriage. It seemed meaningful then. It was a synonym for *important*, for *cherished*. Wife as in *Let me ask my wife first*. Wife as in *Please take care of my wife*. That was seven years ago. Now she is twenty-five, a mother of two, and she doesn't feel like a wife. She feels like a person with a husband.

The last straw: George discovers that her husband has invested in, of all things, a ship that doesn't exist. Faced with George's fury, he is full of protestations: he could not possibly have known, the whole thing was so convincing, so expertly done. She should be comforting him rather than berating. He thought it was a good thing for him, for both of them; she should be thanking him for trying to do such a good thing.

The gentleman who arranged the investment, her husband says, was respectable-looking and entirely plausible: the cousin of a wife of a friend of a friend. The two of them went hunting and had a long dinner; the topic of the ship arose completely naturally, as they were talking more generally about money. The gentleman simply mentioned his own excitement at the investment opportunity offered by the ship; it was sure to be a grand success and the reward would be considerable. It might be possible for her husband to put a little money in, he wasn't sure, would need to check; it was probably too late. They drank more wine. They smoked their cigars. The gentleman seemed to have forgotten the ship altogether when, as he was taking his leave, George's husband mentioned again how interested he was in the venture. *Oh, the ship? Well, I'll make some inquiries. I wouldn't get your hopes up, I'm afraid.* What a surprise when, two days later, George's husband was invited to join the scheme after all!

How can it be, George asks, coolly, *that you did not immediately see this for the scam it is? Was there no information given to you in writing? An address, perhaps, where you could direct inquiries, requests for authentication, reassurances that any discerning investor would surely desire? Was there any pledge of authenticity from a bank? None of this? And without any material to suggest this ship, this extraordinarily lucrative ship, was anything more than a ridiculous fantasy, you sent 25,000 francs off to the pocket of an utter stranger?*

They are arguing in the garden room of their house—*her* house, George thinks; it was her grandmother's before it was hers; her husband is really only visiting; he is a guest who has outstayed his welcome—with a view of the grounds. He is staring out of the window with an assumed air of nonchalance. In the distance, a gardener is cutting back roses and somewhere out of sight Maurice is playing with one of the servants: high-pitched shrieking, sweet peals of giggles. George experiences it all with a sort of shock: that this is her life, as though it has happened to her suddenly and all at once.

But she is old enough now, and smart enough, to know when

her husband has been a fool. The obviousness of the boat scam is what irks her, the tenuous connection the gentleman claimed to her husband, the copious amount of wine involved. This is far worse than the loss of 25,000 francs; worse even than the hypocrisy of the way he talks to her about money while spending his own so ridiculously. The whole thing was so glaringly, patently, a scam, and in falling for it, her husband has revealed himself to be an imbecile. She thinks of all that she has suffered, everything she has ignored or pretended to ignore, for this very stupid man.

George can tolerate being married to a brute, or to a philanderer, but not to a fool. That is, surely, too much to bear.

Or perhaps the last straw comes earlier, three days after Solange was born. The baby is lying crumpled in her crib, fists raised to her chin like a boxer. George is weak and stiff from labor, bleeding heavily, and nauseous. Everything takes five times longer than it used to and everything is ten times more boring. The rush she felt after giving birth to Maurice, a thrilling sucker punch of devotion, is absent now. When she looks at her daughter flailing and mewling, George feels tenderness but not much more. She is restless and exhausted, a nightmarish combination which makes her want to scream.

She hauls herself upright and pads away from Solange to the hallway. She has the vague idea of finding tobacco, smoking being a way of doing something and nothing at once. While she is casting around for a servant to ask, she overhears thumps and grunts from the other side of the wall. The door to the room is wide open, as though nobody has anything to hide, and when George looks through it, there they are: her husband, trouserless, and the Spanish maid with her skirts up around her waist. Neither of them notices George hovering in the doorway: she stands there longer than she wants to out of surprise and stubbornness. She can hear everything: the girl's moans (overly theatrical, amateurish), her husband's little snorts, but also the slick of body fluids, the clap of their skin coming together and apart. She can even smell it: God, unmistakable, that biscuity, musky sex smell.

Her husband and the maid do not give any sign of noticing when George leaves. She pulls the door sharply shut behind her.

And, truly, it isn't the cheating that bothers her. The cheating has been understood and undertaken on both sides. George has not been waiting at home while her husband makes his conquests; she is fairly sure Solange is not his. So, no, not the cheating, exactly, but the flagrancy of it, the shamelessness, the wide-open door and jubilant grunting—all of this while George is alone, shut up away from friends and lovers with only this scrap of a baby to care for. She feels trapped by her body, her still-swollen, pudgy belly and the perineal tear that bleeds afresh whenever she moves and makes her scared to pee. Her milk has just come in and her breasts feel weighty and thrumming, hard as stale bread; her shirt is drenched and sticky. She is all seepage, bloat, and frayed edges. She can go nowhere. She can seduce nobody.

She thinks about the smell of the Spanish maid's vulva. The audacity of filling a room with an odor like that when your wife is next door, foreign to herself, full of milk and boredom.

George can tolerate being married to a brute, or to a fool, but not to a reckless philanderer.

The last straw, after the boat, after the baby, is actually this: there is a day when a servant asks George a question about a millinery bill—the milliner is claiming an outstanding amount to be paid—and George cannot remember the status of her account. She looks through her own papers and finds nothing, then turns to her husband's desk. It is a mess, covered in half-written letters, records of work done and money due on the estate, jotted notes on hunting parties and dinners to attend. George sifts through it, opening drawers, paying no attention to anything that isn't a household bill, until an envelope catches her eye. It is addressed to her, and it says, under her name, *Do not open this until after my death*.

George is no longer interested in following instructions from her husband. She opens the not-yet-posthumous letter.

She stands at the window to get the last of the day's light.

Her husband's handwriting skitters across the page like birds flushed from undergrowth.

What he has written is vile.

George reads every word. She thinks: *I am dreaming; I must be dreaming*. The document is an account of why her husband hates her. He hates her because she is not a normal woman. She does not behave as normal women do. He appears to have added to the screed anytime he was angry: a line here about her bad character, a line there about her perversity, her intractable weirdness. The tone and shade of ink change, the legibility of the scrawl, according to how much wine was drunk at the time of writing. He accuses her of everything that has a name: frigidity, adultery, unnatural insouciance in the face of his infidelities, so unlike the behavior of an ordinary wife. Some things there are no names for, and he accuses her of those as well: he cannot stand *the way she is*.

This is what her husband wants to leave her, as a keepsake, after he is gone: contempt, a catalog of the many ways she has failed him.

George folds the paper neatly in half when she has finished. She digs her thumbnail deep along the crease as though she is going to tear it. She feels dark, angry, betrayed, her heart racing, cheeks reddening, and then, suddenly—light. She takes a breath. Thinks it all through. Her husband hates her, which means there is no point trying anymore, and what could be more freeing, a greater relief, than no longer having to try?

Hasn't she had enough? Seven years of trying and trying and bargaining and cajoling. She made declarations, set out manifestos for how their marriage would be. She promised she would listen more, flirt less, fantasize less, see less of other men. In return she extracted from him a commitment to read more and to talk to her about philosophy, politics, interesting things. Anything, really, that wasn't his hunt or his dinner. He too had tried in his own way.

She settles in a chair in her husband's study and lights a cigar. It is not dark yet; he will be gone awhile longer doing whatever it is he does with his days. She feels calm. She feels occasional bursts of giddiness, excitement. She feels a little regret about how much time they have wasted and how little love has proved to be worth. The room smells strongly of her husband; she fills it with smoke, flicking ash onto the floor. She thinks, vaguely, that they once had sex on that floor, and now it is just wood, a little dust that has been missed, stray strands of tobacco.

She considers all the last straws, and in particular the very first last straw. It happened when they were newlyweds—or was it later, she struggles to remember the time line, perhaps it was when Maurice was a baby—and she was still in a state of exuberant infatuation with her husband. They were staying together in Paris, and her husband returned to the country house before her, saying he wanted to have it perfect for her. She thinks, now, that this was an odd excuse, since it was—God, how many times has she been over this in her head—*her* home; she had lived there most of her life before he arrived in it, so what could there have been to do, reasonably, to perfect it for her? It was already exactly as she liked it.

She didn't think that way at the time. At the time she thought: *My husband is taking care of the kinds of things that husbands take care of.* Those things were houses, land, money, wives.

And then, when she finally got home, it was to discover he had killed her dog. He tried to say she hadn't cared much for it. When George said she had cared for her immensely, her husband snorted and asked how he was supposed to have known: the dog was old; it was badly trained.

George explained that a man with ordinary human feeling would not need it spelled out to him that his wife was fond of her dog.

What more is there to say, now, about this incident? It speaks for itself: the man is a brute, has always been a brute, and while George can tolerate being married to a fool, or a philanderer, she cannot tolerate et cetera, et cetera, et cetera. She did not realize it at the time, but it was impossible, after the dog incident, for her to love her husband the way they both wished she could.

What would have happened if she hadn't found the letter? Her husband is only nine years her senior, and he is in wonderful health: all that hunting, fresh air. She tries to imagine the years passing before his body begins to fail him: she will be an old woman by then, which is a thing she cannot imagine being. There will be decades of effort and failure, of being a person with a husband, and for what? To find, at the end of it all, this miserable piece of writing waiting for her. No, it is simply out of the question to wait.

A small hubbub erupts outside: dogs barking, a few raised voices. George sits up a little straighter. Footsteps approach the house. She hears the door open and slam. In the hallway, her husband says, as he always does, *Get me food. I'm famished. I'll eat at once.* A murmured assent from the servant. Another door opening and closing. Her husband's footsteps are getting closer, closer, and now here he is in the room, jumping when he sees her and saying, *What the hell are you doing in here?*

He doesn't wait for an answer.

He says, *Damned stable boy let the tack rust. I've given him a piece of my mind. The horses can't stand it when it's rusted.*

I expect the horses don't give a damn, says George.

Her husband looks at her closely. *What's going on?* he says.

She speaks slowly, choosing her words with the care of Solange taking only one sweet from the tray. *I do not have the patience to wait to be a widow.*

Don't be sassy, he says. *I can't stand it when you're sassy.*

Sit down, says George, and he sits at once, despite himself, then looks surprised.

What's going on?

George lays it out as clearly as she can. The marriage has concluded. She will go to Paris. He will not try to stop her. She will have a modest allowance to support her living independently. He will not seek to curtail this, or her, or any of her social interactions. Any rumors about her that might reach him should be met with nonchalance and indifference. He can remain in the house for now, but it is her home, as it always has been, and not his. Maurice and Solange will stay with him until it is decided that their interests would be best met elsewhere, either with her in Paris or away at school. He will not speak ill of her to them. She will not interfere with his life any more than he will interfere with hers. They will be completely free. There will be no discussion about any of this. It is over. It has already happened.

She expects something from him now: anger, an outburst, self-pity. Instead he chews the inside of his lower lip, which contorts his mouth into a downturned pout. She wonders if he will say the word *sassy* again. He does not. He stands up.

Well then, good night, he says, though it's not yet late and there is still a meal to be eaten, an evening to be endured.

Good night, says George, before she can catch herself, and then they both realize the mistake and George wonders if they might be about to laugh.

HUNGER

They were so oblivious! Behaving like innocents, frolicking around the cell as though it was the Garden of Eden, naked and stupid! It had never before occurred to me how irritating Adam and Eve were. How insufferable it was to be so naïve, not to notice the way things were so clearly going to go, to stare at a wide, blue sky and think, *The sky is blue, so it will always be blue.* I wished I could spell it out for them, shout, *There will be storms!* over and over, until they finally understood. But they acted as though there was nobody in the world but them, certainly nobody in the cell, nobody who was trying her best to protect their interests, only to have her efforts roundly ignored.

I was annoyed, of course, because I was worried, and being worried about someone makes you angry with them after a while. I had experienced it before, mostly with my family, my various grand- and great-granddaughters. Those girls drove me wild. In this instance, I acted out a little in my irritation: the day after they played truant from Mass, I knocked over George's inkpot in a fit of pique, ruining the uppermost few pages of her story about the monastery. A black lake obliterated a paragraph about sand running through an hourglass as a dying man meets his own ghost, over which she had labored for several hours. She blamed Solange, who, outraged, stomped out to the garden wall where Maurice had left his sketching things and systematically snapped each of his sticks of charcoal. Maurice, perplexed and likewise enraged, ran straight to his mother, demanding she discipline Solange, and a shouting match ensued that became so loud and high-pitched it set off an explosive headache in Chopin, who retired to bed, curled up like a fetus, hands clamped over his ears. All this was briefly soothing to me.

I hadn't left the family for any meaningful amount of time since they arrived, but it felt necessary then to take some time apart: to calm down, primarily, but also to check what was happening behind their backs, to see how far the ripples caused by their absence from Mass had spread. I left, following nobody as I crossed the square and drifted towards the village; it was drizzling faintly as I passed the dentist making a house call and the fishmonger arguing with a customer over an outstanding debt.

I looked in on the house of Doctor Porras and found that his wife had gathered her friends around her and was saying, "In my husband's expert opinion—and there have been doctors in his family for six centuries—the foreign gentleman certainly has consumption." Outside, a cluster of children perched on steps and giggled and squealed as they told stories of the witch who lived in the Charterhouse. And there, to my delight, was Bernadita, my last surviving relative, hobbling along beside her friend towards the market. In her head: nothing whatsoever, occasionally interrupted by sensations of the rain on her face, the fabric of her clothes against her skin. A fragment of a thought about her mother. A glancing memory of her husband, dead twenty years. I had, over time, felt less and less connected to my descendants, but still I felt a surge of joy to see her again and to visit the bleached calm of her old, old mind. *What a joy,* I thought—a stab of jealousy, I can't deny it—*to be so vague, so smooth, to drift away from your life as though in the cool ocean on a hot day.* And then I found I was at the Sacristan's door, and I stopped, and Bernadita shuffled onwards.

I made my way inside. He had been less present at the Charterhouse since the family had moved in, which was one reason amongst many that I was happy to have them there. He was awkward around them, self-conscious. Chopin's nice shirts and kid gloves and black necktie made him uncomfortably aware of his own coarse trousers. George made him feel confused to the point of derangement: a glossy-haired, dark-eyed woman who carried herself so brazenly, who dressed so bizarrely, who smoked and did so many unreasonable things as though they were all entirely reasonable. For hours after any encounter with her, he'd be twitchy and annoyed and faintly, humiliatingly, aroused.

When I dropped in to see him that day, he was alone, waiting for his sister to get back from visiting a friend. He was doing, it seemed, nothing whatsoever with his time: walking from one room to another, sitting down, standing up again. Without the Charterhouse in which to strut unimpeded, he was lost. I didn't bother to spend much time with his present thoughts, which I knew would be both mundane and offensive. Instead, I turned to his past, scanning for acts of antagonism. What had he said about George and her family, and to whom?

I found: several agitated conversations with his sister, in which she pressed him to get rid of "those foreigners," and he said the money was good and who else was going to pay to live in that drafty cell through the winter, and besides, if they were to send the family packing it would be as good as accepting responsibility for them being there in the first place.

I found: an extended and essentially unspeakable sexual fantasy about George. *Good,* I thought, *at least she's an appropriate age for you. Though she'd never have you, she'd never even look at you.* But who was I to judge, after all?

I found: repeated attempts from his neighbors and acquaintances (it would not be true to say he had friends, exactly) to get information from him about the new residents of the Charterhouse. These would begin in casual tones, as though it had just popped into their heads that moment to ask—"So, what's this about some foreigners living up at the Charterhouse?"—and then, when he refused to answer, became more direct. "No but really, who are these people? Enough's enough, surely. What business do they have here? There must be something you can do." The Sacristan shrugged and said it really was nothing to do with him; he knew no more than anyone else.

I found: almost by accident, that his heart was weak. I recognized the signs: the stuttering beat and light-headedness and occasional shooting pains. This was of no importance to the matter in hand, but of great importance to me. *Oh, Sacristan,* I thought. *Your days are numbered, you weakhearted bastard.*

Before leaving, I put bread crumbs in the coffeepot and a great deal of salt into the stew his sister had left beside the hearth. Just as I departed, I heard his footsteps as he crossed the floor, hauling himself out of one chair and going to sit down in another, which had a better view out towards the market, where young girls were going to buy soap and fruit, and where—what a shock! I was taken aback—I saw George, carrying a basket, looking sprightly and undaunted, with Maurice at her side.

What are you doing here? I asked, but I knew the answer. They were hungry. They wanted food.

María Antonia's cooking had been a source of great tension during that first week. She had offered to do the food shopping, and George had handed over money. When María Antonia returned with supplies that would last, at best, a day or so, George challenged her but received only a shrug in return. Food in Valldemossa was clearly more costly than food in Paris, María Antonia replied. George, distracted by her children and her writing and her lover, sighed but continued to pay María Antonia over the following days.

Then there was the chicken incident. "Buy meat," George had said. "We all need to get strong here. The vegetables are not enough." So María Antonia pulled out all the stops. She bought a whole chicken for roughly two thirds of the money she had told George it would cost. The bird was skinny but big enough to feed them all and she spent the whole afternoon bent over her stove. Her cell was full of sticky, pungent smoke. She hummed as she cooked and she ate as she hummed, lifting little pieces of skin off the carcass and digging out the flesh underneath, then covering the hole back over. When the chicken was ready, she moved it to the corner of the room and busied herself with making candied pumpkin for dessert.

I didn't see where the fleas came from. I wasn't paying attention and my best guess is that the stunt was Amélie's doing. She had been brooding and cross for days and I had spent enough time in her head to know that it was very much the sort of thing she had been pondering: inviting stray cats to rest in María Antonia's bed, on her clean laundry, or beside the stove; shaking out infested blankets over the pot. But I couldn't say for certain either way. Perhaps it was someone else entirely. It was easy enough to come by fleas in Valldemossa. All the goats had them.

What I do know is that there was a moment, as the chicken was set down triumphantly before the family, when they were impressed. It looked golden. They had not eaten meat for a while. It smelled peppery and rich.

Then a single flea sprang up from the breast and landed on Chopin's plate. Astonished stares. María Antonia, irritated but not deterred, tried to brush it away with a sleeve and commence carving. But the fleas wouldn't stop, began leaping from the carcass as though it was a hot pan spitting fat, a flea fountain, as though it had a never-ending supply. The little leggy specks sprang around the table and onto the diners' laps and Solange began to scream and stamp and shake her arms to get them off her and the whole thing descended into mayhem.

And so it was understandable that George had decided to relieve María Antonia of her culinary duties and take over the acquiring and cooking of food herself. I could tell she was looking forward to it. The George of the nighttimes had faded and in its place was the George whose head was full of whatever it was that the others wanted, their needs, their desires, whims. She clutched her basket and eyed the market stalls, and everybody in sight eyed her back.

The staring, the sudden lulls in previously lively conversation as they walked past, the occasional whisper: all this was to be expected. George noticed it, but no more than she had on her first exploratory stroll with the children. She made a point of smiling at anyone who accidentally caught her eye, which provoked blushes and stutters. People spun and walked in the other direction.

At her side, Maurice seemed unaware to the point of rudeness. He didn't notice the stares, the smirks, the grimaces. And he didn't notice the wide, desirous eyes of Fidelia, who had appeared, as haphazard and persistent as a butterfly on a lilac, as soon as word got round that the foreigners were at the market. When Maurice and George approached, she stepped forwards so that she was slightly in his path. She bit her lower lip and smiled. But Maurice, still stewing over the fight with his sister and concocting the perfect comeback should the same exact argument arise again in future, did not see a pretty and yearning girl in his path. What he saw was simply an obstruction, which he stepped deftly around, muttering, "Excuse me," in a language Fidelia could not understand.

The humiliation Fidelia felt was sudden and powerful. It hit her like a rock. Her friends were watching her, had egged her on, and she was left standing in the street as though she were a fallen tree in Maurice's path, as though she were nothing at all. She should have tripped him up, she thought. She should have sworn at him. He was a good-for-nothing heathen foreigner and she should have listened to what everyone was saying about him and his family of oddballs: they were no good and would infect everyone with whatever disease it was they had and they should be made to leave at once.

George and Maurice, oblivious, oblivious, oblivious, strolling amongst the stalls. Bulbous loaves of bread stacked high like a drystone wall. The olives and olive oil sold by every other vendor. A chestnut seller bent over a fire, to which, though it wasn't yet particularly cold, people nonetheless were drawn. Oranges, of which they already had an unlimited supply at home. Vegetables: some wilting greens, robust tomatoes, mushrooms clumped with dirt and smelling of the farmyard.

George stopped at the bakery and gestured at a loaf. "How much?" She spoke Spanish in an appalling accent.

The baker crossed his arms, eyed the size of George's purse and named a figure roughly five times what he normally charged.

George laughed. "No," she said. "Really, how much?"

He trebled his asking price.

She laughed again, though her eyes didn't smile. "How much?"

He named the amount his brother-in-law had recently paid for a large house in Palma.

"Fine," George said, and turned on her heel. "Then I'll go elsewhere."

"Good luck with that," the baker muttered, but in Mallorquín so only the locals understood.

"What happened, Mama?" Maurice whispered, as they hurried away, but George only shook her head and wouldn't answer him.

It was the same everywhere: pumpkins, squash, coffee, fish. All laughably, ridiculously priced at one hundred, two hundred times the normal amount. Whenever George protested, the price went up, and when she switched to the next stall to try a different vendor, the first asking price simply picked up where the last had left off.

The color in George's cheeks was rising to an indignant pink. Her features stayed immobile, betrayed no feelings of humiliation or panic, but red blotches appeared on her neck and around her mouth. Everybody knew what she must be feeling.

Maurice began, finally, to understand the basics of the situation. "It's better for servants to do the shopping, Mama," he murmured. "These people aren't comfortable selling to a lady."

George shook her head. "That's not it."

The vendors were unanimously hostile. The other shoppers gave them a wide berth. George picked up a carrot to examine it, then gave up trying to buy it for the extortionate asking price and set it down. The grocer made a great show of digging out a rag from his back pocket and using it to remove the carrot. He held it at arms' length and waved it at some children, who giggled and ran away. Then he marched over to the chestnut seller and dropped the carrot into the fire. People stood back, covering their mouths and noses. The chestnut seller gathered up his wares, looking affronted. Nobody went near until there was no sign of what had once been a vegetable in the flames. Several people performed coughing fits as though they had inhaled something poisonous.

George watched all of this, expressionless and bright red. Then she took Maurice's hand and left the market at speed.

Her breathing was shallow as she climbed the track back up to the Charterhouse. I could see that if she had been a fraction less *George-like* than she was, she would have burst into tears. Instead, she found a boulder at the roadside, sat squarely down on it, and pulled out a cigar from the inside pocket of her jacket. Maurice stood awkwardly beside her, looking around for a second place to sit and seeing nothing.

It started to drizzle again as she smoked. Absentmindedly, she trailed her fingers around the tip of an asphodel spear. Maurice kicked the low grasses and tried to think of something to say. He considered: *I actually like María Antonia's cooking,* which was a lie and too on-the-nose for his mother's state of mind. He considered: *What do you want to do tomorrow?* but that too felt like it had the potential to annoy, putting pressure on his mother to be in charge of everything, as she always was. He considered: *I love you.* He considered silence. George's eyes glazed as she smoked.

I had a sudden memory of that very same spot as it had been when I was little, the knotted carob tree overhead and the feeling of dust in my shoes and something—what was it?—that I was looking forward to; the sensation of being about to eat something delicious. Meanwhile, George's stomach rumbled and I wished, I really wished that she could feel me the way I could feel her, that I could lend her the sensation of being about to eat good food: tantalizing, teetering, more delicious than the food itself.

I REMEMBER

Ham and I have sex all the time now. We can't stop doing it, rarely even bothering to swim until afterwards to wash off. Months have passed since the brothers processed through the village and now it is almost winter and still we meet and get naked in the open air and leap into the water afterwards. It's a sort of craziness that comes over us the minute we see each other— even before I see him, in fact, on the walk from the village to the beach, just thinking about him, the blood leaves my head, I feel giddy and driven, propelled, breathy. At home, I am preoccupied, nauseous with excitement. I excuse myself after breakfast, after lunch, before dinner, to find some quiet, private place where I can touch myself and relieve the pulsing, urgent feeling I have constantly now.

I start to see things differently. Previously uninspiring objects are transformed. Courgettes. The round end of a chair leg that broke off years ago and has been leaning against the wall in the corner by the fire for years. Mushrooms remind me of the rounded head of Ham's penis. I am so agitated by it all I feel sick to my stomach.

The kitchen is a minefield.

Peel these, says my mother, thrusting handfuls of carrots in my direction, and I can feel my whole face turn red.

What's wrong with you? she says.

Nothing.

What's different with you, then?

I stare at the carrots, with seams of brown soil pressed into their wrinkles and grooves, frothy green fronds erupting from the tip. The whole truth not a possibility. A half-truth: *I can't stop thinking about beautiful men.*

Oh, she says, *I remember that phase. Well, you'll be married soon enough to someone or other.*

I nod. This I know to be true.

It took Ham and me several attempts to get it right, and after each failed try he got moody and quiet, would either stomp back up the cliffs or swim so far out I'd lose sight of him. And then one day, after his usual fumbling, he made a strangled, exasperated sound and said, *You do it,* and I found that I somehow could do it, could guide him to the right place, could make his eyes widen, could make my own body tense up with pain, an absolutely wrong feeling, as though this thing we were doing, which surely everybody did, was entirely incorrect. And then that feeling faded and I took long, tight breaths and Ham's face was focused and bright and we figured out, clumsily, how to move in the right ways, how to assume the right positions, how to make it work.

When María comes by to talk about her husband she says, *Do you want me to tell you about sex?* and I'm not sure I can bear it, even thinking about it more than I already do, let alone listening to María talk about it.

Why? I say.

So you will know what to do when you get married.

No, I say, *it's okay,* but she carries on anyway, about making sure he touches you in a certain way before he starts, about using spit if it's painful, and I can't stand it, want to put my hands over my ears until she stops talking. But it's too late, I can feel my body become alert, interested, and before I can stop myself I am scanning the room for something I can use once she's gone: the neck of a wine bottle, elegant and long and suddenly irresistible.

The next day is a Ham day, and I tell my mother I am taking laundry to the river, bustling out with an armful of sheets and then stashing them in the bushes before scurrying to the shore. Ham isn't there when I arrive and I can hear my own pulse, loud and deranged in his absence. I begin to undress, with the idea of creating a tableau for him to arrive to: I will lie prone and naked against the rocks, a washed-up mermaid, shipwrecked princess. The wind has risen and it's colder than I'd like once I'm in position; the rocks dig into my shoulder blades and buttocks. It starts to drizzle and my skin erupts with goose pimples, and eventually I see Ham's head appear over the edge of the cliffs, his face exactly as I want it to be: eager, surprised.

As he descends and approaches, however, his delight recedes and in its place is confusion, brows furrowed.

Ham, I say, *I'm here.*

But instead of falling on me, shrugging off his clothes, he takes a step back and says, *What's wrong with your body?*

What do you mean?

Your body, he says. *Looks different.*

I look down at myself, trying to see what he's seeing. Breasts, stomach, blur of pubic hair, thighs, knees, feet. My feet are dirty. I push myself upright, then walk to the water's edge to paddle. It's cold.

You're pregnant, Ham says. *Aren't you?*

I laughed. *Why would you say that?*

Didn't you wash yourself afterwards like I said? I told you to rub between your legs in the water to get rid of the stuff. Didn't you do that?

I can feel myself, for the very first time, getting annoyed with Ham. *I did,* I say. *You've seen me do it. I'm not pregnant.*

Well when was the last time you bled? he asks and I have no idea. *You're pregnant,* he says. *Just look at you.*

I really can't see, at first, what he's seeing. I have never spent a huge amount of time looking at my own body, which I have experienced for the past couple of years as a changeable, unreliable thing. Breasts appeared, first as hard lumps beneath the skin, and then gradually fleshier. Sometimes bright red spots turned up on my chin and forehead, sore as bee stings, crowning with bright, white pus that was half horror, half relief. Sometimes I was fat, sometimes thin, sometimes bloated, sometimes furious. I tried to ignore it. I was as unreadable as a book.

Now I stare at my nakedness: breasts crisscrossed with blue veins like the cracked glaze on a pot. Nipples hardened into rubbled lumps, dark. Is my stomach rounder? Perhaps it is. Beneath it, my feet in the rippling water are blotchy with light and shade.

Well now what? says Ham. *What are you going to do now?*

I might not be, I say. *Who knows, really? I might not be.*

We still have sex, although he seems irritated throughout, not meeting my eye, turning me away from him as though I have got pregnant with the express purpose of annoying him. Periodically he says, *I told you to wash the stuff out afterwards.* When he is finished and I head into the water to do just that, he says, *Well there's no point now, is there.* I do it anyway.

I feel nothing except a need to make him pleased with me again. I try to smile at him, try kissing him lightly around his ears and neck, until he shakes his head and leans away from me.

Tell me what to do, I say. *I'll do whatever you want. Just tell me.* It is impossible that Ham does not know the answer. Ham, my future husband, wise, funny, caring Ham, will know what to do.

He shrugs. *Just go.*

I wriggle back into my clothes, feeling suddenly that being naked is inappropriate, noticing for the first time that perhaps my skirt does feel tighter around the waist than it did. When I go to kiss him goodbye he shakes his head again and stares out to sea, arms crossed against his chest. He stays that way as I climb the cliffs, though I stop periodically to turn back. Once I'm near the top, he twists around to see if I'm still there, and when he realizes I am, instantly reassumes his position, glaring at the horizon.

I cry all the way home, thinking more about the misery of Ham being angry with me, Ham being disappointed, Ham being annoyed, than about the other thing, which in the moment somehow seems less catastrophic. Occasionally I remember to press a hand to my stomach, to locate the root cause of my upset. I think of how nauseous I've been lately, how unsteady. I can't remember the last time I got my period. And it's true, isn't it, that there's a new breadth to me that didn't used to be there? But all the pregnant people I've known have been so much older than me, so much wiser, so much more married. It seems impossible that I could be one of them. I return to Ham's words, Ham's glum expression, Ham with his back to me, staring at the water.

Where have you been? my mother asks. *What have you done with my laundry?*

I stare. I have no idea what she's talking about. In my

brain, the statement *Ham hates me* sounds over and over like a church bell.

Where are the sheets? she says. *What have you done with my sheets?*

Oh, I say, and before I can think of a lie: *I put them in a bush.*

My mother screeches. Wants to know what's wrong with me. Wants to know why I am trying to ruin our bed linen, to ruin our whole family. Wants to know what I'm trying to prove by acting like a lunatic these days. Wants to know exactly what I was thinking, putting our sheets in a bush.

I'm pregnant, I say, surprising even myself, but she's still talking angrily about the sheets.

I'm pregnant, I say again, and this time she hears me and stops midflow, then suddenly deflates, sinks to a chair, and pulls me towards her lap. *Oh,* she says, *that'll do it all right.*

SOLANGE

So María Antonia bought the food again (taking a large and unauthorized commission) and resumed cooking. Amélie did the housework (but cleaned only visible surfaces; she didn't make the beds so much as rearrange them, didn't wash the sheets as much as shake them out in the garden once in a while and spritz a little lemon juice across them). Chopin played the clunky, pitchy piano (but coughed more and more frequently until the coughing began to sound like percussion: trills, flourishes, deep-low chords, then that rasping, retching *honk*). Maurice studied from books that George piled up next to his bed. George glanced over his work, showering cigar ash all across the pages, and then returned to her own. And Solange? Solange was very, very bored.

Drizzle sometimes turned to downpours, and then became drizzle again.

This rhythm lasted undisastrously for three full days in a row. Not a single thing went wrong. I dipped in and out of the family's heads, kept an eye out for the Sacristan, thought my private thoughts about George, surprised the occasional sparrow; I could feel myself beginning to relax, to enjoy myself again. Until, that is, the undisastrousness started getting to Solange. She was thinking: *I can't stand it I can't stand it I can't stand it.* She drummed her fingers against walls, trees, her thighs. She sucked the ends of her hair. Things had not gone wrong for so long that she began to worry that the rest of her life would be like this: peace, contentment, lethargy.

She looked up from her arithmetic and said, "I can't stand this. I'm going out." She had been toying with long division all morning, moving numbers around on the page as though they were dolls in a dollhouse, solving nothing. She had sighed loudly several times and received no attention whatsoever. Her mother had fallen asleep, her brother was absorbed in whatever he was reading, and Chopin was in his room with the door closed, piano stop-start jangling. "I'm going out," she said, again, and nobody said anything in return.

I was uneasy. It was natural that she would want to roam—of course she would, she was young and bored—but her first jaunt through the village had hardly been a great success. She had a perverse kind of boldness that bothered me, a way of catching people's eyes that was awkward in a ten-year-old. It was cause for serious concern, though none of her family members seemed to realize it. Perhaps Chopin did. If she was going out, then I was going with her.

The part of me that was not worrying was looking forward to spending quality time with Solange. For a child who was often the center of attention, she was singularly lonely and I hoped my presence might, on some subconscious level at least, make her feel more visible, make the space between the edge of her body and the start of everything else seem less vast.

She was treated by the other members of her family as a kind of barometer: if Solange's mood was good, the day would be good;

if bad, bad. She was always the first to point out injustice or to notice something was wrong, but more often than not she was scolded for noticing: always making a fuss, being overdramatic. "My little black cloud," George would say, looping Solange's hair through her fingers as the child was falling asleep. It took me some time to understand this was intended as a term of endearment. Maurice was always: "my little cub," "my bear"; Solange: "cloud," "thunder," "little tempest." How many times do you have to call a cloud a tempest before it turns stormy?

It's true that Solange was often in a huff. Sometimes she had good reason, though often she had no ostensible reason at all. She was in a huff as we left Cell Three that morning, stomping down the corridor past María Antonia's cell, and I settled inside her mind like a cat into a box. The door thudded closed behind us as we stepped into the square.

Solange, walking: the melody of one of the preludes thrumming through her head in time with her footsteps (no. 1 in C major, agitato). She sped up, breathing in the soft, herby smell of the world outside the Charterhouse in bright sunlight. Solange, walking: thinking about a little girl called Laure, who lived near her grandmother's house in France and made up scary stories based on her dreams. Laure, Solange thought, would want to hear about the Charterhouse, with its old abandoned chapels and its creaks and clanks and clatters and the way the wind sounded when it howled through the arches at night. Solange, walking: huffing and grumbling about how hungry she was, how bored she was in Mallorca, how her mother never paid attention to her, though in reality she was full to the brim with oranges from the garden, and had plenty to do, and was spending more time with George than she had in years.

She clambered across the mountainside, first down into the valley and then up the neighboring peak, as though she wanted to consume it. Big strides. Heavy steps.

I peered back through her life: it was brief, there was not much to see, and I went slowly to make what there was of it last. I looked through in reverse: the summer of that year, in Paris, when her mother had been preoccupied with Chopin. Solange coughed and whimpered and feigned weakness, but was told to sit up straight, to stop joking around. "I don't feel well," she said, repeatedly, but her mother said, "Well, you look well." Solange stamped her foot, enraged, her cheeks glowing pink.

It wasn't even a lie—*I don't feel well*—it was really very true. She did not feel well in the world; she did not feel well taken care of; she did not feel well loved.

Sometimes, when Chopin noticed her glowering in the corner, he would say, "Come over here, little cloud," and she would sit in his lap as he played the piano and watch his kid-gloved hands leaping like white rabbits across the keys. He always smelled like confections: candied verbena, violets, rose petals. She liked how large he was because he always acted as though he was small, and she liked that he liked her. The feeling of being enveloped and cherished and entertained brought her an electrifying kind of calm. When he had finished playing, she would press the keys with each finger of her right hand: C-D-E-F; *I-am-So-lange*.

Then there was the previous year, when her father of all people, a man she barely knew, had not seen regularly since she was three years old, appeared at her mother's country house and told her she was finally allowed to go "home." "This is my home," she said, pointing at the doors and windows, the gardens and the fields beyond them, hoping to imply with that gesture that within all of this were the things she cared about: the farm animals that came right up to the fences, and the wooden animals in the nursery that her tutor had painted blue and pink and green to make her laugh; her clothes. "No, no," her father said—and Solange noticed as he spoke how horrifyingly thick his eyebrows were—"you've never seen your home." (*Where was George?* I wondered, as I saw all of this. She was not there when Solange's father bundled Solange into a carriage, was not standing beside the bemused servants, the irate tutor.)

Solange's new home, once she finally saw it, was inhospitable and strange and unnerving and she determined she would fall in love with it. She would fall in love with the severe-looking woman who claimed to be her grandmother. She would fall in love with the horses and the dogs, which everybody seemed to care so much about there. And most important, she would fall in love with her father. She waited for him to pay attention to her, spend time with her, take her out for a walk or a ride, give her any opportunity whatsoever to love him. But he never came. He had simply scooped her up and deposited her somewhere unfamiliar with strangers who claimed to be family. She wrote a letter to her mother: *Mama, I have had enough of being here now thank you.* A woman who called herself Solange's aunt promised to send it, but Solange knew this was a lie. And then suddenly her mother was there, accompanied by police and bailiffs and a crowd of onlookers, producing a document that everybody handled with extreme care and that, Solange understood, decreed that she belonged to her mother and not to her father.

She held her breath as she watched her father read it, waiting to see his explosive rage, his passion, his declarations of love for her. He would never let her leave! He adored her! She was his! But instead he simply smirked and said to her mother, "Well, Aurore, I'll find a way to take Maurice instead. Watch out." As though Solange and Maurice were interchangeable. As though all this had been about hating George and not about loving Solange.

Earlier: There was Solange with George and a man, not the one Solange called "Papa", and not Chopin either; they were in a carriage driving bumpily through Paris and George was pressing muslin over Solange's mouth, telling her not to breathe the air directly. The word *cholera*. A glimpse, through the window, of a corpse being carried out of a house and Solange beginning to dread the end of the journey, wherever it was they were going to end up. But then they arrived and were nowhere terrifying at all: the zoo at the Jardin des Plantes. Solange fed Angora goats from her hand. The sticky lips and the rough hairs on their chins tickled her palm. When she saw a giraffe stumbling around inside a rotunda, taller than the trees beside it, ungainly and completely out of place, she felt a rush of recognition and ran towards it.

"What do we call the giraffe, Solange?" George asked, and when Solange said nothing George finished the joke: "Her *Highness*."

Solange nodded seriously. "I've seen her before," she said, and when the man with her mother asked her where she could possibly have seen a giraffe before, she felt confused and shrugged. "At home," she said. "In a field."

I went back and back through Solange's memories until I found the moment George first left her, or at least first left her in the most literal sense: Solange, with no idea at all what was happening, waving merrily from the window of the large, formal country house where she had lived all her life. Her mother was stepping into a carriage. Two years old, not yet coherent even in thought, Solange was full of conviction, the expectation of needs being met: *My mother will be back soon;* certainty running through her small, freshly unfurled veins. This conviction would not go on to fade so much as crystallize and then break into pieces when her father said, casually, over breakfast, "Oh, no, your mother lives in Paris now. She wants to write books. She doesn't want to be a mama anymore."

(But then, I thought, who was I, of all people, to criticize absent mothers? George and I—we both had important work to do elsewhere.)

I was so wrapped up in baby Solange, plump-faced and even more plumlike than she was at age ten, that I missed all the warning signs. I was toddling with her through the country house; I was eating whatever she could get her hands on; I was distracted. And so, by the time I was aware of what was going on it was already too late. In the real world, the present world, on the mountainside just outside Valldemossa, Solange was surrounded.

It was a group of local children. I recognized all but two of them, who must have come from the next village, or the village after that. There were a few others who I knew were from Valldemossa, but less familiar to me; I couldn't readily name their parents or say where they lived. They were all wide-eyed, in a circle around Solange, who, I now realized—how could I have forgotten how odd it was? How had I already adjusted to it?—was a little girl wearing trousers and a blouse and thus appeared to her aggressors like a lunatic.

I could tell the children were scared, though Solange could

not. They held stones up ready to throw, and when Solange said, "Who are you? What are you doing?" they released their ammunition all at once, as though they had rehearsed it.

Thuds and shocks and horror: the stinging impact against her body, her head. She crouched down and threw her arms up to protect her face. A stone hit her squarely on the elbow and the pain was hot. Her heart was hammering; adrenaline crackling. She squeezed her eyes shut and held her breath and waited for it to stop.

At some point during the attack, the object of the children's fear shifted from Solange to themselves, to the thing they were doing, and they became afraid of the situation they'd created and turned and ran as though it was she who was pelting them. Little clouds of dust and kicked-up earth in their wake.

Solange listened to the sound of their feet in the dirt, and to the sounds of the mountainside once they were gone—goat bells, birds, crickets—but it took her a long time to persuade her eyes to open. When she did dare look, she checked her arms and legs and hands and saw that they were more or less as they had been before: bruised and bloodied, but not broken.

She put her hands to her face and felt her nose: still straight. There was a trickle of blood running down her wrist, already starting to dry. Her heart was racing. She shook her hair out of her eyes. Long, lip-trembling exhale. There was nobody around, but she felt as though she was being watched, still, that the second half of the ordeal was the humiliation of its aftermath. She was determined to give nobody the satisfaction of seeing her upset. She jutted her chin out and pushed her shoulders back the way her dance tutor had taught her, back when she had lived in the big country house, and had things like dance lessons and hot baths.

She began the walk home, dragging her feet with each step to slow herself down and stop her legs from shaking. She did not want to appear to be rushing. She processed across the hillside, humming another of the preludes to keep the pace: no. 20 in C minor, largo.

ADÉLAIDE

Take your eye off George for half a day and the next thing you know there's a goat called Adélaide living in the Charterhouse.

I became aware of Adélaide's presence only gradually. I was still hovering around Solange, who had kept her chin up all the way back to the Charterhouse and then, the minute she got inside, burst into tears. She was crying in soft, unassuming little hiccups—none of the theatrics I'd seen from her before, when, for example, Maurice had inadvertently drawn in her notebook instead of his own—and she was desperate that nobody see her. She snuck off through the cloisters, prized open the door of one of the old, disused chapels, and crouched down in a corner amongst the spiders and dead leaves.

Stupid good-for-nothing country, she was thinking. *Stupid good-for-nothing Solange. Stupid, awful, too-much Solange who everybody hates, even Mama, even Maurice, even stupid good-for-nothing children who don't even know good-for-nothing me.*

Solange, I murmured back to her, *that's not how it is at all!*

She continued to cry.

And then a godless shriek reached us through the old stone walls.

Whatever had made the noise wasn't close by. It was faint, for all its shrillness; I thought perhaps it was somewhere beyond the Charterhouse. On any other day, in any other circumstance, I'd have known exactly what it was. But out of context like that, with only stone and dust and crucifixes and crying little girls as far as the eye could see, I had no idea. It could have been a demon, for all I knew, or a particularly indignant ghost. (Surge of hopeless excitement at the thought, though after centuries of disappointment I should have known better.) Solange looked up with a pinched little frown, then went back to crying.

I ignored the noise when it happened again, and again, and then it got louder and louder, shrieks coming every few seconds. And then I became aware of Maurice's voice, and then George's: giddy peals of laughter. They were somewhere nearby. And then it became very apparent that they were somewhere nearby with a goat.

I left Solange and went in search of them. They weren't hard to find: George and Maurice in fits of laughter as they tried to cajole the goat along the cloisters. They had a rope around her neck and were taking turns pulling on it and walking behind offering support in the form of taps either side of her tail. The goat was reluctant, to put it mildly, planting her hooves on the tiled floor and shrieking her objections. She was a sugary shade of brown, with eyelashes so long they drooped over her eyes and ears that flapped when she shook her cross little head.

"This way, sweet one," George was saying, when she caught her breath. "This way, my love, my darling, my goat, my dear." (In her language, these three words—*darling* and *goat* and *dear*— sounded very similar, *chérie* and *chèvre* and *chère*, which set Maurice off laughing again.) She thrust a handful of hay towards it and shook it. "This way!"

"My dear goat," Maurice said. "My dear, expensive goat."

George wafted the hay near the goat's face again, and said, "Eat well, my dear, expensive goat," for which I can offer no sensible translation but involved another word that sounded like "goat," like "dear," like "expensive": *fais bonne chère, ma chère chère chèvre.*

And so on, and so on. They made slow progress, giggling and punning their way around the cloisters. I could see where they were aiming: the courtyard where there was a little patch of scrubby grass, and in which the goat could be contained. It was not, I thought, an appropriate place to start a farmyard: it hardly ever saw the sun, and had a lonely sort of unkemptness to it. But I supposed the seclusion was what drew them. The goat would be sequestered, safe from thieves, who could easily scale the garden wall. They could keep her away from María Antonia, even, who was as guilty as the delivery boys of watering down Chopin's milk.

Once the goat was finally installed in the courtyard and released from her halter, she urinated firmly on the grass and did an awkward little trot from one side to the other. She was looking bemused and wary, as though expecting a shock.

"You're free!" said Maurice.

"You're home!" said George. "Be happy!"

The goat did not look happy to be home and emitted a shriek that made Maurice flinch. "She'll be all right here, won't she?"

George nodded briskly. "She has hay, she has all the old fruit she can eat from our trees, she has us for company."

"Do you think she's missing her baby?" Maurice pressed. The goat's udder was bulbous and pink.

"Of course not," said George, whose smile faded at the suggestion. As though to ease the tension, the goat began to defecate against a wall, fixing her eyes on Maurice.

"Look," said George, "she's feeling quite at home."

The goat shrieked again, and this was when Solange shuffled into the courtyard, looking forlorn and disheveled, and began bleating, "Mama? Mama? Maurice? Mama? What's going on?"

"Oh," said George. "Solange."

"We've got a goat," Maurice said, pointing at the goat. "Mama paid a lot of money to a very stupid boy for one and he didn't seem to like it at all but he took the money and let us take the goat, so here she is and she's ours now."

"Why do we need a goat?" Solange forgot, for a second, that she was feeling fragile, and spoke with her usual sharpness.

"I'm sick of paying through the teeth for that watery piss they call milk," said George. "It's making Chopin sicker than ever and I've had enough of it. So I've gone straight to the horse's mouth. To the goat's teat. We'll milk her ourselves and it's going to help Chopin get well again. What happened to your head?" George glanced distractedly at her daughter, noticing for the first time her dishevelment.

"I was attacked," said Solange. "By about a hundred people on the hillside." She began to cry again.

Maurice went over to her and pulled her into a hug. He stroked her hair. "Of course you were, little sister," he said. "Of course you were."

George cast an eye over her daughter. She noted what was real (the bruises, the trail of dried blood crackling on her wrist) and what was exaggerated (the chest-heaving sobs, the tall tale). She wished her daughter would, just for once, be truthful; it would make it so much easier to sympathize. As it was, there was something in Solange's neediness that repelled her, and then she felt shame for feeling so unnaturally towards her own child, which in turn made her angry with Solange for making her feel bad.

"Any broken bones?" George said. Solange shook her head. "And the people who attacked you, were they adults or children, and did you fight back, and did you have the last word?"

"I did," Solange said. "I did have the last word." It was what her mother hoped to hear, and Solange wanted, more than anything, more than sympathy, to make her mother proud.

George, reassured that whatever Solange had been up to was something childish and therefore unthreatening, turned her attention back to the goat. "What shall we name her?"

Maurice said, "Catullus."

George said, "Mallorquina?"

Solange said, "Solange."

"Let's think. What do we know about her?" George said. "She is brown. She is pretty. She is very, very sweet."

"She has milk," offered Maurice.

"She shits in our house," said Solange.

"She has milk," echoed George. And that was how the name came about.

She has milk, the way George said it, was *Elle a du lait. A du lait; Adélaide;* it amused them and they kept playing with the words, tossing them up in the air and catching them, tying them in knots. They said, *Elle a du lait* so many times it stopped having any meaning at all, became nonsensical. They added consonants and meanings. They laughed a lot.

Elle a de l'aide. She has help.

Elle a de la laine. She has wool.

Elle a des laideronnes. She has ugly women.

But most important about Adélaide was that she really did have milk. None of them knew how to milk her, but they dragged Amélie from María Antonia's room to show them how to do it. Adélaide was a good sport about the whole thing, and muted her bleating to a few reluctant huffs as Amélie tugged and twisted at her udder.

"This goat is an angel," said George, watching the sharply etched frown on Amélie's forehead soften as she worked and sniffing the air for the sharp smell of fresh milk. She pulled Solange and Maurice closer to her side. "This goat will solve all our problems."

PRELUDE NO. 9
IN E MAJOR, LARGO

Chopin's longing for his Pleyel piano became almost romantic. He pined for it as though it was a lost lover, sitting with his knees tucked under the inferior Mallorcan model. He thought about the way the keys had met his fingers with pressure, as though touching him back. It seemed to him that he was being punished for abandoning it in the first place, that the piano would never forgive him, would not come back to him after such a betrayal. Sometimes he would think he heard it, a single crisp note played from somewhere behind him, and would spin around, heart aflutter, to find only the bare walls of the cell and the vaulted ceiling.

There had been no news of the piano since they arrived at Palma to learn it was still in France, and he feared something had happened to it on the voyage. He had written to friends in Paris demanding news, but all they knew was that it had been shipped from Marseille. Chopin began to dream about water, his piano plunging through clouds of seaweed, past fish. The texture of piano strings and the texture of fish scales. Deep-sea creatures. Tentacles grasping the pedals. Air bubbles rising from a depressed F-sharp.

He was working on a prelude he had begun in Paris and this made the contrast between the two instruments particularly glaring. On the old piano, *his* piano, the piece had sounded sonorous and significant, melancholy enough not to seem too grand, bright enough not to seem waterlogged. On the Mallorcan piano it was reedy and insubstantial and bogged down. He persevered nonetheless, hands clustered together on the lower half of the keyboard, feeling their way over the black keys like crabs across rocks. Chopin was drawn into a place where there were no walls, no doors, nothing was contained, and the prelude swelled and ebbed, wave upon wave, crescendoing loud enough to drown out, for example, the sound of a goat shrieking as it was led down nearby cloisters. By the end of the piece, if he was really immersed, Chopin could feel almost uncomplicated: sanguine and clear-sighted and content.

"Chip-chip?" Solange, disheveled, dusty, skin striped with dried blood, was standing in the doorway of his room.

She waited for Chopin to register her. Her bruises were throbbing like hearts and the realization of what had happened on the hillside kept coming to her anew. Having found no consolation in her mother and brother, she had left them behind with the goat. The pain began to burrow deep, hot and vague, so that her bones started to hurt and she wanted more than anything for Chopin to turn around and look at her. He seemed elsewhere, his back to her and his fingers spread across the keys, though he had stopped playing.

"Chop-chop? Chopin? It's Solange. Chip-chip?"

Her voice had reached Chopin on the ocean floor, but it was taking some time for him to rise to the surface. He found his way towards the light and then, slowly, looked over at her.

"Solange?"

He started at the sight of her, recoiling on the piano stool, gripping its edges. When Solange saw his reaction she burst into loud tears.

"Solange? Where's your mother?"

"With Adélaide," she said, without explanation. "What happened to you, Solange?" Chopin asked.

She went to him and pressed her dirty face against his shirt.

"What happened?" he asked again, but in response she only burrowed deeper into his armpit.

George and Maurice arrived in Chopin's doorway, still thrilled by the milk, triumphant, swinging a pail between them.

"You'll never guess what I've done!" said George. "What I've done for *you*, my dear!"

Chopin did not guess. "What has happened to Solange?" he snapped.

George's smile fell. "Oh, she's all right."

I had never seen Chopin so angry. He was brittle with rage, jutting his fingers into the air as though daring them to snap. He was gesturing at Solange, who was still pressing herself against him, and I realized for the first time how much he loved her.

"What?" George asked. "Is she not all right? What is it?"

Chopin peeled Solange off his chest and waved his hands at her face. She stood there, limp, watching her mother.

"I was attacked," said Solange, in a rare moment of good judgment deciding less was more and opting for the truth. "By some children. Mallorcan children. With rocks."

George surveyed her daughter and saw her afresh, how small she was and how outraged and hurt. She had assumed that Solange had simply taken a tumble and decided to dramatize it. Now she saw that her daughter was injured and telling the truth. It became suddenly easy to care for her. "Oh, darling." She gathered Solange up, squeezing her shoulders, placing a palm across the back of her head. "Oh, darling. Was it very bad? We should put you straight to bed to rest."

"Wash her!" Chopin's voice sounded girlish and odd. He swallowed. "Wash her first. She's filthy."

"Of course I'll wash her first," said George, not looking at him as she ushered Solange out of the room. "I know how to care for my own child."

George pushed Solange past Maurice, who was standing in the doorway gawping. He hovered in her wake, unsure what to do with himself. He wondered why it was he felt so angry with his sister, why the image of her throwing herself upon Chopin had made the blood rush straight to his cheeks. She was just a child, he told himself. She wasn't doing anything. He stayed in the doorway, watching Chopin brush dirt off his shirt. He imagined striding over to Chopin and punching him: the way Chopin would crumple to the floor like wet laundry snatched from the line. Maurice had a clear, horrifying vision, of Chopin's head cracking against the corner of the piano lid, limpness, a slumped body.

Chopin loves Solange, I thought.

Maurice hates Chopin, I thought.

It would be too simple to say: I wished they could all get along. But even after hundreds of years of experience, I was still naïve enough to think it was at very least possible. I certainly felt, then, that it was more likely than not they would be all right. I considered Chopin and Maurice as they considered each other. *What sort of men are you?* I asked. *What do you have in you?*

Not for the first time, I felt the urge to dip into their minds and look forward. *What sort of men will you become?* I imagined future-Maurice, grown tall and broader-shouldered, his nature crystallized. Gentle, sweet Maurice, who liked to sketch his sister while she played. Vicious, jealous Maurice, who clenched his fists as he imagined Chopin's skull connecting with the lid of the piano.

When I tried to imagine Chopin's future, I saw nothing at all. A vacancy. Blank as the white keys.

From the other room: the sound of George ordering Amélie to bring water for Solange. "Hot water, Amélie. I mean really hot." Solange was whimpering a little. There was a thud as Amélie dropped something. "Careful," said George, and then a little murmuring from Amélie in response.

Maurice loitered between the two rooms, staring at Chopin, ignoring the scene behind him.

Chopin, satisfied that Solange was, for now at least, being cared for and wishing to signal that his involvement with the situation was over, pivoted back to the piano. He wanted to return to his prelude, to slide back into the water and let his body sink. He let the fingers of his left hand settle across the E major chord. But he could sense Maurice behind him, staring, emitting hostility like a strange smell.

Chopin pulled back. "What is it, Maurice? What do you want?"

Maurice twisted his lips. His heart beat hard. He should say something, he thought, and wished the blush in his cheeks would pale. He wished that, faced with Chopin's immense foppishness, he felt commensurately strong.

"You should be kinder to my mother," Maurice said in a voice that broke halfway through the sentence. "She bought you a goat."

GEORGE REMEMBERS

There's a thick seam itching against George's inner thigh. She wants to reach between her legs and scratch. She glances at other people on the street: nobody is looking at her, nobody would notice. Men do it all the time. And yet she finds herself incapable of making the movement; she imagines her grandmother watching her, imagines the scrutiny of every passerby. She cannot do it. The itch starts to feel like a burn.

The cost of wearing trousers: this niggling crotch irritant.

And this is the reward: that nobody looks twice at her as she hightails it across Paris in the rain. Her boots keep the water out and she adores them for it—sometimes wants to fall asleep in them because taking them off feels like a kind of defeat. They are solid, their iron heels thudding on the pavement. When she plants a step, the ground grips her back. She feels bigger now, and more justified. She can go anywhere.

Why did nobody tell her, she wonders. When she first arrived in Paris, she spent almost all the allowance from her husband on the kinds of clothes she saw Parisian ladies wearing: feathered hats that made it hard to turn your head quickly, brittle little pumps. But she tore through shoes and overshoes, petticoats,

coats, and overcoats as though she was deliberately destroying them. The dresses got spattered in mud thrown up by vehicles in the street; the shoes wilted off her feet like dying flowers; the headwear was impossible from the start. Why did nobody tell her that the clothes she bought were made for sitting in, for stepping gingerly from drawing room to carriage and back? They were not made for marching along the Rue de Seine up to the river and into the Mazarine Library, or across the river to haggle over firewood at the market. Once, on her way to the salon of a person she knew only slightly, wearing a particularly complicated hat, fronds of which were constantly getting in her eyes, she ran into an old friend who looked at her quizzically and said, *You look like a boy dressed up as a woman.*

Why did nobody say: *Take off that silly hat, George.* Why didn't they say: *Men have been wearing boots all along, you know, with solid soles and metal heels; you should try it; you might like it.* Why didn't they say: *Put on a pair of trousers and see how fast you can run with the wind between your legs—it will blow your mind.*

Now, she is head to toe in thick gray cloth. The frock coat she ordered is long, in the fashionable style; it reaches her ankles. It flaps vaguely and generously around her lower half, transforming her buttocks and calves into an assumption of masculine flatness. From behind, she is confident, she looks the part. The front, admittedly, troubled her at first, where the coat flares open to reveal the air between her legs. There was this sudden hyperawareness of her crotch—worse, of her genitals—that made walking, even taking a leisurely stroll, feel obscene. Where once was a froth of skirts and underskirts and stockings, there was now this giddy void.

They can see right through me, she caught herself thinking.

She remembered her father bellowing at her half brother, *Boy, you walk as though there's nothing between your legs!* and her brother blushing pink before assuming a broader stance. She thought it to herself then: *Boy, there is nothing between your legs.* Negative space like an arrow pointing directly at her vulva.

Now, she stands a little taller. She sets her feet wider apart. The feeling of being exposed has washed away, leaving only this tide line of doubt: the fear that scratching an itch between her legs might somehow give the game away. She takes a breath and plunges her hand down, digging her nails through the fabric of the trousers. The relief is orgasmic and nobody is watching. She feels powerful, almost invisible, as she scratches and scratches like a flea-ridden stray.

Hey! Excuse me! The child's voice behind her is urgent and George freezes in place, like a pickpocket reaching for a purse.

She lifts her hand away from her crotch. She turns around.

Excuse me, the boy says. There's something wild in his face, as though he's sleepwalking or mad. She would think he was drunk if he weren't so very young. He looks to be Maurice's age, seven, maybe younger. He is wearing a coat much too big for him, tatty and unwashed. He starts to open it and for a dizzy moment George thinks he is going to reveal a female body underneath. She takes a step back and looks around, but even now nobody is watching. The street is full of people not noticing her, not noticing this ragged little boy who is digging into the innermost pockets and producing something, a squirming lump of something, white and brown and pink, and saying, *Sir, please, I found this. Would you take her, sir? I can't keep her and I think she'll die.*

A puppy wriggles in his hand as he holds it out towards her, its eyes barely open.

That dog should be with its mother, George says.

She shouldn't have been left alone, the boy says. *She was alone when I found her. I think she'll die.*

So now George has a dog.

She has been in Paris for three weeks. She has taken a lover and rooms on Rue de Seine, Saint-Germain. The lover, Jules Sandeau, is only nineteen, a writer, incredibly sensitive and intriguing. She plays with his hair and he says he has had an idea for a story. *Stay there, just like that,* he'll say, as though he's about to paint her. He dashes to his desk to start scribbling and she does her best to freeze in place wherever she is, on the sofa or standing by the fire, wobbling slightly like an unfinished statue still in the clay. After a while she says, *Did you still need me like this?* and he looks up, blinking, and says, *What? Oh. No, no, I was writing about something else.*

Her lover is dramatically, emphatically talented. This is what she tells him and herself. A lightning conductor, except the lightning is good writing. *As adorable as a hummingbird,* she writes. Everyone says, *There's Jules, the genius,* and he smiles wanly. He is very young and will be more brilliant than anyone else, or would be, at least, if he would only focus and snap out of his bad moods. George takes care of him with all of the energy no longer sapped by Maurice and Solange, though she thinks of them, both of them, all the time, back at the country house without her, and that in itself is draining. She considers sending for them, but when she tries to imagine being who she is now and a mother to them all at the same time, her resolve falters and she doesn't ask them to come.

She spends so much time with Jules that it makes more sense just to move in with him. She keeps his rooms tidy, and when he needs money she helps him write his articles for *Le Figaro*, *La Mode*, and *L'Artiste*. With George behind him, Jules becomes prolific.

George, for her part, finds herself suddenly ignorant. It was easier to feel clever in the countryside with her husband. Here in Paris, she and Jules attend parties full of intellectual young men who have read everything before it is even published, who have seen the latest play, it seems to her, before the opening night. They talk about *tone* and *emotion* and *feeling* in art as though those things were utterly divorced from real emotion, real feeling. They are impossibly cultured.

It occurs to her in a vague, panicked sense that the claims these young men make about their erudition and learning are *literally* not possible. Their art is, above all, that of exaggeration. But why would anyone lie about something as simple, as essential, as reading?

Have you read the new Hugo? they say, and she wants to reply: *I will read the new Hugo when I can afford to buy it without going hungry.* She cannot understand how these men, who have as little money as she does, or less, afford themselves so much knowledge.

Have you seen the new play at the Porte Saint-Martin? they say, and since women aren't allowed into the pits of the theaters, where the tickets are cheap, this is what first tips George into ordering her gray frock coat and trousers and boots.

In the days that follow the nights at the salons, she sits on the balcony of Jules's apartment, taking in the view of the Seine and all the little bridges crossing it like stitches over a wound. Across the river, the Louvre is bright yellow in the sun, crisp against the spring sky. She wants to reach out into the city and grab a handful and stuff it into her mouth. She wants to walk down every single one of those streets, march into every theater and demand to be entertained. She wants to lift the rooftops off the houses like covers from books and rifle through the rooms. She wants to read everything.

She takes her new puppy to the parties and wears the new gray coat and trousers. Jules doesn't mind—likes it, even—and it's fun to have people come up to pet the dog, introducing themselves to George as though for the first time. There's a funny little start they give when they look away from the animal to her face and realize who they are talking to. She lights a cigar and shakes her hair loose and laughs. *It's just me,* she says. *I have taken on a new form.*

She puts the puppy on the floor, where it scrambles about, chewing shoelaces and chasing heels. She judges people by how they react to it, remembering those who avoid or skirt around it and remembering those who play. The world is full of cowards, she thinks, and it turns out that sometimes the opposite of cowardice is playfulness.

What do we think about the new Musset? says a young man she knows only from literary gatherings like this. He has been working on the same poem for the entirety of the time George has known him and has never once remembered her name. He has caught a cold on the journey over; in the sudden heat of the room, his skin has come out in blotches.

Everyone says the new Musset is wonderful or awful or disappointing or groundbreaking.

What about you? He turns to George. *Have you read the new Musset?*

She has indeed read it. She got hold of a copy in draft, borrowed from a friend of a friend two weeks before it came out in the *Revue des Deux Mondes. Yes,* she says, *I've read it,* and realizes, looking at the faces of the men in the circle, unstable in the flickering light of the salon, that she is the only person telling the truth.

She tucks this knowledge away into the breast pocket of her new coat like a half-blind, half-furred puppy: she is not more stupid than anyone.

What did you think of the ending? she says to the poet. *I would love to hear, in detail, your thoughts about the ending.*

She leaves the party early that night, and alone.

PARIS

Adélaide grazed in the courtyard, teats swinging low to the ground. When she climbed up the little steps that led to the locked gate to the cloisters, her nipples brushed blades of grass and the edges of the stone. She was, by nature, an optimist: every morning she would do a circuit of the courtyard, seeking a way out that she might have missed the day before. Finding no escape route, she bleated softly and bemusedly. The sound went right through me.

At night, she huddled in a corner under the dubious shelter of a dead seedling and closed her eyes. I tried, pointlessly, to get inside her head. As with all my other attempts to understand animals, this failed. The closest I could get was a bleary, fuzzy redness: the shade of the insides of eyelids.

I imagined that Adélaide was dreaming about the hillside. I imagined that her body hurt with worry about her kid. I imagined that she felt suddenly deaf, suddenly mute, suddenly invisible, secluded as she was, as though she had died and been reborn in the Charterhouse, very alone and friendless. I found it easy to imagine these things.

She had me, of course. I tried my best to entertain her by ushering birds in her direction. Sometimes she noticed and directed her bleating at them. She had Maurice, who sketched her from the top of the steps and said things to her like, "There's a good goat" and "Dear little goat." Solange came by and gazed adoringly at Adélaide, and sometimes, in the middle of the night if the moon was bright, George would wander through the cloisters to the courtyard and stand silent under an archway watching Adélaide sleep or shift her weight from hoof to hoof.

Adélaide had all of us, but her real friend, it turned out, was Amélie. Amélie alone could persuade Adélaide to hush her cries. When Amélie appeared in the courtyard, Adélaide would skip towards her and head butt the backs of her knees. It seemed to me that Adélaide sensed and recognized Amélie's indentured gloom.

Amélie couldn't find a milking stool. She inspected the steps, which were moss-slimed and damp and permanently in shadow. When she pressed the moss with a foot, water bubbled up as though she was squeezing a sponge. In the end she used a pile of hassocks she had found in a corner of one of the old chapels. They were fraying and moth-eaten and smelled of mildew. Before sitting down, she laid one of Maurice's shirts across them. It was a precarious seat: she had to keep Adélaide stiller than Adélaide ideally liked to be; she had to splay her feet to keep steady as she milked. Any time Adélaide took a step forwards the pair of them would wrestle, Amélie by turns grabbing, cajoling, and steering Adélaide backwards towards the hassock pile, Adélaide harrumphing and snorting and shuffling side to side. This happened every morning.

For all that they tussled, Adélaide seemed to have as good an effect on Amélie as Amélie did on Adélaide. Amélie smiled to herself when Adélaide ran to greet her, an unassuming little uptilt at the corners of her mouth; I looked back over everything that had happened since the family's arrival and realized that nobody was ever particularly interested, let alone pleased, to see Amélie. Compared to Solange's tantrums and constant small needs ("Can I have an orange from the garden, Amélie? No but can you *squeeze* it for me, Amélie? No but I don't like the *bits*, Amélie!") and María Antonia's supervision, Adélaide was a breeze.

The goat milk was well received by Chopin, who drank it mixed with almond milk that George and the children made themselves, and really did seem to think it helped him. Amélie would bring it directly to his room, and he would perk up at the sight of it. For the first time since Chopin had joined George's household, he met Amélie's eye and thanked her.

Amélie began milking Adélaide more than was strictly necessary, and within a few days this "milking" had come to involve a lot of sitting on the hassocks stroking Adélaide's beard and humming. At first it was only a few minutes, then it stretched to a half hour, then a full hour spent daydreaming about her return to France. She fantasized about wearing different clothes to the two dresses she wore in rotation in Mallorca. She pictured sleeping in a room where María Antonia was not: how quiet it would be, how fresh it would smell. She sat with a dopey little smirk on her face, in bright, cold sun, and in the drizzle, and in the early morning fog.

I felt guilty, watching Amélie soften and sweeten in Adélaide's company, for paying so little attention to her. *Poor Amélie,* I whispered to her. *Poor Amélie, so far from home and so utterly pissed off about everything.*

Each morning she sat down and considered the date: counting how long they had been in Mallorca and how long until spring came. She had it in her head that the family would return to Paris in the spring. And so she made a point of keeping track of the shrinking number of days until the winter was over and she could go home.

I liked Amélie's Paris memories. She was so good at savoring small pleasures: the sweetness of a stray sugar crystal from George's plate dissolving on her tongue, the arrival of gas lamps at the Place du Carrousel and how the new, frothy light clung to curls of fog rising off the Seine. I liked walking with her around the Square d'Orléans, where George's most recent apartment had been, to the Rue Saint-Lazare, where milliners and dressmakers kept their shops, and where, on their half day off, Amélie and her friend Sylvie would play a game of "What would you steal?"

Once, Amélie really had stolen something: a shawl, dropped by a lady stepping into one of the shops. It was unthinking. Amélie didn't even hesitate, just pounced like a street cat hunting sparrows. She didn't dare look at it until she was home, but later, as she inspected it, she realized she didn't even like it: the colors were brash and there was mud on it from where it had fallen on the street. The next day she took it out with her when she went to buy the little marzipan fruits that Solange liked and dropped it at the feet of a beggar, who snatched it up as quickly as she herself had done. It was funny to think of it, wherever it was now, passed and snatched and thrust from person to person, making its way across the city to God knows where.

Memories of Paris pleased Amélie, and her pleasure was so pleasurable that this was where both of us spent the most time. But we were always disturbed, eventually, by George or Maurice or Solange stomping into the courtyard reporting that María Antonia needed help with cooking. Amélie's body would change when this happened: it felt as though she were being crushed by her own skin. She would be cold suddenly. She would realize she had lost the feeling in her fingers, that she had pins and needles in one foot.

And then there was a time when the interruption came from beyond the Charterhouse walls. It was the day after Christmas and Amélie and I had been milking and reminiscing, enjoying in particular a memory of the sky over Paris just before snowfall, velvety as the clothes of the women who called on George and fawned over her and drank her tea. We were engrossed; the bells ringing from the church barely registered with us. But then the sound of footsteps and voices on the other side of the Charter-house wall found their way through the cloisters to the courtyard. There was no mistaking it, the pitch of the conversation, the pace of the footfall: a funeral. Amélie's skin tightened a little. This was how I discovered that she was very afraid of death.

Don't be scared, I said.

It's fine, I lied.

As for me, I was alarmed. I was caught off guard. I wondered whose corpse was being borne up the hill towards us, running through likely candidates: the Sacristan (optimistic), the elderly father of the butcher, the sickly baby of one of Señora Porras's friends. Except it wasn't any of them, and I began to know that somehow.

I left Amélie and went to watch. The men carrying the coffin appeared to find it very light, as though they had forgotten to put the body inside. I scanned the faces of the mourners and knew all at once who it was.

Bernadita? I called. I sort of howled it. *Bernadita!*

I knew it was her because the faces of the mourners indicated sadness but not too much. They were mourning an old person. I knew it was her because her best friend was walking alone, carrying some lace that Bernadita particularly liked, waving it like a flag. I knew it was her because she was not amongst the mourners, and because eventually the mutterings of the mourners confirmed it. I felt a strange sort of narrowing, lightness, the closest I have ever felt while dead to the sensation of being about to faint. I kept calling her name, pointlessly: *Bernadita?*

I had not even known her well, which made it worse. I had, as centuries and decades passed, lost interest in my family. I had kept an eye out for them, and generally made a point of looking in on them as much as I could, but my visits to Bernadita had grown less and less frequent, and my last glimpse of her, shuffling towards the market the day I had checked up on the Sacristan, had been fleeting, inconsequential. When was the last time I had told her I loved her, was proud of her, was grateful to her for showing me what life was like when lived at length and gently?

Bernadita was gone. I could find no ghost of her. As I followed the procession to the graveyard, where they had already dug a hole beside the other members of my family, beside—how peculiar, every time, to imagine it—me, I caused a ruckus. I yelled loud enough for birds to notice and take flight, lifting off in a rush and causing all the mourners to look up. I hurled some fruit around, grabbed a woman's scarf and threw it on the ground; I kicked a baby, who burst into the sort of tears I felt I deserved.

I don't want to be alone, I said. *I don't understand why I am here alone.*

I REMEMBER

I wait for Ham. He does not appear. It's raining and there's no shelter on the beach. Since I'm wet enough already I swim, floating about aimlessly and squinting at the cliff tops. What I imagine is Ham's head appearing over the top of the rocks turns out to be: a bird, a branch, another bird, a particularly dark cloud. I think, *Ham is coming, Ham is coming, Ham is coming,* in time with my foot kicks. My brain responds, *Ham hates you, Ham hates you, Ham hates you.* For a brief moment I am angry like I've never been in my life: how dare he leave me like this, not knowing whether he's all right, not knowing what he's thinking, how dare he just— And then the rage is gone, as suddenly as it appeared, and in its place is a great remorse, the knowledge I have let him down, that this was not what he wanted, that really it is no wonder if he doesn't come today, because after all what I have done—what my body is now unmistakably doing—is unforgivable.

I swim until my fingers are wrinkled, and then I sit on the rocks, naked and shivering, and when I realize I'll never dry off in the rain, I dress, my hands so cold that I fumble with the buttons, the fabric sticking to my skin. Still he doesn't come. The anticlimax, the downpour: unbearable, truly, and I want to find some small cranny in the rocks to curl up in, would rather be anywhere, really, than back at my mother's house, but since there is nowhere else to go and I'm hungry, I trudge home, dragging my feet through the mud.

Well, my mother says. *What did he say?* She has been anticipating this meeting, if possible, even more hotly than I have.

I look away. Can't bear to meet her eye. *Nothing,* I say. *He didn't come.*

Oh, Blanca, she says. She deflates towards a chair. *Oh, Blanca.* She has been talking about my next rendezvous with Ham all week, ever since I explained what has been going on, with the feast day procession and the swimming and beach and all the sex Ham and I were having and now, the sudden inconvenient fact of my swelling up the way I am. She pinned all her hopes on it, resolutely refusing to worry.

He's not a monk yet, is he, so he'll just have to never be one, and marry you instead, she said.

Yes, I said. *That was the plan anyway.* I did not mention that this is a plan of which Ham has always been unaware.

He'll explain the details to you next week, she said. *He'll have had time to think about it, and then when you see him he'll explain when he's going to leave the Charterhouse, when the wedding will be.*

And now the reality is that she was wrong, has got this wrong. Her face, when I can bring myself to look at it, has crumpled a little.

Even worse: she has already told everyone all about it, that I am getting married, that she can't share any details just yet but that the young man is very educated and interesting and good looking and that the wedding will be very soon. She has told my sister, the neighbors, the people she meets at the market. She left out the pregnancy, to everyone except my sister; she left out any information about when or how my future husband and I met, but still, it is now common knowledge and the horror of Ham's absence is magnified when I think of this: everyone in the village watching as my body balloons and then bursts, all the questions about this husband that will fail to materialize, about the baby that *will* materialize, uninvited and unknown, a stranger hammering at the door. My sister is already interrogating me, incredulous that I have somehow leapfrogged her, that I turned out to have already known what she was so desperate to tell me.

I'm going to lie down, I say to my mother, because talking about it will only make it worse now. I can't bear to listen to her attempts to make sense of it, to excuse Ham, to concoct a hundred different reasons why he didn't show up that absolve him of any responsibility.

Alone in the bedroom, I contemplate my body more energetically than ever before. Body: which has carried me to the beach and back all those times to see Ham. Body: which Ham appreciated, or really seemed to, which he touched and moved and shunted and bent and sweated over. Body: which has ideas of its own now, is at work on its own project, nothing to do with me at all, thrumming and busy and announcing, in the form of my rounding abdomen, its intentions. Hand on my stomach, I press down, almost expecting something to push back, indignant.

Blanca? My mother is standing in the doorway. I groan, cover my eyes.

Come on, she says.

Come where?

We're going.

I roll over to face her. She looks resolute. Has put on her best clothes and a stern expression, as though she is going to go to Mass, or to battle, or to the house of a friend she particularly dislikes.

Going where?

To the Charterhouse, she says. *If that boy won't speak to you, we'll just have to speak to him. We have to make him see some sense about all of this.*

I GAVE MYSELF A BODY

I curled up in George's dirty clothes like a mouse. It helped calm me, the smell of skin and tobacco smoke on the fabric. My many-times-great-granddaughter had been buried alongside the rest of us, and the mourners had processed back down the hill, and after hours going full tilt in my anger, I was empty. It was early morning, still dark.

I had taken to squirreling away George's shirts, hiding them in the rafters above the cell so I could visit them alone. I liked the feel of things she had felt against her own body. I felt stronger just being near the smell of her. I felt more like myself and less familiar to myself all at once, as though in all my years of being dead there had been this small, living seed that was only then starting to germinate.

I imagined, sometimes, that they were *my* clothes, that I could be as real and sharp and clothed as George, could straddle a wall and smoke a cigar and write a book. That night, though, I was so tired and so alone that I imagined the clothes were George herself, that she was enveloping me, pressing back when I pressed her. I had been lonely for centuries, and now, without Bernadita, my last tangible link to the living, breathing world was gone. There was no more of my flesh and blood walking around; I was untethered entirely. I clung to George's shirts as tightly as I could, wrapping myself up in the smell of her, hoping that she could keep me moored and in one piece. I peeped down through cracks in the plaster at the top of her head: she was writing at her desk, hand barely pausing as she passed it across the paper. I could see the blue pale of her scalp where her hair parted.

I love you, I said, nuzzling a cuff.

Below me, George's concentration broke. She sighed in a way that reminded me of Adélaide: guttural. She put the pen down, stretched her arms above her head, laced her fingers together, and flipped her palms faceup. Her knuckles cracked.

I love you, I said.

She stood up. The chair legs scraped the floor.

I love you, I said, and what I saw through the ceiling cracks then was a sliver of eyeball. George was looking up.

My heart—where my heart had been—quickened. Eyes— where eyes had been—prickled with instant near-tears. Skin— where skin had been—suddenly very hot. George was looking up at the place where I was and she was therefore—it was not too much of a stretch to say, surely?—looking at me.

Deep breaths where breaths used to be, I told myself. *Savor it.*

I was all aflame, ignited, cheeks—where cheeks had been— flushed.

What is desire, without a body to have it in? All I can say is that to me it was like the kind of hunger people get in dreams. It was formless, gutless, all-consuming because unconfined. It had no edges. I say it was like a dream, but the truth is that I no longer dreamed—I no longer slept—so the analogy is approximate. Back then I missed dreaming almost as much as I missed the things I used to dream about.

What I did to make up for the loss of dreams was teach myself to fantasize freely and loosely. At first this had seemed like an effort, as arduous as learning to read, but over time it came easily, naturally, often unexpectedly. I would find that hours had passed and I had been elsewhere entirely, thinking about the taste of bacon: the sting of salt on the tongue, slivers of fat stuck between the teeth, and the tingling wide-open sensation on the gums when, the day afterwards, the scraps came loose. Or I thought about my mother, hot-breathed and earthy and annoyed after a day of tending pigs, arriving home and stroking my cheek and saying, *Get me a drink, would you, Blanca?* I thought about all the people I used to love who were dead. I brought them back to life. I asked them how they were.

Often there were revenge fantasies: monks who did unspeakable things, the men in the village who never seemed to notice the damage they were doing to women. The Sacristan. The man responsible for my own death, too: I thought about him plenty. I imagined fates that none of them, in real life, received. Torrents of blood. Elaborate torture devices. A little speech I'd deliver while they were still conscious enough to understand, explaining that they were bad, that they were being punished for being bad, and now they were going to die. It was a nasty, brilliant kind of pleasure. It felt very pure.

But never had my fantasies been as vivid, as overwhelming, as delightful, as the fantasies I had about George.

In those, I gave myself a body—not the body I'd had when I was alive, but an older, stronger, better one. I gave myself outfits, too: the kind George wore, trousers, shirts, sturdy shoes. I gave myself a swagger as I walked into the room where George was sitting and said, *Hello, darling.* And George would look up and see me (See me! The thrill!) and say, *Hello, you,* and we would find that we were speaking the same language.

The body I gave myself was visible, tangible, and so it was easy to think, when George locked eyes with me through the ceiling cracks, that the next thing she'd do would be to beckon me down into the room and draw me towards her with a hand cupping the back of my head. It was easy to feel her fingers entangled in my hair. To taste her mouth, really taste it, the dusty tobacco taste of her saliva. A spit-glossed tooth sliding across my lip. Her tongue, rough and firm and granular. I spent a long time on her tongue, imagining its textures, its directions.

In my fantasies, having sex with George was loud and unrestrained: she would make noises from the back of her throat, gripping my arms hard enough to bruise them. She was the same wild, cagey George she was at night, when only I was allowed near her, only me with my mouth trailing over her breasts, stomach, thighs, and my fingers inside her where it was hot and as smooth as the inside of a shell. All of this was possible in the seconds that passed when George was looking up at the ceiling.

And then she looked away. It was beginning to get light and birdsong in the garden drew her attention to the window: a view of faintly lightening mist, interrupted by branches of the pomegranate tree. Sparrows were hopping from twig to twig, chattering. And then, from the blue-gray haze, a dark bulk emerged, growing and blackening as it approached. It was a bird of prey, wings broad as palm leaves, coming in at speed. George stiffened, imagining the moment of impact, the window frame shattering, the claws against her face. At the last second, the bird swerved towards the tree and plucked a sparrow from the lowest branch. Quick: as though it were twisting a fruit from its stem. Too quick to see the sparrow struggle. And then it shot upwards into the mist, out of sight. The rest of the flock took off. There was a sudden silence in their absence.

George sat and looked at the empty tree. She shook her head as though to wake herself up, as though questioning whether she had seen anything at all.

I wanted to grab her face and point it up towards me again. *No*, I said, *come back. Come back like you were before.* I wanted to return to the fleshiness of the two of us.

Come back and touch me. Turn your big black eyes right on me and see me from the inside out. Put out your cigars on my lungs. Spit coffee into my mouth. Write your spidery words all over my stomach.

I was being a creep and I knew it. What right did I have to judge the Sacristan, the way his eyes always trailed so slowly over the backs of the girls who stood in front of him in church, when I was behaving positively lecherously with George? What right did I have to haunt the monks of the Charterhouse, back in their day, punishing them for their callousness and possessiveness with other people's bodies—with women's bodies?

I was a hypocrite: a creepy, dead hypocrite who couldn't keep her creepy dead hands or thoughts away from George. Constantly fluttering around her like a moth at a candle. Stealing her clothes away for my own personal enjoyment. It was embarrassing.

But then, who was I bothering with my obsession? My creepiness was as ineffectual as a storm too far out to sea for anyone to notice.

The moment was slipping away from me; the day was beginning in earnest, and it was a day in which Bernadita was dead and I remained unembodied and George was still unreachable. There were footsteps growing louder, approaching the door of the cell. Easy enough to recognize María Antonia's irregular shuffle. She knocked, and when George didn't answer, she pushed open the door. She crossed to George's desk and set down a pot of coffee and a letter, murmuring a "Good morning" that George left unanswered.

George didn't appear to know anyone else was there. She continued to stare forwards out of the window at where the birds had been. But when María Antonia had gone, she flipped the pages of her story facedown, poured the coffee, and picked up the letter, turning it over and over in her hand. I took the opportunity, in this final moment of quiet, to slide down from the ceiling and push my lips—where lips had been—against George's neck—where neck definitely and deliciously still was—and taste the salt and tobacco and dead skin cells amongst the downy hairs.

GEORGE REMEMBERS

Every time George's stomach rumbles, she wonders if she's getting sick. If she gets up too quickly and makes herself dizzy: she must be getting sick. If the smell of rubbish outside the front door of her building is strong enough to make her gag: she's sick. It's exhausting, the constant scanning of her body for signs of malaise, the sudden fear of breathing when other people are around, the urge to exhale twice as much as she inhales. She feels the same way about Solange, who she summoned to live with her and who arrived in Paris shortly before the epidemic. It is an experiment in mothering and worrying and writing all at once, and one George is determined to make work. If Solange so much as burps, George's mind starts racing. Solange is three years old and George tries to imagine that she will die. She forces herself to picture it, what would happen, what she would do.

The illness—vomiting, diarrhea, racing heart, death sometimes coming within hours—has spread across the city like sunlight crawling over the rooftops at dawn. George stands on her balcony and watches the day start, the edges of the buildings hardening, the sounds of the street drifting up to her fifth-floor perch, and the bodies being dragged out of the houses. There are vehicles waiting like taxis to collect the corpses. It seems to George that the whole of Paris now has a feeble diarrhea stench to it: fecal miasma drifting along alleyways and through windows. Even rich people have cholera now. There may be no escaping it.

At first there were only cases on the ground floor of her building, then it was the first, then the second. Now six of her neighbors are dead and the illness is rising.

There is no point in fearing it. That's what annoys her about all these twinges and worries: if she *was* sick, what then? She would simply recover, as strong people do. And the same for Solange. Her daughter is fierce, unnervingly so. Nothing should scare them and least of all this. She is not going to die and neither is Solange but still her brain plays it out, over and over: *if I die, this will happen, and then this, and then this.* She rehearses for disaster.

And if it wasn't for all of this—she feels bad for thinking about it; it feels indulgent now but she can't help it—it would have been a glorious spring. It was supposed to be a sort of arrival for George. She has a book out. It was published just as the cholera took hold, and now it seems less real, obscured by all the other stuff, the bodies being wheeled away, the hearses cluttering the streets, the smell everywhere. Who cares about books in a time of death? (George does.) She hears from people who have read her novel, slowly at first, their letters interspersed by others saying so-and-so has died, so-and-so got it but is on the mend, so-and-so's little son was taken at only three weeks old. She separates out the ones about the book, and tucks them in her breast pocket. When she clutches her chest to check for a racing pulse, she finds the reassuring crunch of paper.

She wrote the book over the course of six weeks while she was back at home in the countryside with her husband and children, barely paying attention to anyone while she was doing it. She missed Paris, she missed Jules, but it was good for Maurice and Solange to have her back, however briefly; writing the novel was a way of staying in touch with herself while she was there. She wrote the story of an unhappy marriage, the young wife caught between a tyrannical husband and an inconsistent lover. She told herself she was not writing about *her* marriage exactly, but about marriage in general, which deserved to be exposed for the torture it was. It was not hard to come up with ideas, to imagine the wife's horror at her husband's cruelty to her dog; to imagine the young wife's tempestuous passion for a man not her husband.

She wrote to Jules occasionally, in between chapters, but his responses were vague and unsatisfying. She had hoped he might be as enthused by her project as she was—he had been excited by her first novel, and had even lent a version of his name to the cover, to indicate it was their joint project: J. Sand. This time, though, he seemed indifferent.

As though to fill the gaps in Jules's letters, she started dreaming a lot about Paris: about the pink-gray sky, thick and soft like felt. She dreamed about the parties and about Jules in his tattered artist's coat and crumpled shirt, his cravat coming undone. He took up space in her dreams as he did in her life: sprawled across three chairs while others stood awkwardly around him; he had to be reminded to let other people sit. She dreamed about the walk from the apartments to the library, the way in summer the air seemed to draw you towards the river. She dreamed about the stone-colored pigeons that nested on the stone hair of the gargoyles on the Pont Neuf.

Her publisher wrote, asking what name was to go on the cover of her new novel. She asked Jules: did he want to do the same as before, with the first book, and use the name they had created together? He wrote back: no. The book was nothing to do with him, he said. She should use a name of her own choosing. She was hurt but not entirely surprised. She replied to the publisher: this new novel was hers and hers alone. She chose a name close enough to the original pseudonym to reassure readers of continuity, distinct enough to announce, to herself as much as anyone else, a departure: George Sand.

A friend wrote suggesting Jules's attentions were becoming increasingly focused on a German girl who had entered their circle.

George finished her book at speed and returned to Paris, promising the children she'd see them soon.

And now, here come (finally, after the papers were full for weeks on end of death counts and cholera misery) the reviews. After the tentative few letters she received in the immediate aftermath of publication, it is a shock to see the novel's title in print on the pages of *Le Figaro, L'Artiste,* the *Revue des Deux Mondes;* a shock to see the name she chose for herself in print beside the title. Most of all it is a shock to see terms like *exquisite* and *brilliant* and *delicious* in the responses to her work. She reads and reads and rereads the reviews. She can't stop reading them.

Word of her book spreads like a rash. Reviews beget more reviews. The letters about cholera are now few compared with letters in praise of her novel. Now she stands on her balcony looking at the rooftops of her neighborhood thinking not about the dead bodies behind all those walls, but about the copies of her books, the unknown readers turning pages, all these people who have come to know her without her knowledge. She feels superpowered by the novel's reception, as though the good reviews and the sales numbers and delighted words from her peers are padding her out, making her bigger inside her clothes. Sometimes she finds that whole days have passed in reading, writing letters, receiving visitors, answering requests from journalists and readers and other writers— and as she is falling asleep she realizes she has not thought about cholera at all. Sometimes she realizes she has not thought about Jules either.

There are moments, though, when she crouches on the balcony with her back to the city and asks herself, *What have I done?* She tries to think straight. There is nothing wrong; nothing has gone wrong. What she has done is only what her nature and interest dictated; what she has done is put in words something that, it turned out, was felt by lots of people; what she has done is a tremendous success. Still, there is this latent sense of dread accompanying the thrill of praise, the feeling she has unleashed something that will come back, somehow, to bite her. She feels disrobed, as though she is wearing neither skirts nor trousers and has emerged from between the pages of the book stark naked. What goes up must come down, thuddingly, and she cranes her head to look over her shoulder at the little figures of people moving around on the street, a single corpse being dragged from a house onto the waiting cart, and thinks, *What have I done, what have I done, what have I done?*

PALMA

Chopin was asleep when George strode into his room and planted a kiss on his cheek. It was a little bolder, a little firmer than usual. He twisted in the sheets.

"Wonderful news," she said, waving the letter at him. "Your piano is here."

It was the fastest I had ever seen Chopin move. He sat bolt upright as though waking from a nightmare and said, "Here? Really here? Where?"

"Not *here* here," said George. "But here in Mallorca. This just came from the consulate. It has arrived in Palma port. We have to pay duty before they'll release it to us."

Chopin sank back down, pulling the sheet up to his chin. "I thought you meant it was really here." He wouldn't meet her eye. "But really you are telling me the opposite. That nothing has changed. It is still *not* here." He turned away from her, as though they had ended the conversation and he was about to go back to sleep, though we all knew this was a pose.

"I thought you'd be pleased," said George.

Chopin placed a hand atop the covers and splayed his fingers. "Well I'm not."

"Good morning," said Solange, and we all spun around to see that she and Maurice were standing in the doorway, rumpled from sleep but wide-eyed at the news.

"How much duty are they charging?" Chopin asked, rolling over to face them all.

"Seven hundred francs." I couldn't tell from George's tone whether this was outrageous because it was so little, or so much.

"Seven hundred francs! We might as well tell them to send it back to Paris. If we all left now we might arrive home at the same time as the piano and forget this ever happened."

That is the first good idea Chopin has ever had, thought Maurice.

"I'll go there today," George said. She was full to the brim with resolve. A stirring of excitement at the thought of a challenge. Preemptive pleasure imagining how pleased Chopin would be. "I'll reason with them. They can't possibly want so much. I'll fix it for you."

Chopin gave her a watery smile.

"Darling," George said, more forcefully, "I will speak to them and I will fix it."

Which was why we ended up going to Palma that day.

It had been a couple of decades since I'd strayed that far from the Charterhouse. There had been a time, in the middle of the sixteenth century, when I was an avid traveler. I had gone all over the island, had even, once, boarded a ship for Barcelona, though I lost my nerve before we set sail and disembarked. At first, I was astonished by how vast Mallorca was. My fourteen years of life had been contained within a tiny corner of the island. I had missed the chance to smell for myself the salty pine needles floating across the bay at the Platja des Coll Baix and instead had to borrow the nostrils of fishermen. I had to rely on the stomachs of tradesmen to flip, thrilling, when they peered over the edge of the ravine on the road to Sa Calobra. I had never even been to Deià, just along the coast from Valldemossa.

For a long time after I died I assumed, perhaps out of habit, that I was limited in where I could go, what I could do. I did not think to question that eternity for me was the Charterhouse, was Valldemossa, was—at a push—the hillsides surrounding the village and the cliffs plunging down to the sea. It was a shock to follow a party of traders out of the village one day and find that without quite meaning to, I had accompanied them and their donkeys all the way to Sant Elm, and that the sun was setting; it had taken us the whole day. It was as unnerving as: discovering there was no longer ground under your feet; finding you can breathe underwater; waking from a dream in which something dreadful had happened and realizing it was not a dream.

That night I gorged on Sant Elm. I tasted octopus in the mouths of rich women in a big, fusty house by the water. I felt the appalling and brilliant itch of bites from the mosquitoes that swarmed around the traders' children. I sat inside a nine-month-old on the beach, who stuffed his face with sand and ground the grains between his half-erupted teeth, then coughed so hard he threw up his milk. I considered not going home but I left in the end: I was dealing with a complicated situation in the Charterhouse at the time involving a monk and a married woman, and I felt duty bound to return to it. Still, the thrill of travel stayed with me and I spent the next few decades roaming the island, always returning to Valldemossa to check on things and then taking off again.

I explored less and less over time: my second great realization, after discovering the vastness of the island, was to understand its smallness. By the turn of the seventeenth century I knew it all by heart and its limits began to depress me. I did consider going further afield. The ships to Barcelona departed from Palma twice a week, after all. But my family was in Valldemossa. My descendants kept me close to them, without meaning to. I was scared I would lose track of myself without the reminder of who I had been, where I had been, how I had been. I stayed at home. I watched my family reproduce and age. I undermined my enemies.

I had always promised myself I wouldn't get too comfortable in death, that I wouldn't fall into smaller and smaller days, taking up less and less space, covering less and less ground, the way I had seen my descendants do towards the ends of their lives. And yet centuries had passed and it had happened to me nonetheless: I was a creature of the Charterhouse.

So when George looked around at her family and said, "Who's going to come with me to Palma to rescue the piano?" I was the first to speak up.

I will!

The rest of the room was quiet. Solange and Maurice eyed the weather. It was a mild gray day with brief flickers of sun breaking through the clouds. Earlier, a little rain had spattered against the window and it was still wet, though the air was dry again.

Solange said, "Not me," at the same time as Maurice said, "I'll come."

And so the three of us set off from the Charterhouse half an hour later, with fruit in a bag to eat along the way and shawls to keep out the cold and every single note of George's money in a pouch tucked into the waistband of her trousers.

The driver they found in the village was reluctant to take

them. He looked skeptically at the gathering clouds and shook his head. He was skeptical too of the pair of them. Without Solange or Chopin there to dilute the effect, Maurice and George looked disconcertingly similar: the same black hair and long noses, the same way of holding themselves up and away from the world, slightly imperious. George, in her jacket and slacks, looked as though she was attempting to pass herself off as her son's brother: a pair of staring, sallow, foreign boys. The driver took all of this in and preferred not to get involved.

"It's not raining," George said. She mimed it: fingers fluttering down through the air and her head shaking. "It's fine."

"Bad weather and worse coming," the driver grunted.

"It's very important," said George. She fished into her jacket and slid the money out from under her belt.

The driver stared in silence, chewing the inside of his cheek, then said, "I'll take you to Palma but I won't wait. I'm coming straight back after, and you'll pay me double."

George, understanding almost nothing, agreed and handed over payment in advance, having no sense of a reasonable fare in any case. They set off as soon as the deal was struck, George firing questions at the driver he barely understood: how long would it take to get to Palma, why was he taking this route and not that, what was the name of this type of carriage and was it commonly used; what was the name of his mule, what did he feed it, how much rest did he give it, and so on. Sometimes he hazarded a guess at her meaning and tried to respond. Mostly he glowered at the track ahead and steered around the endless obstacles the winter's storms had blown into his path. George stopped trying to engage with him and instead let her eyes rest on her son.

Maurice sat close to his mother and thought that this could

be the best day of his life. The countryside was flashing past them: red earth and yellow grasses and occasional glimpses of blue water, a primary palette. He was too old to wriggle into George's arms the way he wanted to, but her proximity and her attention thrilled him. She was staring at him more than she was looking out of the window and every time the carriage jolted over a rock or hole in the track, she gripped his hand so hard her knuckles turned white.

"What's the plan, Mama?" he asked.

"I'll go and speak to them at the customs office," she said. "I'll explain that what they are asking is unreasonable. I'll tell them it's Chopin's piano. Surely they'll know who he is and make an exception."

"What if they won't?"

"They'll have to," she said. "We can't afford what they're asking, and we can't afford for Chopin not to have the piano. So they will make an exception."

"Are you sure?"

"Perfectly," she said, and reached over to pat his wrist.

Maurice settled in closer to his mother, dropping his head on her shoulder—black hair crushing softly against black hair—and I settled into him. I had spent less time rooting around in Maurice's memories than I had in Solange's or even Chopin's. I knew Amélie's history better than I knew his. There was something sweetly ignorable about him; even his jealousy of Chopin was endearing, giving me the impression that Maurice was very simple. Of course none of this was particularly fair.

Maurice's mind: intricate, like the inside of a travel clock. Everything was pieced together very neatly, like the little details in his drawings. Even in the time that I was witnessing his thoughts, he was busy ordering and arranging them and cleansing them of unpleasantness. He refused to notice, for example, that his feet were damp from the walk between the Charterhouse and the market square, where they had found their transport. He was willfully ignoring the way that, whenever the carriage lurched or thudded, his head slammed against a sharp bone in George's shoulder. As Maurice would have it: he was having a wonderful time. He was alone with his mother. It was one of the happiest days of his life.

Still, I did not have to look far back in his memories to find an incident he had failed to whitewash. It was in Paris, sometime in the spring. He was walking under an archway; the street was behind him and ahead was the main quad of his boarding school. He was thinking about an incident he had just witnessed on his way back—a beggar had been singing a folk song and from across the street a woman had started singing the same song in a different key, and the two singers had faced off against each other; a horrible cacophony—when he heard his name being called.

"Dudevant! Hey, Dudevant!"

He looked around and saw a group of boys turning the corner towards him. They were a few years older than he was, spotty and half-mustached.

"You're Maurice Dudevant," one of them said.

"Yes."

"Your mother is La Sand."

"George," said Maurice. "George Sand. She's a writer."

This answer entertained them. They asked him to say it again, which he did.

"Do you know who your father is?" they asked, and Maurice said he did.

More laughter. "You're wrong," they said. "You're wrong! You don't know."

"Don't know what?"

"That your father isn't your father, and your sister isn't your whole sister, and your mother isn't a writer, she's a whore."

Maurice wondered whether he should fight them. There were several of them, they looked larger and stronger than he was, but he was probably angrier than they were, which had to count for something. He clenched his fists. He imagined swinging a punch; even in his mind's eye it seemed implausible. He turned on his heel and half walked, half ran, to his room.

He wrote a letter to George: "They said all sorts of things, because you are a woman who writes, because you are not a prude like most of the other boys' mothers." He chewed the end of his pen. "They call you—I can't tell you the word because it is too wicked." He thought about the word *whore*, about the prostitutes he had seen leaning out of windows as he walked between the school and the river, about the one who had called out to him in particular, using all sorts of embarrassing names, and how he had quickened his step to get away from her whilst also wanting to stay and hear what she would say next. He imagined his mother in one of those windows, calling out to men passing by. Was his mother a whore? He knew he should be angry at the idea—he was angry at the boys for calling her one and for acting as though it made him a laughingstock—but he did not entirely mind whether or not she really was. Whatever she wanted to do was the right thing. She was his mother. He thought she was wonderful.

A short while after the letter was sent, George arrived at the school and took him away with her. She would teach him herself, she said. She told him everything he wanted to know, about who she was sleeping with, and what rumors people were spreading about it. She showed him snide articles about her in the press, laughing at the more salacious details. When Maurice asked if she needed him to do anything, she shook her head and said, "What on earth should we be doing?" and they went back to his studies: Montaigne, Condillac, Bossuet.

The memories became yellower, happier; they were in the large country house, eating a lot of meat, sharing in-jokes I didn't completely follow. When they returned to Paris, he and George and Solange lived in an apartment next door to a painter and there were always adults around who spoke to Maurice as though he were the same as them: mature, intelligent, wittier and wilder than other people.

A second shadow in Maurice's memory: the day he found out Chopin would be joining them in Mallorca. Hearing the news had been like stepping into a chilled room. He had been under the weather for months: a series of colds that his mother blamed on the rain and grime in Paris. Her idea of Spain, of a holiday, of taking off, just them and Solange, had been a treasured, hopeful one. And then she had said that Chopin would be coming as well, and Maurice had wanted to cry like a little child.

For all Maurice's efforts to notice and remember only good things, his memories of Chopin tended towards the ghoulish. Chopin limped through Maurice's memories, vampiric and sickly. His cough was amplified, his gloved hands always reaching out for George, pulling her further and further away.

"You don't mind, do you, if we bring dear old Chopinet along?" George had asked.

Solange had jumped at the idea and said, "Not at all!" before Maurice could think how to express the disappointment, the loss, the betrayal, without using overblown words like *disappointment, loss, betrayal.* He thought about saying, "But wouldn't it be sim-

pler, Mama, if he did not come?" but bit his tongue. By the time
he regretted it, it was too late. They had already packed up their
household, the plans had been made, everything was set in motion.

So the trip to Palma that day was what he had imagined the
Mallorca trip would be, before Chopin was added to the mix:
Maurice and George against the world; new places and strange
feelings and the undivided attention of his mother. When we
arrived in the city, the noise and smoke made him grin. The carriage was full of the smell of oranges; they had eaten all of the
fruit they had brought, and built a tower of peel on Maurice's
knee. As we neared the harbor, fishiness mingled with the cit-
rus. The driver dropped us at the edge of the port, where a tide
of fishermen were dragging ashore nets wriggling and hopping
with silvery bodies. The place stank of seaweed and urine and
still Maurice was smiling. He stepped lightly down from the carriage and offered his arm to George, who landed heavily and
sent up a spray of mud.

They asked around for the customs office, for anyone who
might have heard about a very expensive and somewhat famous piano that had been shipped from Paris. It started to
rain again and nobody seemed to know anything. The streets
were already boggy; Maurice kept losing his footing, sliding
and grabbing George's arm for balance. George scowled at the
sky and palmed wet hair out of her eyes. "I need to pay duty
on a piano," she kept saying, to anyone who'd stop long enough
to listen. There were a lot of shrugs, a lot of bemused smiles,
a lot of stares at this man-woman who was speaking a strange
language, and no answers.

They came across the right place by chance, turning a corner and recognizing one of the customs officials they had spoken to when they first arrived. It had been he who had initially told George there would be duty to pay both when the piano left France and when it arrived in Mallorca. He recognized her too, and said, "Madame Sand! You've come at last? The office is just this way." He put a hand on her arm in a way that made her step back from him.

She turned to Maurice, took a deep breath, and said, "Right."

"Do you need me to come with you?" Maurice said.

George looked her son up and down. There was mud all over his trousers and the cold had made his cheeks flush; he looked like a child who had been left unsupervised somewhere dirty for an afternoon. "No," she said. "You wait here. I won't be long."

She went in alone and Maurice waited for her, sheltered under the eaves of an abandoned shop across from the offices, nervously tying and untying the bag that had held the oranges. He wondered, even though George had told him not to, whether he should go in after her. Briefly, the older boys from his former school came to mind, the laughter, the sense that his mother was a joke. He thought about the hand of the customs man on George's arm. He took a step forwards, then back again. He was used to people staring at his mother, but even so. He entertained a slightly lackluster fantasy of throwing punches in the direction of anyone who smirked, whistled, catcalled, or disrespected George, but the target was too vague and Maurice was too cold, too wet, too hungry to keep it up for long.

The rain began to fall more insistently. The ground between our waiting place and the customs office became first muddy and then a shimmering gray as a puddle formed. When George finally appeared in the doorway and called something out to Maurice, the sound of water pounding the rooftops and the ground and his own head made it impossible to hear. He splashed his way across to her.

"What?" he said. "What happened?"

"They won't budge," she said. She swung a kick at a plank that was protruding from the puddle; it barely moved and she pulled her foot back sharply. "Fuck," she said. "Fuck. We can't get it."

I REMEMBER

We are standing outside the Charterhouse, staring at the dark wooden entrance. My mother knocks, a sharp, restrained tap, and when nothing happens she starts to hammer, and after a while I join in too, and now we are both pounding maniacally, slapping our palms against the door as though we could push it down.

And then suddenly the surface I am hitting is not there. The inner door recedes and I almost hurtle through it, towards a person who is staring at us on the other side of the threshold. I stop still, palms raised, and look into the face of the man. He is not dressed like a brother, but he's not someone we know from the village either.

Who are you? my mother says.

What do you want? says the man. He looks bemused. He doesn't say it unkindly. And then, registering my mother's question, *I live here. I work for the brothers. What do you want?*

It dawns on me, horrifyingly, sickeningly, that I do not know Ham's name. I know it's not really Ham, of course, but whatever he said that I'd misheard is a mystery to me. Standing here, after making all that ruckus, tasked with answering this man's question, I have no idea who we should be asking for.

We want to speak to Ham, says my mother.

Mum, I say, *no. His name's not really Ham.*

Well what is it then?

I don't know.

The man in the doorway is looking from me to my mother. *If you want the apothecary,* he says, very slowly, *he will be at the market on Thursdays like always. You can't just come here and see him whenever you want.*

He thinks we are idiots. He thinks we are mad people who need to see the apothecary.

Is there a novice here, I ask, *whose name sounds like 'Ham'?*

The man's mouth cracks ever so slightly into a smile. *Ramón?* he says. *You want to see Ramón?*

Yes! I say. *Probably!*

My mother launches into it at once: how this Ramón has got me pregnant, how he didn't turn up to see me as planned, how he must of course leave the Charterhouse at once so he can marry me, how the clock is ticking, how I'm swelling up fast and this all needs to happen before it's too late (to clarify what "too late" would be, she mimes producing an infant from between my legs—both she and the man on the threshold are interacting as though the other doesn't speak the language very well), how she needs to see this boy at once to talk some sense into him.

You have come here to speak to Ramón? the man says. His expression remains mystified. The smile has gone. *You have come here to speak to Ramón about this girl who is having a baby and wants him to marry her?*

Yes! my mother says. She seems excited, relieved to be understood. *Yes! Exactly. Could you fetch him?*

You can't just come here and speak to the brothers, the man says. *You can't just—*

He's not a brother, my mother says.

He's studying. They are all busy in study and prayer. Even the novices.

He wasn't too busy to get my daughter pregnant.

I'm entirely certain that he was. A hard edge is creeping into his voice now. He is losing patience. *The brothers never leave the Charterhouse. The novices never leave the Charterhouse. There is simply no way this could have happened as you are telling it. I think you should leave now.*

My mother looks on the cusp of something. I can't tell, in the moment, whether she is about to explode or shrink. She is contemplating—I just know it—pushing past this man at the door and charging through the Charterhouse in search of Ham, but somewhere else inside her, resolve is fading, doubt is creeping in, because who is she to contradict this quiet-spoken stranger who acts on behalf of all the learned, holy, sweaty brothers?

Mum, I say. I pull on her sleeve. Easier for her if she can be seen to give in because I beg her to. *Mum, let's go. He's not going to talk to us.*

Blanca, I really think—

Let's go.

The man in the doorway has stepped backwards, is starting to close the door.

If it was down to me, my mother is saying, *I would not leave until that boy answered for what he's done. But since my daughter—*

The door closes. My mother stares at it, emits a frustrated growl, and then aims a kick squarely in the middle of the hard wood. I can tell it hurts her foot but she won't admit it. On the way back down to the village, she limps and says nothing.

I am miserable, and in the moment all I can think of is that my mother feels humiliated. I have forgotten to think about Ham, about the baby, about everyone in the village knowing and talking about it all. Instead I feel my mother's shame for her, her indignation, her throbbing foot, her fury in the face of closed doors.

Mum? I say. I put a hand on her arm. She won't look at me and continues to shuffle towards the house. *Mum? I'm sorry.*

The stone hits me square in the back of the head: a sting, surprise, a clatter as it falls to the ground. I wheel around, one hand to the spot where it struck, the other grabbing my mother, and there is Ham in the middle of the path, red-faced and trembling, panting slightly. He looks disheveled, as though he hasn't slept well. His novice's cape has slid off his shoulders and looks feminine, like the kind of shawl old ladies wear to Mass. His arm is raised, aiming another stone.

Blanca, what were you thinking? he says. *Why would you do this to me?*

NO, NO, NO, NO, NO

If I ever had cause, in the years since my death, to fear I might die all over again, it would have been on that journey back from Palma to the Charterhouse. Perhaps it was just that everybody else was so scared. I was surrounded by racing hearts. I became as deranged and terrified as the rest of them.

The storm had broken before we left Palma. The rain, which had been steadily worsening all day, was no longer really rain so much as a wave crashing over the port. Everybody was breathing through open mouths, gasping for air. Thunder made the horses panic; men were dashing to get them inside; the animals were kicking up high plumes of mud. Only the fishermen were calm in their oiled jackets and hats, watching their nets hop and writhe, fish briefly revived by the downpour. We dashed past all of this towards the thoroughfare back to the town, but when we reached a line of carriage drivers huddling in their own vehicles, they ignored us entirely.

"Valldemossa," George was saying. Water was filling her mouth. She stopped to spit. "We need to get to Valldemossa." Her hair was plastered to her face, making her head look small and oddly pointed.

The drivers ignored her or pretended to be asleep.

"Please," she said. She hammered on the woodwork. "Please."

Maurice had been standing behind her, shielding his eyes from the rain with his hands and slowly sinking into the mud. He occasionally took little half steps forwards and opened his mouth to butt in, but never spoke. George turned to him with a face I hadn't seen before; I realized at the same time he did that she was about to burst into tears.

"Hey!" he howled past George to the drivers. His posture changed. It was as though he was doing all his growing up in the space of a second, getting taller and braver all at once. He bellowed. "Hey! Hey! Wake up! My mother needs help!"

The only driver to stir was the only one who really had been asleep. He was at the end of the row of carriages and smelled to Maurice of the tramps who used to accost him at roadside inns on his journeys between Paris and the country house: alcohol and urine and dirt. The driver came to with a start, looked blearily out at the downpour and at Maurice, and said, "Where to?"

George and Maurice bundled into the vehicle at once, both repeating "Valldemossa."

"Tomorrow?" said the driver.

"Valldemossa," George said.

The driver, still sleep-addled and half-drunk, stumbled off to fetch his mule. By the time he had returned, the rain seemed to have woken him up to the folly of the enterprise, and he began to state his case to his passengers: it was dangerous and cold, the hillsides between Palma and Valldemossa would be like waterfalls, they would arrive long after nightfall, perhaps they would all die. It would be better not to, he said. It would be better for everybody to go back to sleep now.

George, understanding little, simply said, again, "Vallde-mossa."

The driver again shook his head. His mule was lame; she might not last the journey. His axle was in fact broken.

"Valldemossa," said George. She reached into her belt to retrieve her sodden money, jabbing it wetly in his direction, and so, reluctantly, precariously, we began the journey home.

It would have taken three hours on a good day. It would have taken five on a bad one.

Six hours into this journey, we were so deep in a river that the mule was having to crane her neck so she could keep her nose above water, and George and Maurice and the driver were up to their waists.

"This is not a road," George shouted. "This is not a road!"

The driver gestured at the river, which he and I both knew was where the road had once been, and said, "It is the road." It was the road and it looked, in the downpour, like the ocean. Worse: the last of the light was retreating behind the mountains.

We pressed forward, the mule half swimming and the driver shouting miserable little instructions, more for his benefit than for his animal's. Maurice had turned blue and was shivering. George, gripping him close to her, was white. Adrenaline was surging in her body.

It was so loud that we didn't hear the crack. The driver continued to attempt to steer the mule. The mule continued to swim and stumble. George and Maurice continued to sit in terror. And then we all became aware at once that we were sinking. The axle, which may or may not have been damaged when we set out, was definitely broken now, and the weight of the waterlogged passengers was driving the whole cart downwards.

At the same time, a boulder slid loose from the hillside above us. It missed the carriage, but released a battering ram of water that tipped us sideways, and in a rush we were everywhere, spluttering; we had nothing solid to hold on to and I was in nobody's mind or body, I was alone, I was underwater thinking, like a child, *Please don't let me die! Please don't let me die.* I watched plants and branches and a ragged boot float past in the murkiness.

We flailed for seconds, not even a minute.

By the time we had come to a standstill and George and Maurice and the driver had hauled their bedraggled bodies onto the tallest rocks they could find, the driver was a broken man. He stared at his wild-eyed mule and at the wreck of his vehicle, and shook his head and said "No, no, no, no, no, no, no" so many times it seemed as though he did not know how to stop saying it. He couldn't bring himself to look at his erstwhile passengers, who were both shaking violently and missing their shoes. Maurice's jacket was gone, and his shirt covered in grime and blood, though from where it wasn't clear.

"What are we going to do now?" said George, holding her jaw to stop it from shaking.

"No, no, no, no, no," said the driver, still refusing to look at them. He loosed his mule from what was left of the carriage, stroking her face and kissing the side of it in a frenzy. "No, no, no, no, no," he said, as he steadied himself beside her, climbed onto a higher rock, and then swung his leg over her. He steered her away from George and Maurice and, muttering, began to ride back down the mountain in the direction of Palma.

George and Maurice stared after him and the last of the light faded. In the dark, they began the climb, using their hands as much as their feet to guide them up what had once been the road to Valldemossa. Neither of them spoke. It took them three hours to reach the village, by which point the storm had exhausted itself and shrunk to a fitful drizzle. They were numb by then, barely thinking anything at all, covered in scratches and bruises they couldn't feel, couldn't even see in the pitch black. They stumbled through the village like drunkards.

As we rounded the corner of the road and saw the dark bulk of the Charterhouse, the rain stopped. We stopped, too. George put out a hand to steady herself against a wall. Her panting, which had been rasping and harsh for the entirety of the climb, slowed. Beside her, Maurice held his breath.

It seemed to me the village had never been so quiet in all my hundreds of years. Everyone was inside; everyone exhausted from the storm and asleep. Above us, the clouds were thinning around a washed-out moon. Maurice swallowed to keep his teeth from chattering.

Then we all heard it at once. It was faint and sounded further away than it really was: the faltering, pitchy glimmer of Chopin's piano. He was playing the same note, over and over (an A-flat, it turned out), as though he too had been on the hillside, half drowned, and was shaking his head, saying, "No, no, no, no, no."

PRELUDE NO. 15
IN D-FLAT MAJOR, SOSTENUTO

Maurice and George crossed the threshold to Cell Three, wet and expectant. They anticipated a rush towards them. They anticipated dry blankets, warm drinks, giddy questions: what had happened and were they all right and were any bones broken and weren't they both so brave, so very courageous, to have attempted what they did? They were! Maurice had focused on the thought of a hot meal to get him up the last of the hill, picturing the steam rising from one of María Antonia's stews, which had previously seemed barely palatable, the skin of a tomato curling away from the flesh like a scroll, flakes of fish floating in broth, oil droplets clustering on the surface. George wanted a dry place to smoke, she wanted to sink into Chopin's arms, she wanted to be congratulated and reassured. She wanted to begin the work, at once, of turning their disaster into a good story that would cleanse it, and that, over time, would replace the memory of the event itself.

They stood at the entrance to the cell and dripped and shivered and waited for everything they'd been imagining to happen. What came instead was silence. There was no movement. The cell was dark. Water pooled on the floor between their legs. It seemed to Maurice they stood still for a long time.

"Hello?" said George. "We're home."

No reply, but there was a line of weak light under Chopin's door, and they moved towards it. George's chest tightened. She thought at once that Chopin had died, that in all their excitement and terror in the trip to and from Palma they had forgotten the point of it all, which was to make Chopin happy, to keep him alive. She thought about how lovely his hands were, about how beautiful he was, and then she thought about how quiet the rest of life would be if, when they entered Chopin's room, what they found was his body, limp on the mattress, and all the thoughts and words and all the music of him gone forever. It seemed suddenly the most likely thing. Inevitable, even. Those faltering notes we'd heard outside must have been his last. She was scared to push the door and paused. Behind her, Maurice's teeth were chattering.

And then we heard the piano again. It was a single A-flat, but it was enough to fill George with a rush of joy that carried her into the room with Maurice in tow, saying, "Darlings! Chopin! Solange! Darlings, we're home!"

In Chopin's room: the pale face of Amélie, standing by the window and playing nervously with the hem of her collar; Solange, eyes wide, backed into a corner; Chopin at the piano, turning slowly, looking neither excited nor surprised to see them. He took in their wet clothes, bare feet, their bloodied everything, made a strange strangled noise, and said, "I knew you had died." He played the A-flat key again without looking down.

What's going on? I asked. He looked pallid. His eyes were red. He kept playing the same note, though his gaze slid away from George and Maurice and began to dart across the room.

Solange and Amélie still said nothing, hadn't moved. *What has happened?*

Chopin's head was full of ghosts. At first these ghosts were all I could see when I went searching through his mind. I fought my way through them, batting them out of the way to try to get to a single concrete thing. There were ghosts atop the piano, with Solange's body and the eyes of his parents. There were ghosts in every corner, bobbing up against the dusty vaulted ceiling (which was shaped, he saw now, exactly like a coffin) and sliding in and out of the window and door. And then there were the ghosts of Maurice and George, standing limp before him, indistinguishable from all the rest. They were pale and ragged and insubstantial. They slumped and hunched the way the others did.

"How long has he been like this?" asked George.

Amélie blinked and tried to gather herself. She didn't know what time it was, only that it was dark outside and had been dark for a while. "Hours," she said.

As George began the work of telling everyone what to do— ordering Amélie to heat water, bring towels, wake María Antonia for food, fetch Chopin his milk; telling Solange to go to bed, Maurice to find himself clean clothes—I looked back over Chopin's day. There was the firm, abrasive morning kiss from George. The news about the Pleyel piano, a soaring hope that had briefly displaced his pain, and then a plunging black mood, a return of aches and twinges and breathlessness. He had been annoyed. With George. With Mallorca. With the friends back in Paris who were supposed to be handling his finances and correspondence and who had so woefully failed to get him what he needed in order to work. The only thing he really needed: the right piano.

There was: "Darling. I will speak to them and I will fix it."

There was George heading out the door with Maurice and a bag of oranges. Solange flitting around the room like a bored canary, wanting his attention, wanting him to watch her dance. There was the rain coming down hard, and the eruption of a small leak at the corner of the window, water worming its way down the stone inside and onto the floor. Chopin watched in horror as it pooled and grew, reaching out to swallow the flagstones and creeping towards his feet. (Everything hurt: the way the water hurt was a kind of bottomed-out nausea, stomach cramps, and stinging in the bones.) This was the beginning of things going very wrong.

He coughed and there was a spatter of blood across his white glove. The blood appeared to him like the leak. His body: a storm breaking into the room. There was a single red droplet on the middle G key. He pressed it and the blood came off on his finger.

Solange brought in some stew María Antonia had made for lunch and he ate it with her, pretending that nothing was wrong. In fact, he struggled to swallow. The vegetables had the texture of body parts, little organs bobbing around his spoon, livers and hearts, spongy tomatoes like lungs, and rubbery olive eyeballs. When Solange had finished and padded off to her own room, he vomited into a water jug. The taste of the stew in reverse made him retch more. He gripped the wall to keep himself upright. He staggered back to the piano stool.

It seemed to get dark very early. Earlier than usual? Early, in any case. The storm picked up force; lightning flashed jagged shadows across the wall and when it was over left the room darker still. Amélie came in, wordlessly, and lit the candle on the piano. The flame made a hungry, spluttering, tearing sound, drowning in its own wax. When he pressed the piano keys, Chopin could barely hear them, the candle was so loud.

Or: it wasn't the candle. It was the storm. Thunder was rolling down off the mountain like punches. The pain of the thunder was the pain of a full-body blow.

Water was finding its way into the room through new cracks. Reaching in like fingers trying to pry the lid off his coffin.

Or: he was inside an egg and the shell was breaking and he didn't want to hatch, he really, really did not want to. A dark flower of damp opened up on the ceiling by the window. Drops began to fall from it. Chopin looked at it and it was a ghost, exposing a flat, leaking breast. He closed his eyes, opened them. The ceiling again. Probably.

"Hello?" he said. "Is somebody there?" He said it in his mother tongue, which I had never heard him speak before.

The drops from the ceiling were regular, percussive. They fell into the puddle below. Tiny splashes. (The pain of the splashes was the pain of hair being tweezed from the skin one strand at a time.)

A ghost crossed the room and blew out Chopin's candle. A draft. The storm was sending cold, boisterous currents of air through the Charterhouse.

A ghost placed a hand on Chopin's hand and guided it to the keyboard.

A ghost pressed down on Chopin's finger, and the note it played was A-flat.

Chopin began to play. It was something he had begun working on in previous days: a dappled sunlit opening, a break in the clouds, a tentative ray touching the horizon. But the A-flat was running through it now, at first barely noticeable beneath the right hand's melody, and then louder, increasingly insistent. It became the saddest sound I had ever heard: *perhaps you are happy,* the music said, and the A-flat said, *but what about this—this— this—this—*

I understood by then that Chopin's music was the best of him. It was where his loveliness resided. All his better impulses, his tenderness and sadness, were there, in safekeeping away from his body, unhampered by the sharp edges of pain and illness, cranki-ness and frustration and irritability.

The left hand barely strayed from the A-flat. (The dripping from the ceiling continued.) Then the right hand took it up, and how could it be that the same note over and over could convey exactly how it was to be Chopin, to be stuck in a body and a mind that undermined him; how it was to be alone in the dark and leaky coffin of his room on a blustery Mallorcan hillside in 1838, surrounded by a fog of ghosts and loss and worry and no George to be found and no comfort to be found; to know that he was not as good as he might be, not as gener-ous or as kind as he might be, and that he would die without thinking as clearly about things—life, music, love, gentleness—as he wanted? How could it be that the prelude conveyed so precisely how it was to be anyone (me, for example) who has been lost in something (time, for example) and unable to find a way out?

Chopin's hands moved over the piano. It occurred to him that George was dead. It occurred to him that Maurice too was dead. They had been gone so long, and it was so dark. Solange, who had crept into his room and whose mouth was moving as though she was trying to say something, was a ghost. Worse: it seemed likely that he, Chopin, was dead, that his hands were being moved by ghosts because he too was a ghost, he was gone, the room was not *like* a coffin, it *was* a coffin, and what could be more terrible, he realized, than dying and being still, somehow, alive, waking after burial to find nothing changed and everything worse? The servant girl, also a ghost, was there, saying, "Sir, please stop screaming. Please stop screaming," which is just what a ghost might say to another ghost. He kept playing the A-flat and making whatever sound with his mouth he had been making before, and the ceiling kept dripping and dripping and dripping.

Once George and Maurice had dried off and found fresh clothes, once George had smoked and Maurice had eaten and the pair of them, with Amélie's help, had persuaded Chopin into his bed, George slumped on the floor beside him and stroked his hair. She ran her fingers lightly over his cheekbones and nose, waiting a second beneath the nostrils to check she felt his breath.

"Maurice," she whispered, and gestured to Maurice to come closer. "We can't stay here." (Amélie looked up from the fire.) "If we stay here, I don't know what will happen. We'll all go mad. We have to go home."

Maurice, crouching beside his mother, found forming words burdensome. His calf muscles were still shaking. He gripped the edge of the mattress to steady himself. "We can't stay in the Charterhouse?"

"We can't stay in Mallorca," said George.

For the first time I saw it clearly. I didn't need to cheat and look forward to see it, didn't need to skim the pages ahead. It was plain: they could not stay in Mallorca. They could not carry on as they were, hungry and damp and alone and mistrusted and unwell. The villagers were too hostile, Chopin's health too fragile, the weather too extreme. *Someone is going to die here*, I thought. All I had wanted since George first arrived was to know that she would stay, to spend all of her days with her in the Charterhouse and the garden, but I knew that my job from then on would be to help her get out before it was too late.

JANUARY

GEORGE

The following days were subdued. Everything felt upended. Everybody's sleep schedules seemed to change: at eight in the morning, George would be awake, nervously pacing between the bedroom and the garden, and Chopin still in bed; Solange would wake up at two in the morning and have to count spiders to fall back to sleep. Nothing quite made sense, and George was acting as though perhaps it did, or could, as though words said in a firm, cheery voice had the power to soothe the children's malaise and her own. She fidgeted, barely wrote, and compulsively looked in on Chopin. More often than not he'd be sleeping and George's attention would be drawn to stains on the ceilings and walls of his room, left behind by the leaks. The air wasn't healthy, she worried. He was breathing in the damp and dust of the building. They should leave at once; they should just pack up and get out, because the whole venture had been a terrible failure.

I knew she was right. I was ready to do whatever I could to help. But still, I panicked at the idea, as though at any moment she might clap her hands and say it was over, she was leaving me. I found myself wishing for just one more day, one more evening, one more morning, before things were cut short.

Maurice too had departure on his mind. "Are we really going to leave?" he asked, as he chewed dry bread and watched his mother smoking.

George shrugged. "I don't know which is more likely to kill him, staying or going."

Maurice, in turn, shrugged.

George swatted at him. "Let's go to the ocean."

"I did enough swimming in Palma," said Maurice. He was still feeling damp from the inside out, as though even his personality had got wet. The dry clothes and the fire Amélie had lit and his mother's breeziness in the days since were all incapable of mopping up his inner bogginess. He had developed a resistance to blinking, because whenever he shut his eyes he saw the river on the hillside.

"It's a beautiful day," said George, and she was right. She gestured at the window with her smoking hand, showering ash in the direction of the sunshine. The storm had cried itself to sleep, and what remained in the subsequent days were crisp blue skies and a slightly shell-shocked peace, as though we had been granted a reprieve from winter. In the garden and on the lane to the village, a layer of blown, bruised fruit covered the ground: pomegranates and oranges that skittered when kicked and upset walkers. By midday, the whole of Valldemossa would be full of a warmed-up pulp odor; the steepest section of the path would be slimed with juice where people had tripped and slid. If there was no more rain to wash it away, it would start to congeal and ferment and smell like bad marmalade.

Solange wanted to go to the ocean and so Maurice agreed, because worse than being wet was being left alone with Chopin (or were the two in fact very similar, he wondered, Chopin striking him as not unlike a wet blanket or drizzling cloud, a dampener). And while Maurice was not at all against the idea of leaving the island and going home, a kind of preemptive nostalgia was already rising in him. He might never again have the chance to walk in pale sunshine with his mother and sister down the Valldemossan hillside towards the Balearic Sea, and he didn't want to miss his chance.

Just as they were about to leave, George faltered. "We should stay with Chopin," she said. "He's not well."

Maurice grabbed her arm and pulled her in the direction of her boots. "He's never well, Mama. He's not well when you take care of him and he's not well when you don't."

So they left a note for Chopin, who was still asleep, emphasizing that they were all feeling fit and that the sun was shining and that they would turn back at the first drop of rain, then set off. Pace: brisk. Mood: perky. Conversation: playful, a lot of back-and-forth between Maurice and Solange about who Adélaide preferred, which was safe territory since Adélaide was just about the only living being for whose affections they did not actually compete and who, in any case, cared for neither of them.

The route was one I knew well, of course. I tended to avoid it because it brought back bad memories, though most of the landmarks from my living days were gone. The buildings and plants I passed on my sad-solitary-optimistic walks to meet Ham had crumbled or wilted in the centuries since. But occasionally we passed something that had been there all those centuries ago, a twisted little olive tree bending over itself in the sun, a tumbledown portion of stone wall, and it left me feeling giddy and wary all at once.

To distract myself, I focused on the air on George's skin, which made her feel bright and optimistic.

I focused on the stone in her boot, fidgeting between the sole and the stocking, making precise indents into her skin.

A stitch was coming loose in the seam of her shirt, itchy at the base of her spine.

The odd bulk of her tongue in her mouth. The mineral taste of her saliva.

She was beginning to crave a cigar: fidgeting fingers drawn towards her coat pocket.

I was so absorbed in all of this I missed the moment when the path opened out and revealed the ocean. It was always a delicious shock, that section of the route, and even though I had seen it hundreds of times before I was sorry not to have noticed it for myself this time, or seen the children's reaction to it. I was so focused on a brief experience of the bubbling and fluttering of George's stomach (she was getting hungry) that I didn't even glimpse what she felt about the view.

The edge of the island was up ahead, abrupt and staggering: the ground sloped down steeply towards it. The path forked. On the left was the route Ham and I had used, which zigzagged down through the rocks to the water. The family paused, unsure, and then took the right, which led us along the flat cliff edge for another twenty minutes or so, above trees and bushes clinging tenuously to the rock face, and then bottomed out entirely and became air and vertical cliff, pale gray rock and, far below, the booming blue of the water. George and the children were a little way off, still, but the descent was becoming scrappier and more dangerous. Solange skidded on loose gravel and fell backwards, tearing a hole in the back of her trousers.

"Careful," said George. "Let me go first."

It's easier, I said, *if we go back and take the other path.*

Solange was scampering forwards, not listening, and Maurice went after her, and George's heart was thumping very fast; her palms were sweating; she was terrified of something. I clung to her chest, looping through her ribs, searching for the reason she was so scared. I wondered whether she sensed something I couldn't, whether if I broke my own rule and skipped ahead to see what would happen, I'd find something dreadful: Solange toppling off the cliff and Maurice after her and George after them both? I was skeptical. The path was steep but the children were old enough to take care of themselves. George's sudden terror was a mystery to me.

The path culminated at a flat slab of rock, a balcony cut into the cliff face. The three of them stood there breathing in the thick, herby smell of the plants and feeling their skin grow soft from the salt in the air. They stood a little way back from the edge. Far, far below them, waves churned.

"But there's no way to get to the water," Solange said. "There's no way to swim." She was warm and dusty. The newly active sweat glands in her armpits were making her feel sticky. She had imagined hurling herself into the ocean from rocks; splash and spray and playing with Maurice.

Maurice crouched down, then awkwardly tipped back onto his behind. He looked surprised to have landed so heavily, but set about getting out his sketching things neatly: his broken stumps of charcoal, his sketchbook. "It's nice here," he said. "Let's stay."

George, looking distractedly at the rock, the shrubs surrounding them, and the ocean: "We can get lower down. Look, there's a way over here." Her heart was beating faster still. Her adrenaline was pulsing, a singeing pain on the underside of her skin.

Oh, I said, *no, you really can't get lower down.* There was no way. The rock face was essentially sheer. Even goats eschewed it. Even ghosts! But George was stepping forwards, heart hammering and determined.

Wait! Why are you doing this if you are so scared?

George held out a hand to Maurice, who stared for a moment, then folded his drawing away and took it. She hauled him onto his feet.

"I don't see how," he said, but he followed her as she stomped through bushes towards the edge. "I don't think there's a way."

George pointed to a thin ledge.

Oh that, I said. *I can see how that might look like a path, but really it's not safe, it's not—*

"There," said George.

"That's not a path," said Maurice.

"Stay back and let me try it," said George. There was a brittle raspiness to her voice.

I racked her brains, searching for a clue. She wasn't thinking in words. She wasn't even thinking the kinds of thoughts that were just underneath words but bore relation to words. She was all fragments, heartbeat, hungry, adrenaline, sore throat, need to smoke, and then flashes of memory: a horse, up to its chest in water, George straddling it, her feet submerged. Was it from the journey back from Palma? The mule on the mountainside? It felt older, different; George was younger.

I pieced the memory together: George and the horse were in a river. France. The countryside around the big house of Solange's and Maurice's childhoods. George was a teenager. Somebody was on the opposite bank waiting for her to get across, but George had pulled the horse to a standstill at the deepest point, and the animal was losing its footing in the current. She knew she should ride on, ride forward, lead them both to safer ground. A voice in her head was weighing up her fate, asking, *No? Yes? No? Yes?* like a metronome. Which was which? It wasn't clear. Was it *No, don't kill yourself*? or was it *No, don't live*? Was it *Yes, I should drown* or *Yes, I should survive*?

Her feet were losing sensation in the sharp, cold water. She started to laugh and she stayed like that for a long time, laughing, the horse stumbling on the riverbed. Her friend on the bank called out to her, and instead of answering, she steered the horse to face the current, sharply. The horse lost its footing and fell, and they were both underwater, and she was buffeted out of the saddle and away, and there was no horse anymore and she had done it on purpose to die.

This was when I understood something crucial about George.

She was the kind of person who feels the need to throw things from high places.

Including, now, herself.

That is to say: she was a person with urges. There were all her regular urges, of course, for caffeine, nicotine, sex. There was the urge to laugh at awkward silences, to smirk when nervous. There were more nefarious urges, too. The urge to trip up a passing toddler. The urge to steer her horse into the force of the current. All of this I understood very well.

She had thrown a shoe, once, from the window of a top-floor Parisian apartment. She could not explain why she had done it. It had been entirely deliberate. She hadn't dropped it, she had hurled it and taken pleasure in its speed and in the bemusement of the boy whose walk was interrupted, abruptly, by a lady's shoe thudding onto the ground in front of him. The boy picked it up and looked around. He peered up at the sky as though the shoe was a kind of weather. Rain, snow, hail, shoes. George had been delighted.

She had thrown coins from bridges into streams.

She had thrown a wet slab of quince tart down a stairwell.

She had thrown a hat down a crevasse of a glacier in Switzerland.

And now she was about to throw her own body off a Mallorcan cliff.

As she scrambled down the ledge, the metronomic voices started up. *Yes? No. Yes. No?* They were very loud and her own pulse was loud and her blood was moving so quickly through her veins that it made a screeching noise.

George is fine, George is fine, I told myself. *This is just a blip. A weird impulse which will pass. George is fine.*

The ledge was so narrow that she had to grip plants in the rock face for balance. Maurice and Solange had stopped further up, horrified, and were shouting.

"Mama, stop!"

"Mama, what are you doing?"

Solange had a terrified squeak in her voice. I could feel even from far away her small heart pounding, frenzied as a fist. Maurice was red-faced and red-eyed and furious.

"Come back," he yelled. "What are you doing?"

George didn't hear. She had forgotten her children were there. She had forgotten they had ever been at all.

She stopped shuffling forwards and looked down. I did too, and felt dizzy at the nothingness under us, the plummet, the long rocky void that stretched between the edges of George's feet and the water below.

She could just step forwards. There would be a rush. Fear spreading wide as wings.

The biggest gulp of air.

She would go headfirst, down.

Down, and then a little splash.

There would be a gloopy *thunk* as the water swallowed her.

That would be all.

(That would just be the start.)

She loosened her grip on the weed she'd been clinging to. Took a breath.

Yes?

No?

I braced myself to catch her. Perhaps I was strong enough to slow her descent. Perhaps I could hold her back just long enough for her to come to her senses.

She breathed a gasp of sea air.

She swallowed.

And then she began, unsteadily, to reverse up the ledge, back towards her children.

The stones underfoot were digging through the soles of her shoes. The wind felt very cold, even in the sunshine. Pulse subsiding. Blood flowing a little more serenely.

"What was that?" Maurice demanded, as soon as she was on solid ground. "What was that? What were you thinking?" He was so angry he was struggling to breathe properly. Beside him, Solange was cowering. She started to cry.

George looked from one to the other, perplexed. "What do you mean?" she said. "I don't know what you are talking about."

She sat down, pulled her children down either side of her,

and stared out at the water. They were all suddenly exhausted. George's mind, now, was just a single question—I realized it was what she was asking in her book, what all her monks were worrying and talking and praying about—which was: *What am I to make of life?* She dug out a cigar and lit it and they sat like that until the sky clouded over and it started to rain and Maurice said, gruffly, that perhaps the Mallorcan climate really had got rid of his colds, not with sunshine and clean air, but simply by washing them away. George smiled to acknowledge the effort at humor, but her mind felt smooth, erased, scrubbed down, almost-but-not-quite-not-there.

I REMEMBER

Ham and I sit on rocks, a little way down the hillside from the path. I watch the back of my mother's head as she limps homewards, turning occasionally, craning to see what's happening between the two of us. She was reluctant to go, would have sat with us and chaired the meeting if she'd had her way. I ushered her off with glares. In any case, there's nothing to see: Ham and I haven't said a word to each other since sitting down. His face has turned from pink to white. He is jiggling one of his legs, sending little ripples down the skirts of his robes, waves approaching the shore.

So? I say.

So? he says.

So what happened to you at the beach? Why didn't you come?

Look, he says, *you can't just—you can't just turn up like that, with your mother, telling everyone everything like that. You can't just—*

They didn't believe us anyway.

Ham's leg stops wobbling for a second. *That's not the point.*

Well what is the point? I ask.

I was busy, he says.

Near Ham's right foot, a lizard pokes its head out from under a leaf. It approaches his toes in stilted, stop-start bursts. It pauses, arm and leg raised, to swivel its eyes around.

Look, I say, *that lizard's going to climb onto your shoe.*

But Ham is distracted, not paying attention to the lizard or even to me, really. He's chewing the skin at the side of his thumbnail, jiggling again. *The thing is*, he says, *it's not as simple as just not-becoming-a-brother.*

That lizard, I say. *That lizard really is going to—*

And then the lizard really does. It scuttles, first onto Ham's foot, and then disappears under his robes. Ham doesn't react for a second, and then leaps into the air as though he has been stung, wheeling around, arms raised, jumping and stomping and lifting his knees in a strange, idiotic dance, all the while making high-pitched little *Ah, ah, ah!* noises that morph into a kind of squeal. He kicks up dust. He looks like a vision.

Where is it? I say. *Where did it go?* But he isn't listening, still twirling and hopping, and there is nothing for it, really, but to laugh. I sense before I start that he will hate this, that nothing would be worse than laughing at him, but somehow knowing this makes it all the more appealing, and the more he prances and shrieks, the more I lose control, until my eyes are streaming and my face hurts and my stomach muscles begin to cramp.

Oh my god, I whisper, when I can catch my breath. *Oh my god, oh my god, oh my god.* And then I start laughing again.

The lizard is nowhere to be seen and I think it must have run away, but Ham is too far gone in his panic to realize: he leaps through the air and then pivots as though the air itself is attacking him now, as though it is not just one lizard but hundreds, crawling all over his thighs and groin and stomach.

Ham, I say, when I've regained control of myself. *Ham. It's gone. You're fine. It's gone.*

It takes a long time for him to hear or to believe me. He seems reluctant to stop, now he's started. But gradually the speed of his stomping slows, the whirling stops, the dust subsides.

Ham, I say. *You're fine.*

He is crimson-faced. He sits back on his rock, tucking his robes around his ankles so that nothing can penetrate them. He is breathing heavily. I wonder if he is going to burst into tears.

I don't want you to have a baby, he says.

I'm not doing it on purpose.

I don't want to not be a brother. I don't want to get married or anything like that.

Well, I say, *you have to.* It does not occur to me that he considers this a decision he has to make. It does not occur to me that there are options for him that do not exist for me. *It's simple,* I say. *So it's fine.*

Maybe the baby will die before it's born.

I consider this. It is certainly possible. I have seen it happen on occasion: women in the village who have swelled up and then, mysteriously, deflated again. Black lace and the church bell ringing. Tiny crucifixes in the graveyard, exactly the height that dogs like to piss on. Perhaps this will happen to us—to me—to the baby. I search myself for a reaction. Would I care? Would I be sad? Would I cry like the women in the village, dressed up like dark brides in their mourning clothes, red-eyed, puffy-faced? For now I just think: *that might happen. That would be all right. If Ham would prefer it, perhaps I would prefer it.* (And now a feeling does creep forward: not exactly sadness at the thought of the dead baby, but disappointment that the rosiest version of the future would fade, that Ham and I would not then get married, would not be a family, and beyond that, just out of reach, a stirring panic.)

Maybe the baby will die, I say.

Can you do anything to make that happen? says Ham. And then he seems to hear himself. His eyes widen. His tone is softer when he says, *Nothing that would be dangerous to you. Nothing bad. I just mean, are there ways to make it so there isn't a baby anymore?*

Isn't that the sort of thing you know about? I consider Ham's expertise in this area: if you have sex when you're on your period, you can't get pregnant; if you wash yourself afterwards in the water, you can't get pregnant. He seemed to know all sorts of things about how not to get pregnant. *But then again,* I say, *maybe you don't actually know anything.*

I looked it up in the books at the Charterhouse, he says, *but there's not much there. Some plants that work very early on, but not once you're . . .* He gestures at my stomach. *Not much once you're already big.*

Now we are both staring at my belly. I put a hand on it, pushing it in a little. *Do you know when the baby will come?* I say. *Does it tell you that in the books?*

Ham frowns. *Maybe in the spring? I don't know.*

He has regained control of himself. The lizard is forgotten. The flustered, angry look he had when he chased us from the Charterhouse is gone. His cheeks are cheek-colored again, and something about his calmness makes me very afraid. I realize I'm going to burst into tears. I try to catch myself in time but can't.

Why are you crying? He looks crestfallen. *Blanca, what's wrong?* He shuffles over from his rock to mine, which isn't big enough for the two of us; he ends up shunting me off onto the ground, and then somehow I am sitting in his lap, his arms are around me, somehow we are kissing, somehow his hands are under my dress, skirting over my stomach, touching my breasts.

We have sex on the ground, barely hidden by undergrowth. I lie with my back on the dirt, silty earth running through my fingers. It's uncomfortable when Ham presses down on my stomach, but I don't say so. It's not like the times before, by the sea. I watch him as though I am barely involved, as though I don't know him at all, his thrusts and heaves a little ridiculous, and when it's over I look around for a pool, a puddle, or a pond, anywhere I can wash.

Don't worry, silly, says Ham, heaving himself onto the ground beside me, taking a strand of my hair between his fingers. *We don't need to worry about that anymore.* We lie like that, Ham murmuring nice little things and me hearing them, until it starts to rain and I realize that I'm going to cry again.

Will I see you at the beach? I say. *Like normal?*

I'll let you know, he says. *I'll tell you soon.* And then he shrugs into his novice's cape and scuttles back up the hill to the Charterhouse, which has been glowering at us from above the whole time, like a particularly dark cloud. He moves so quickly and lightly up the path that I think of the lizard again, Ham's whirling and the dust, and it is only this that distracts me from another fit of tears.

My mother is standing in the doorway when I get home. I wonder if she has been waiting there the whole time.

Well? she says. *Well? What did he say?*

I stop to consider. What did Ham say? I can't now remember a single thing we talked about, a single resolution reached. There was the idea about the dead baby, but this doesn't seem worth mentioning. *Nothing,* I say, *not really.* I rub my hands together. A curl of dirt peels off the skin. And then I think about Ham's hands in my hair, about lying side by side on the ground, not having to worry about washing after sex now, his meaty breath on my cheek. *Oh,* I said, *no, actually, he did say something. He said everything will be all right, not to worry about it.*

My mother's mouth straightens into a grimace. She claps her hands together and grips them in front of her stomach as she surveys me. *Well,* she says, *isn't that a relief?*

BLANCA

A confession: what scared me most about George on the cliff—more than Maurice's face, or Solange's little pounding heart—was how it made *me* feel. Maurice felt rage, Solange felt fear, George felt the fractured tick-tock-yes-no of the inconsequence of her own existence, and what I felt was that I would like to die. Not that I might. Not that I feared it. But that I wanted to. Which—ridiculous, obviously. It was a feeling I had never, since my death, allowed myself to engage with. If I thought about it there would be no unthinking it, I sensed; if I went there, there'd be no going back.

A door I had kept bolted. A precipice of my own that I had never before peered over. I had intended to keep it that way forever, but out there on the cliff, I briefly lost myself in George, and there was a moment when what George wanted and what I wanted were one and the same, namely: nothing whatsoever.

I was tired. I had been conscious for 379 years. Fatigue, condensed, was a death wish: a death-of-death wish as clear and sharp as a chip of ice.

Yes? No. Yes. No? went George's internal metronome, and I thought to the rhythm of her monosyllables: *George-is-not-fine.*

I thought: *I-am-so-tired.* I thought: *I-hate-this-life.* I thought: *I-want-to-die.*

There was a version with a caveat: *If George is going to die, then I want to die too.*

But there was also this, simple: *I want to die.*

When I first died, I came to at once and discovered I was not dead entirely. At the time—I was fourteen, and somewhat stupid—I was reluctant to see my condition as contradictory to the teachings I'd received while alive. There had been no mention of ghostliness in church beyond the Holy Ghost, which did not feel relevant to my state. There had been Jesus, of course, back from the dead. And eternal life, naturally. But there had certainly been no indication from the priest that life after death might take place exactly where one's life before death had left off. And so in those early days, I drifted through the cloisters confused and newly pious, chanting my mantra, *Trust the Heavenly Father, Blanca; Trust in the Heavenly Father.* It was, I told myself, part of a grander plan, the ultimate goals of which remained unknown. God surely knew what was up.

After a while my confidence in God's plan wavered, and I began to suspect that what I was experiencing—disembodiedness, a great reduction in strength, apparent invisibility—was a kind of glitch. Something had gone wrong in the divine system, and soon this would be discovered and rectified. I was like a coin that had fallen between flagstones. Someone, sooner or later, would pick me up.

I gave up on trust and put my faith in mercy: *Mother Mary will have mercy, Blanca.* She would, I promised myself, take pity on me and relieve me of my nothingness one way or another: she would either give me my body back, or transport me to wherever it was that well-behaved little girls who had nonetheless had the misfortune to get tangled in knots with men called Ham were supposed to go. I knew full well that what had occurred between me and Ham was a cardinal sin on both sides, and I was grimly prepared to discover my real fate was eternal hellfire. Even that, I thought, would be preferable to this slipped-through-the-cracks existence, this haunting, this going-nowhereness. And in any case, there was still part of me that believed in and yearned for heaven, which I imagined involved a lot of good seafood and gentle harp music of the kind I had never actually heard while alive.

Once I got over the mercy thing, I went on a positive thinking kick, and tried to convince myself that what I was experiencing was in fact a wonderful gift. *You have been given a second chance at life, Blanca.* Most people just died. I had seen plenty of deaths: gasps and falls and thuds followed by nothingness. My own death being so equivocal, so porous and unsure, was therefore a tremendous thing. I had lost nothing, not really. I could still smell orange blossom and wet earth after rain, could hear little children laughing, and could see the gluttonous blue of the ocean on the horizon. (These are the kinds of things that you try to convince yourself are what matters when the things that actually matter have gone horribly wrong.) It was true that I was utterly friendless and mute; time, by that point, had taken on a vertiginous, slimy quality. But nevertheless: a second chance at life! How lucky I was. It was the sixteenth century. I took up travel.

You are here for a reason. I stuck with this one for almost the entirety of the seventeenth century—and beyond, I suppose, since I kept up with the habits I had developed over those years. Ham was long dead by then, but I had found the process of haunting him and the other brothers so gratifying and so necessary that

I simply transferred the focus to the men who followed in his footsteps. There was always somebody. I simply could not leave. There was Brother Pablo, who snuck into the village and poked sticks through windows to hitch curtains aside and watch women undress. I was careful in my efforts with him, wanting to be proportionate, not to overdo it. I made everything prickly. He could never sit down without finding something sharp on his seat. His bed was always full of grit and sand, no matter how many times he brushed the sheets clean. And then there was a voice in his ear, saying, *You are being watched.* It made him paranoid. It made him wonder if he was going mad. It made him cautious and nervy, never wanting to be naked, even when he was alone.

Then there was Tito, the butcher who supplied the Charterhouse and who tormented his own daughters. I was swift, direct. His wife, who relied on her rosary at all times, woke one morning to find it missing. On the floor by the hearth: a single bead. And there, on the threshold: another. She followed the trail from her cottage to the outhouse behind the butcher's shop, where she saw her husband with her sixteen-year-old. The next day she invited him on a clifftop walk with her; they stood together on the very edge and she looped her arm behind his back; she laid her head, just for a moment, on his shoulder, and then she pushed him. That was the crowning achievement of this period of my existence.

And so on. *You are here for a reason* was a very helpful thing to believe. I meted out punishments and took my revenge and generally kept an eye on everything, and was more or less content, or at least resigned, to be doing so. I tried not to let doubt creep in. I tried not to ask questions, to think it through, to attempt to understand. But being there for a reason did imply that somebody had done it on purpose, cast me as a bit player in a grand plan. But after a hundred years of considering this, the logic faltered. If it was God's plan, or really anyone's at all, it was a terrible one. I was a solitary, ineffectual child-ghost. My success with the butcher was a one-off. I was not up to the task of policing the sex lives of the living. I was not up to the task of anything, if truth be told. I just did my best.

Do your best, Blanca. Short-lived. 1698–1701. My best was depressing.

It is not so bad, Blanca. Similarly.

One day at a time, Blanca. This one stuck. I stopped looking forward. I only looked back. I never anticipated. I never hoped, just was. Day by day. I still had things to do, of course. I kept up my avenging role. I looked in on my family (more or less, and as time went by, less and less). But mostly I measured the days in the smallest ways I could find. A pomegranate seed, nudged in the path of a sparrow. A spider scaling a pane of glass. I watched medicine congeal in jars at the back of the apothecary's shelf; cork stoppers drying, cracking, crumbling into the liquid.

If ever I slipped up and began thinking about things like *tomorrow* or *the day after that,* I distracted myself. There was no need for it, I told myself. All I had to do was watch the paint on the shutters of the bakery peel and flake and expose the rotting wood beneath. There was Brother Samuel, who was handsy and voracious. To him I whispered: *There is no God.* There was an elderly man who invited young girls to his house to look at the flowers in his garden. I hid his walking sticks. I poisoned his flowers. There was the Sacristan, and all that business with the bread crumbs.

And then there was George, and I fell in love with her, and the mantra changed again, became *George is fine.* George being fine made everything else seem fine.

She was the most interesting thing that had ever happened to me.

I stopped caring about paint and seeds. I started caring about her, and the little gaggle of people she cared about.

And then George was not fine and the words in my head became *I want to die* and I was confronted with the enormity and impossibility of my own existence, and the only thing that might have helped relieve me was to have a body that could vomit or faint or spontaneously combust, and even that had been lost.

I cycled through everything that had ever given me comfort:

Trust the Heavenly Father, Blanca.

Mother Mary will have mercy, Blanca.

You have been given a second chance at life, Blanca.

You are here for a reason, Blanca.

It is not so bad, Blanca.

One day at a time, Blanca.

George is fine, Blanca.

Still I found myself spinning around like a top: *I, Blanca, want to die.*

I thought about the solid, regular thud of a heartbeat. I thought about Adélaide's beard. I thought about bones underground, dry and hard, the soft coil of an earthworm looping a femur.

I thought about a conversation George and Chopin had once had, early in their stay when they were still making time to talk to each other and Chopin was well enough to listen. They had just had sex and George had squeezed next to Chopin on his narrow little bed.

"If I believed in Hell," she said, "it would be a place where nothing happened. It would be a house, somewhere in the provinces, with the best housekeeper in the world. She would make everything run smoothly and nothing would ever be out of place and nothing would ever break. They would never allow a dog inside in case it pissed on the carpet. That is the closest I can get to an idea of eternal damnation. Tidiness, but forever."

Chopin played with a curl of her hair. "It sounds nice," he said.

(I knew then that they would not stay together.)

"It's just as well I don't believe in Hell," she said. "Sometimes I feel I can't believe in anything eternal."

Here I am, I said. *George, George, here I am.*

I thought about how, when I said that, her body changed. How her eyes narrowed a fraction, lashes almost meshing. How I felt, just for a second, for the tiniest fraction of anything eternal, that maybe she knew I was there.

GEORGE REMEMBERS

George first sees Marie at the theater. It's a crowded night, a popular play, and everyone who you might think would be there is there. The stalls are a who's who of the men of the literary set, and George is there amongst them, casually disguised in coat, trousers, and boots. Above, women occupy the balconies: a halo of ruffles. It's January and the weather is freezing but it's clammy inside; everyone is pink-nosed, rubbing their hands together, and the women are fanning themselves unnecessarily, which gives George the impression of being in an aviary, surrounded by wings.

George has heard of Marie, of course; it would be hard not to have heard of her. She's in the papers a lot. She's the sort of person that people George knows boast about knowing. But tonight is the first time George will put a face to the name, and she goes into the experience with curiosity, nothing more: a chance to see a famous actress performing in her prime. It is a Hugo play. Marie has the eponymous role, Marion de Lorme, a courtesan. George expects a good night. She expects to be entertained. She expects, she supposes, to be impressed.

And then there, sauntering onto the stage, is Marie. She is

in her mid-thirties, a few years older than George, pale, relaxed. She moves with an artlessness that makes the other actors on-stage look like puppets. When she speaks, it sounds louder than the other voices, though the volume is roughly the same. There is something about her nonchalance that reminds George of her old friend Boy, of the nights spent scratching at the walls of the Convent of the English Augustinians. George straightens her back, pays more attention. It happens over the course of maybe fifteen minutes: George falls in love with her.

George understands herself well—at least she believes she does. She is twenty-eight, an emancipated wife, a woman living independently in Paris; she is used to people and the ways she reacts to people. She remembers the flush of recognition she felt on seeing her future husband for the first time, that day at Tortoni's, as though they both remembered their own futures, as though all that was going to happen was stored somewhere inside their minds already. She remembers how her early encounters with Jules left her in a state of hot restlessness; she didn't know what to do with her hands and smoked incessantly. Sometimes a stranger's face across the street will strike her in the same way: a pleasing jolt of attraction. She is used to this by now. It is part of being alive, of being in Paris, of being George.

The feeling Marie provokes is familiar, therefore, but also wildly surprising. George mistakes it, at first, for anger—thinks, *Who is this woman taking up all this room?* Thinks, *I can't see anything else on the stage with this woman so loud and distracting.* Thinks, *I can't follow the play, I can't follow the play.* She fidgets, cranes her neck, checks the faces of her peers to see if they too are aggravated by Marie.

And then it settles on her like nausea: desire.

It is as though I am watching my soul, she thinks, *walking around in clothes and boots, outside of my body.*

It is a terrible, agonizing, unbearable experience and she goes back to the theater night after night to feel it again.

George writes Marie a letter. She decides from the start to be unrestrained. That was the joy of women, after all, that you could say exactly what you meant, and they'd only think better of you for it. So she writes that seeing Marie was like seeing her own soul, and that she could not think, of all the experiences of her whole twenty-eight years of her life—she couldn't think of *one* that had shaken and delighted and absorbed her as much as seeing Marie on the stage, and now she couldn't be satisfied, or even really relaxed, until she had made the acquaintance of—no! more! become *friends* with—the woman who had made her feel like that. And so, she writes, would it be all right, would Marie be willing, to receive a visit from George Sand?

It seems she has only just sent off the letter—she is still feeling elated, a bit giddy, at having put all her feelings on paper so freely—when there is a knock at the door of her apartment, and, in a swathe of fabric and feathers and noise, Marie is suddenly there, embodied and perfumed, dashing across the floor to where George is standing by the fire, throwing her arms around George and saying, in just the same voice she uses to project onstage, *Here I am!*

Marie is the first person George has loved who makes her feel stupid. It is not something Marie appears to do on purpose. It is just an effect of her presence, as though she gives off a kind of stunning gas. She renders George clumsy, slow-thinking, almost mute. They meet in the evenings, to go to the theater or have supper, and then sit by the fire in George's rooms until the early morning. When Marie says, *What did you do today?* all George can think to say is *I thought about you.* This isn't even true: her brain is working, constantly; she is writing a new book, but if Marie asks her to talk about it, all she can say is *It's a story about a woman.* Faced with Marie, George finds herself tantalizingly simplified: she wants to do complicated, impressive things for her new friend, but Marie never seems to notice any lack.

In the aftermath of Marie, however, really the minute she leaves the room, George becomes electrified. Her thoughts feel crisp, everything about her feels clear, and she writes through the night in a frenzy, wanting to get down on paper how it is a person can transform a room, a building, a whole city, like a sudden new season. Winter, spring, summer, autumn, Marie. Marie makes George ambitious the way that spring does; she makes George determined the way that winter does.

George is aware that some people feel their feelings less and less intensely as they grow older; her friends talk about how music once affected them more powerfully than it does now, how seeing a painting or reading a poem at sixteen years old was a kind of shock to the body in a way they no longer experience. George has wondered, listening to them, if this is something that is happening to her, too. Now she knows for a fact it is not. If anything, she is aging in reverse: the world feels more and more astonishing with every year that passes. It is as though she is shedding skins, becoming rawer. Before Marie, there was nothing in the world that struck her as thuddingly, as immensely; and now there is Marie, and George's days are an onslaught of sensation that winds her: God, the birds! God, the taste of coffee! God, the faces of absolutely everyone she passes on the street!

Then Marie appears in her rooms, and George becomes smooth and quiet and absorbent again.

They arrange to go to dinner, George with Jules, and Marie with her lover, Alfred. Once they have all arrived and been seated, it strikes George how terrible an idea it was. She and Marie formed the plan in a mood of giggly mischief, when the thought of dragging the men along seemed entertaining. *I will shoot glances at you whenever Alfred talks about himself,* Marie said, *so I'll be shooting you glances the whole time.* Now, George looks from Jules, who is twisting his lips into an almost-pout, to Alfred, glowering at his wine. The men have sensed at once, or have been well aware for some time, that something threatening is happening between the two women. Normally, George would fill the silence with stories of her own, but because Marie is here her brain is sluggish. When she tries to speak her tongue feels too big for her mouth.

They run out of small talk over the soup. There is a thick silence amongst the four of them. George spoons her food around the bowl, as though an idea for something to say might emerge amongst the lumps of potato. Jules pushes back from the table an inch and his chair scrapes against the floor. Arthur belches, very quietly, into his hand. When George looks up, it is straight into Marie's eyes, which are glassy with tears. Marie's face is bright pink. George realizes Marie is struggling to suppress laughter, is losing the battle, is about to crack. On seeing this, all the solemnity and awkwardness of the occasion lifts off her shoulders and she cackles, a delighted, maniacal hoot. This sets Marie off in turn, and the two of them are irrepressible now, beside themselves entirely, shaking and crying and rocking in their chairs. George thinks she might wet herself.

Oh no, oh no, Marie gasps when she manages to catch her breath. *This is awful! Oh no!*

The men sit still and silent until George and Marie manage to get ahold of themselves, wiping tears and occasionally lapsing into aftershocks of giggles.

I'm sorry, says Marie, flapping her hands at her face to dry her eyes. *I just couldn't.*

Alfred leans towards Jules, acknowledging absolutely nothing, and says, *I have been working on some new poems. I plan to publish several in the autumn,* as though answering a question he feels he should have been asked.

When the ordeal of the dinner is over, they go out to the balcony to smoke. The couples divide, Marie with Alfred looking out towards the river, and George with Jules on the other side, facing the city. George watches Marie, who appears to be remonstrating with Alfred, caressing his cheeks and neck, pressing kisses onto his hands. George wishes she hadn't seen it.

Jules remains silent, as he has been for the whole evening, and George feels gaspingly, dizzyingly alone.

What's wrong? she asks. She is being disingenuous. *Don't you like Marie?*

He doesn't answer for a while, and then says, *It's not about how much I like her, is it?*

Later, the men go inside to drink. George and Marie are left alone for the first time all evening. Marie kisses George's cheek and George feels instantly drunk.

What a disaster, says Marie, beaming out at the dark rooftops, reaching for George's hand. Marie's skin is cold and George presses it against her thigh to warm it.

Catastrophic, says George.

Alfred says you have no grace. He says you are like a man.

George lights a cigar. *God forbid you spend time with someone like a man,* she says. It is one of the cleverest things she has managed to say in Marie's presence, but Marie laughs exactly the same amount as she does at George's duller jokes.

He's jealous, says Marie. *I told him of course he has no need to be, that I love him more than anyone in the world, and still, he rages, calls me Sappho, calls* you *Sappho. Imagine!*

It stings. George says, *I love you.*

Marie grips George's hand tighter. *I'm miserable,* she says.

You know she sleeps with women, Marie Dorval? says Jules. *I've heard all sorts of things about her.* Jules is looking tetchy and thinner than ever, strutting restlessly around George's rooms, picking things up and putting them down in different places. George follows him, replacing objects he has disarranged. A few days have passed since the dinner with Marie and Alfred and he hasn't kissed her once. He seems unsure whether or not to do so now.

You should be careful, Jules says. *People might talk.*

It is true that people, including Jules, might talk. It is also true that they do anyway. George has become aware of a strange disjunction in the way her friends mention the matter: instead of saying, *I heard something is going on between you and Marie Dorval,* what they say takes the form, always, of a warning: *I heard you should be careful of Marie Dorval. People might talk.*

Who had they heard this from, George wonders, if people were not already talking?

She wonders if Marie is hearing the same about her: *Be careful around that George Sand. I've heard she sleeps with women.* Of course, Alfred will be saying that, and worse. Except most people don't even come right out and say *sleeps with women* either. They say: *she has a passion of the same nature that Sappho had for the young Lesbians.* As though comparison is more discreet.

George veers between caring what they think and forgetting what it felt like to care. Some days, she is full of a kind of disgust she can't stand, to imagine what people are thinking about her and Marie, to *know* what George herself is thinking about her and Marie. The idea of it, two women together: so unnerving it settles on her as a kind of sadness. The rest of the time, however, she can't recall what on earth might have led her to that kind of melancholy. She tries to remember what it felt like, the shame. It is very faint, like a memory from a night of drinking. She can't piece it together into something meaningful, and in the absence of clarity, what can she do but shake off the fragments and resolve to be more herself than ever? She feels willful. She wants to live up to the gossip, to give people something to talk about, to give Alfred a real reason to be jealous. She wishes she actually was sleeping with Marie.

In fact, it happens only once between them. Jules has gone off to stay with friends—he is barely talking to George anymore, and they both seem to know that whatever they had is no longer there—and Marie appears in George's rooms after supper. She stands in the doorway looking glassy-eyed, tired, perhaps a bit tipsy, and instead of collapsing into a chair by the fire as she normally does, proclaiming that someone or other is a bastard, that nobody has had a fouler day than she has, she crosses the room and stands with her face inches from George's. Her gaze flickers side to side; she is looking from one of George's eyes to the other, checking.

George's heart stutters.

It's not that she hasn't imagined this, hasn't tried to think through exactly how it would work, who would do what, what would go where, whether props would be required, the mechanics of the thing. It is not as though she hasn't stood naked in front of a mirror and inspected herself, amused and frustrated to think she knows less about how to please someone with a body like hers than she does men with their alien protuberances. She has tried to picture, as graphically as she can, a vulva that is not her own, summoning its textures and folds and odors, its curls of hair and wrinkles of skin, and asked herself: *is this what you like? Is this attractive? Appealing? What do you do with this?* She suspects Marie knows the answers to these questions, and George does not.

It's just that, despite all her attempts at preparation, she really has no idea what to do.

She wills Marie to show her. Except that now, Marie is doing nothing, just standing there, lips parted around breath that smells of wine, and so it is George who ends up taking a step forward, moving her face just close enough to kiss her. It is tentative, a sort of sip. George pulls back and searches Marie's face, wondering if it was the right thing. Marie, still distant, presses her lips together in a knowing little smile, breathing out a small laugh through her nose, and then leans forwards to kiss George back, and George almost wants to sink to the ground with relief, because now it's all right, she thinks, now it doesn't matter what she knows or doesn't know, it's all right to be ignorant and strange, talked about or not talked about, a man or a woman, stupid or clever. Her body loosens, a sigh, and her hands find their way under Marie's clothes as though a seal has been broken.

A BLEEDING WILL KILL HIM

And then Adélaide's milk ran out. Her supply had steadily declined since she had arrived at the Charterhouse, and she appeared, now, to be gripped by a deep depression. She barely lifted her head when Amélie, carrying the hassocks and milk pail and singing a song about a cow and a gray donkey, appeared in the courtyard. Amélie was in a spectacular mood, sashaying across the flagstones, and she did not notice at first that the goat was limp with misery.

She interrupted her own song to call, "Adélaide! Adélaide!" Her head was full of what she had heard George say two nights previously: "We can't stay here. If we stay here, I don't know what will happen. We'll all go mad. We have to go home." It had taken the form of a promise in Amélie's mind. They were going to go home to Paris. And that was why she felt like singing Christmas carols and folk songs about donkeys. "Adélaide!"

Adélaide turned her back.

"Adélaide!" Amélie persisted. "Come here, sweet thing! I have something for you."

What Amélie had for Adélaide was only a persimmon from the garden, but it was enough to lure her. The goat shuffled forwards to take the fruit and consented to settle beside the hassock stack while Amélie commenced twisting and squeezing her teats.

Nothing came.

"Adélaide?" Amélie said. Her voice dropped to a murmur. "Adélaide? Are you all right?"

Adélaide seemed not to see or hear. Amélie stroked her ears, her neck, her beard. And then Adélaide lay down and closed her eyes.

She was not dead. Her stomach rose and fell over her breath. She pushed her nose into the ground, as though trying to get even lower.

Amélie looked, for a moment, as though she was going to burst into tears. She knelt beside the goat and took a long, ragged breath, then exhaled slowly through pursed lips. She shook her head. It was just a goat. She didn't care, not really. She was going to Paris. She was going to Paris.

Adélaide seemed to sense both the wave of sympathy and its sudden withdrawal. She nuzzled the ground. She kept her eyes shut, long eyelashes clasped over the squeezed-tight lids.

Amélie left her, returning to the cell empty-handed, explaining that Adélaide had dried up and become downhearted.

"No milk?" said George. There was a crackle of panic in her voice. "None?" She had been at her desk writing a letter about the piano. She was imploring the French consul in Palma for help reasoning with the customs officials. There must be something somebody could do. And now there was no milk. Amélie tilted the pail to show it was empty.

Chopin had regained some of his senses since the day George and Maurice had gone to Palma, but not all of them. He remained listless and vacant. The hope of the piano and the milk may or may not have done any real good, but the ritual of mixing Adé-laide's contribution with the homemade almond milk had been helpful to everyone, had given us all the impression that, on this small scale at least, things were under control. The prospect of doing without it made us all anxious.

As George and Amélie were having the milk conversation, Chopin was in his room coughing and clutching his throat. His teeth were all falling out, he believed. He had inadvertently breathed them in. He was coughing and coughing to dislodge his teeth from his throat, but all that came up was blood.

George listened to the spluttering from Chopin's room and stared into the empty milk pail and said to Amélie, "Go and fetch the doctor."

As she waited for Doctor Porras to arrive, George sat down and stood up again four times. She crossed to Chopin's door and then spun around and made instead for the room where she and the children slept. She poked her head in and saw that Maurice was lying on his bed reading and Solange was dozing. George withdrew before either noticed she was there. She paced to her desk and took out three cigars, which she tucked into her jacket pocket. Then she turned on her heel, and went into the garden.

Amélie ushered Doctor Porras in while George was smoking outside, and by the time George realized he'd arrived, he was in Chopin's room with the door closed. She put her palms and ear flat against the door. She heard: a low voice and the sound of her own skin brushing against the wood. She knocked and pushed the door open a crack before anyone replied.

"Doctor Porras?" George said.

The room had a musty, damp smell to it. Chopin was lying on his front with his shirt lifted up to expose his back. Doctor Porras was prodding him in between his vertebrae, occasionally bending down to press his ear to Chopin's shoulder blades.

"Doctor Porras?" George said again. "Chopin?"

When Chopin turned his head to look at George, his lips were bright red. He had been coughing facedown in his pillow and blood had transferred from the linens to his skin. I noticed his hair had grown long, how, with his gaudy red lips, he looked girlish. His skin was pallid, almost blue, and the sight of him like that stirred something in George. She crossed the floor to him and kissed him, on the mouth, right under Doctor Porras's jowls.

George pulled back, wiped her lips, and retreated to the piano stool.

Doctor Porras's expression: concern. A hint of horror.

"What have you found, Doctor?"

Doctor Porras wiped his own mouth with the back of his hand, as though he had been the one doing the kissing. He cleared his throat. Frowned. "Well," he said. He wiped his mouth again. "It is a clear case, now, of contagious consumption. I suspected as much initially, but it is fully evidenced now." He recovered his composure enough to point to the swelling in Chopin's neck (neither George nor I could see it) and the bright glassiness of his eyes; there was a general limpness about him. Chopin was flaccid and pale and on the brink of tears.

Doctor Porras lifted one of Chopin's hands and splayed the fingers. He showed the reddened fingertips and pronounced them engorged. Chopin's blood was stagnating, he explained. It had ceased to flow. It was pooling in the lungs, the hands, the throat; this was why Chopin was coughing up so much. Urgent measures were needed.

"Are you certain?" George said. "I just feel so sure, Doctor, that if you saw him when he was well—and he is well as much as he is ill—you would reconsider." An exaggeration. "If it were consumption, surely we'd all have it by now. He is with me and my children almost constantly."

Doctor Porras's hand darted back to his mouth. "There have been doctors in my family going back six centuries," he said. I swatted him and he bristled a little. "I can assure you I am not mistaken. I know a consumptive when I see one, and if you and your children have not yet contracted the disease, it is only a matter of time." His eyes lingered then on George's lips, as though he could see the sickness upon them, working its way between her teeth.

"I see," said George.

"Furthermore, if the villagers are not infected, madam, it will be down to God's grace. Your husband—your *friend*—is a danger to those around him. We must act now to save his life, and when he is strong enough to travel it would be wise, it would be essential, for you to return to—to wherever it is that you came from."

Chopin had been silent throughout all of this. He had shifted onto his back and was looking at the ceiling, which seemed lower now than it once had. "What do you recommend, Doctor?" he said.

"Bloodletting," Doctor Porras said. "At once." He had come prepared, with his lancet and scored bowl. He flicked open the blade and laid it on his knee. "Only three or four incisions today, I should think. More tomorrow."

Chopin frowned and sought out George's eye. She twisted her lips and rubbed her forefingers and thumbs together; she wanted to smoke. Chopin held in a cough, swallowing and swallowing. Neither of them said anything. They had both known for a while now that everything had gone wrong, that the sunlit winter of clean air and good work had become, instead, cold and stymied and deathly. But now they were both scared, and scared in the same way and at the same time.

Doctor Porras unbuttoned Chopin's cuff, rolled up the fabric, and held Chopin's forearm across his lap. Chopin turned his face away.

Everyone was braced and I couldn't stand it.

That was when I did it. Slipped up. Fell forwards. After holding out for so long.

I turned the page and read ahead. I saw the future in which Doctor Porras pressed his lancet to Chopin's forearm, nicking the vein in three places. Blood draping like a sleeve over Chopin's skin, running into the bowl. Chopin's face white, whiter. He would start to cough, and the pressure of the coughing would make the blood run faster and George would say, "He's going to faint. Watch out, watch out, he's fainting," and then Chopin would faint.

I saw how Doctor Porras would continue the bleeding until blood reached the highest notch on the bowl. Pooled, the liquid would look black. Amélie would be summoned to carry it away. She would walk very slowly so as not to spill it. Then there would be wiping, cleansing, bandaging. Doctor Porras muttering instructions for the night, that he would be back in the morning. Chopin on his back like a corpse and George sitting by his head, stroking his hair, watching Doctor Porras leave, saying almost nothing and staying there all night. Chopin's coughing would get deeper and worse, and around four in the morning his eyes would open very wide, very glassy, and he would twist round on the mattress, hoist himself up, stand. He would go to the piano and sit at it and spread his fingers as though to play a chord, but he would not press down, would just hover there and then get back into bed.

I saw that George would put her hand against his forehead

and find it very cold. She'd take his hand and feel his pulse, which would be quick, thrumming like a trapped insect.

She would think: *He is leaving me. He is leaving me.*

And then he would die.

His death would be to George like the loss of an organ: a sudden dark space inside her where there used to be something vital.

I retreated, tumbling backwards to the present moment, in which Doctor Porras was wiping the blade of the lancet on the side of his trousers.

"You are happy to proceed?" Doctor Porras said.

I was too panicked to think about what I had done, what I was doing. I focused all my energies on George, on saying, as loudly, as clearly as I had ever said anything, *A bleeding will kill him! A bleeding will kill him!*

George looked steadily at Doctor Porras. She did not blink. Her tongue darted out between her lips, then back in.

A bleeding will kill him! I said. I held her face. I spoke my words right into her mouth. *George, listen. A bleeding will kill him.*

"A bleeding will kill him," said George.

"A bleeding will kill him," she said again. "I cannot allow you to proceed, Doctor Porras."

He protested, of course. Something about: pressure. Something about: urgent. I wasn't paying any attention to him.

George? I said. *George?* I touched her hands, I touched her face, I touched her mouth.

She looked right at me. I could have died.

I REMEMBER

At first there is only my stomach, protruding where it used to dip in beneath my ribs, and a slight additional fleshiness to my breasts. None of this is obvious, or at least I don't think it is when I'm dressed and busy with the pigs or shopping or housework. I fasten my clothes as tight as I can. I fight my flesh, scrunching it up, pressing it in.

Then, butterflies in my stomach, jittery and distracting. When my mother asks what's wrong I just tell her I'm worried, I'm so worried, I don't know why. Household objects, friendly greetings, waves in the street: they make my insides flip as though the world is ending. Days of the week: the word *Tuesday* seems laden with foreboding. *Tuesday. Thursday.* The butterflies get worse. My stomach churns.

The sensation coheres into distinct movements. Not butterflies. Some sort of spider. Several small snakes. A lizard.

There is a thing with arms and legs inside of me. The baby extends hands and feet into my body, helping itself to what's mine: a scoop of lungs, a punch of bladder. Sometimes it is so sharp, so precisely aimed, it makes my knees buckle.

Naked in bed, I stare at the dome of my belly. The pummeling from the inside intensifies: a writhing, fidgety little poltergeist in there. And then there it is: a bump in the stretched skin where the baby kicks; next time, even more clearly, a small, brief bulge protruding out of the large, permanent bump. The baby is feeling for an escape route. It bangs and scrapes at the walls of me. I put a hand where the movements are; I try to imagine this is a maternal, soothing thing to do. I try saying, *Hush, hush, little one. Go back to sleep.* But I can't muster the right tone, and what I really mean is *Go back to the kind of sleep you were sleeping before you took up residence in my body, whatever that was. Go back to that.*

I notice babies in the village as though for the first time. Until now, they have been background noise, like wind blowing, or rain on the roof. I peer into the wives' arms at church, at the milky, squirmy faces of their infants, which scrunch up like dried figs when they cry. It makes me shiver to look at them, to think of what I am doing, what my body is doing. The mothers of the village cluster together, rounded or hollowed out and clutching their children. I imagine standing with them, holding my own squirming creature as though it is a normal thing to do, to be, to have happen to you.

When it's cold my nipples turn purple and white; they start to burn. I scurry off in search of something warm to press against them: my mother, my sister, the pigs, stray dogs. It is the only thing that helps: the hot blood and beating heart of another living being.

What's wrong with Blanca? my sister asks as I fling myself upon her.

She's got chilly tits, my mother says, and from now on when my sister visits she strokes my bump, my hair, my cheeks and says, *Sweet little Chilly Tits, what's wrong now?*

Mothers in the village have started to notice me back, of

course, and even the younger, unmarried women now cast their eyes over me as I waddle and heave my way around. I know they are wondering about me. I know they want to ask—about the baby, about the husband my mother has promised is on his way, but who has yet to materialize. But nobody dares and I hold my tongue. *You'll see soon enough,* I think. Which is the kind of thing you think when you are hurtling forwards the way I am, when the future is happening to you faster than you know, when you can see things happening only one way and not millions of ways.

I stop going to Mass. My mother tells everyone I am ill. I tell myself I am ill. There is something very, very wrong with my body.

It won't be tiny and helpless forever, my mother says. *Soon enough it'll be big enough to talk and help with the pigs. And then in no time it'll be sleeping with monks and getting itself into all sorts of*—she pauses—*adventures.*

The walk to the coast each week gets harder. Feet heavy, stomach heavy, bladder compressed, I drag myself anyway. Most of the time, Ham is not there. I sit on the rocks and soak my toes in the water and feel that I'm on the edge of a precipice, and when I get home I tell my mother it was great, he was very loving, he says the wedding will happen any day now, he just has a few last things to get straightened out.

Sometimes, though, he really is there, swimming despite the cold, or lounging, affecting a kind of casualness he never seems to feel.

Ham, I say, *what's happening?*

I want him to say the things I tell my mother he says, or at least some paler, looser version of them: *Everything's all right; everything is wonderful.*

Ham, I say, *the future is happening inside of me.*

I want him to say, yes, he agrees, there is only one possible future.

Instead he says, *You're getting bigger.*

Soon, stretch marks run from my thighs to my nipples so that my body looks like an old, frayed cushion. Ham stops coming altogether, and so says nothing at all.

THE SUDDEN FUTURE

I'd slipped up, obviously. Broken the one rule I still kept. I had seen the future and in narrating it, had changed it.

So often I had wanted to change it! But had never thought I actually would.

Talking to the living was a centuries-old habit by then. How many times had I said, *Mary doesn't like you!* to Ham? And had he ever really got the message? At best, I thought, I succeeded in passing on a sense of malaise. Maybe my messages, little gaggles of words, made it into people's dreams. I had never before believed I could be heard, really heard, like any other voice. And yet there had been something in George that had seemed to hear me, something that had felt, if even for a second, my fear and my urgency and my love.

Now we were living in an alternative world. George should have been about to commence a long, bitter journey back to France with Chopin's corpse. And yet here she was, blowing into a cup of coffee that was too hot to drink. And here Chopin was, sitting up in bed and drinking almond milk and Solange making him laugh with an awkward display of shadow puppets on the wall.

They had no idea.

I said to them all, *You have no idea,* then stopped in case George was listening.

But I couldn't hold back. I looked forward again, to see how it would play out, this new future I had created.

I saw: the journey back to France on a ship shared with hundreds of pigs; Chopin coughing worse than ever and Solange throwing up over the side. Maurice saying, "Is he going to die?" George throwing up her hands, saying, "Well, yes, eventually, my bear, as will I and you and Solange and every last one of these pigs." The wind throwing salty punches into their mouths when they spoke. I watched their arrival in France, disembarking at Marseille with wobbly legs and wide eyes; everything there sharper than Mallorca; the edges of everything looking crisp and deliberate, the blues extremely blue; white-sailed boats in the harbor and everyone very alert.

I saw them rush straight to the office of a French doctor, who declined to poke and prod and inspect Chopin and instead placed the backs of his hands against Chopin's forehead and chest. He scrutinized the rest of the family, too: compared to the people around them in Marseille, they all looked pale and thin.

"He needs sun," the doctor said. "And rest. You all do."

"Is it consumption?" George asked.

The doctor twitched his head. "No. He's tired," the doctor said. "An infection. It will clear up if he sleeps and eats as much as he can of everything he likes."

They took this advice to heart: *as much as you can of everything you like.* They rented a house by the water and set up Chopin's bed so that he woke and saw the cold January sun hitting the ocean. They ate pastries and meat and sweets. Solange attacked an apple tart at such speed she was almost sick.

I saw them getting rounder, stronger, George standing taller, walking with a swagger.

I saw visitors outside their house, asking Amélie to let them in. They had heard that Chopin the composer was in residence; they had heard that George Sand the writer was there.

"They are resting," Amélie said. "They are very tired."

George contemplated faking their own deaths, just to get a moment's peace and quiet from all the people knocking at their door. "We could play dead, just for a little while," she said. "Wouldn't that be a treat?" But Chopin shuddered and refused. He was enjoying the feeling of coming back to life. He didn't want to lose that, even if it was only pretend.

The weather warmed and they traveled north. To Paris. Amélie beside herself, George strutting ever more delightedly, Chopin in raptures about soft furnishings and new waistcoats and clean, bright, white gloves; his new piano, he announced, was finer, even lovelier, than the one whose delivery he had been so anxiously awaiting in Valldemossa and which, on their departure, he had sold to the wife of George's banker in Palma. Solange ate little almond cakes and was called pretty by everyone. Maurice was introduced to George's friends, who claimed to barely recognize him, he looked such a man now, he was so grown up. He was allowed to sit with them at salons. He took up smoking and appeared every morning in a gray cloud, still looking like a lanky, almost-bearded version of his mother.

In the summer they moved to the big country house I'd seen in their memories, which was slightly darker in its future version, slightly less expansive and golden, but still full of fresh countryside smells.

Chopin appeared taller as his health improved.

He and George both seemed to get richer. They stopped worrying about money.

They started having sex again.

They kissed whenever they passed each other in the house, on the grounds.

Chopin published his preludes, and George published her book about the monks. They both got paid.

George still wrote all night, but in the daytimes she would go out riding. In the early evenings she played billiards. She avoided thinking about things that made her want to die. She muffled her metronome.

She wrote: *I find life acceptable because it is eternal. You call that my dreaming. I call it my faith and my strength. No, nothing dies, nothing is lost, nothing ends, whatever you say. I feel profoundly and passionately that those that I have loved and seen depart live on in and around me.*

(*Yes!* I cried. *Yes! That's it!*)

They were all well. They were all happy. They found life acceptable because it was eternal.

I should have stopped there, I knew. I had seen them safely delivered back to France, returned to good health, happy relations restored between them. I had seen Solange eat an apple tart crust-first. What more did I need? They were alive. They were happy.

For crying out loud, Blanca, stop looking now. Don't go any further.

Of course I went on.

THE FUTURE BEYOND
THE NEAR FUTURE

I saw Solange growing up. I saw her face narrow, her breasts fill out, and her waist shrink. I saw the way she carried herself change from flat-footedness to a calculated poise. When she started her period, she didn't panic or cringe as I had done and seen other girls do. She touched the blood with her finger and rubbed it against her thumb until it was sticky and then dry. She was like an ivy plant, taking root and sprouting upwards, gripping onto everything she could.

She gave up dressing like her mother and wore only women's clothes.

She noticed that men could be momentarily silenced by the movement of her eyelids: she lowered them, looked up.

She turned seventeen and learnt to bite her lower lip.

She set her sights, ever more sharply, on Chopin.

He was not her father, after all. He was a friend, she told herself. An unmarried friend.

She asked him to teach her the piano, properly this time, not just to play those tunes he'd taught her when she was a child. She wanted real lessons.

I watched, appalled, as she sidled up beside him on the piano stool while he played, her hip against his hip, thigh on thigh, knees knocking. When he shifted to reach the piano, she let him press right into her. When he reached for the high notes, she put out a hand to rest atop his. He stopped playing, twisted slightly to look at her. He was very serious. She was very entertained.

"What do you want, Chop Chop?" she asked.

He wanted to kiss her. He didn't know why or where this urge had come from. He did not know that this had all been set in motion years previously, when Solange had shown him her bruises in the Charterhouse and he had been so angry at George's indifference, or even earlier than that, when Solange was born, or even earlier than that, when he was born needy and changeable and overly moved by attention. It had certainly been in motion the week before, when Solange, looking at herself in the mirror, had decided she could have whatever she wanted.

It seemed to Chopin that his love for Solange appeared suddenly, from nowhere.

It seemed to George as though she had woken in an alternative world, where everything was wrong and backwards and upside-down and her daughter and her lover were betraying her.

George took Solange to Paris. Solange transferred her attentions to other men.

Chopin wrote angry letters, demanding George return, accusing her of being the unfaithful one.

George took a lover in a fit of pique.

Solange got engaged to one man, and then another, a sculptor for whom she and George had posed for a portrait, and who afterwards, once George had left, made love to Solange in his studio beside the still-wet bust of her mother.

Chopin wrote angry letters asking why his permission had not been sought for the engagement(s).

Chopin wrote angry letters accusing George of no longer loving him.

George wrote angry replies saying she was coming home to sort all of this out.

But when she and Solange arrived back at the country house, everyone was furious with each other and nobody knew how to express themselves. Chopin said he felt ill but in fact he was lonely. Solange said she felt lonely but really she was angry. George said she was angry but mostly she was very, very tired.

Maurice, who had stayed in the country with Chopin, said he was leaving, and he was the only one who really meant what he said.

"You can't leave," said George to Maurice. "I love you, I love you, I love you, my bear."

The sculptor fiancé arrived at the house, drunk, and demanded George pay off his debts before the wedding. He told her the many and various things he had done with her daughter. Solange watched and laughed and tried not to notice that the man she planned to marry was a brute. George told them both to get out and they refused. There was a scene. A hammer was involved. George took a blow to the chest. Somebody produced pistols. And then, at last, Solange and the sculptor left the house.

George said, "I have never done anything to merit a daughter like her."

George said, "I no longer love her, or that is what I believe at least."

George said, "As far as I am concerned she is a cold rod of iron, an unknown being, a stranger."

The country house became very dark. George receded into herself. Chopin started coughing again. George went to Paris and left him behind. Then he went to Paris and even though they were both there they didn't talk.

They didn't talk and didn't talk until they were *not talking*, until they had separated entirely from each other and were talking to their mutual friends about how badly the other had behaved. George told everybody she was relieved. Chopin was domineering, she said, and a drain. She had stayed with him so long out of pity. She saw, now she was free of him, that she had spent the best years of her life tied to a corpse. She did not mention Solange, though Chopin did, saying George had betrayed him and had treated her daughter cruelly. He said she knew nothing about love.

Solange had a baby and the baby died.

Chopin and George ran into each other, once, in the stairwell outside a friend's apartment. Chopin told George she was a grandmother (he did not then know that the baby was dead) and George opened her mouth to say more, to say sorry, even, for how things had gone, but before she could get the words out Chopin had given her his hand, bobbed his head, and left. She listened to his footsteps as he descended, and to his coughs echoing up the stories.

A year later, George received news that Chopin had died. She held herself very still with the letter flattened on the desk in front of her. She was facing a large first-floor window in the country house, overlooking the grounds. It was a cold day, late October, everything was becoming crisp and brittle; the night's mist was lingering on the lawns. A rabbit emerged from a flower bed, pausing to nibble the grass, then startled at some noise George couldn't hear and dashed for cover. George's mouth cracked open and she cried. The sound was a kind of groaning that lasted for hours, for days.

(And once I'd got this far, the only hope was to keep going.)

THE EVENTUAL FUTURE

I forged forwards in search of comfort. And, eventually, what I saw in the future was George at the country house, working in the garden with a little girl. The little girl was Nini, Solange's living child, left to George to raise after Solange and her husband separated. George adored her. The two of them worked outside together, building grottoes, piling earth up into mountains, and planting violets across their miniature peaks. They made foundations and streams. They carried wheelbarrows of soil and rocks to and fro, side by side, for hours on end, for days on end.

It was the happiest I had ever seen George. It was the least complicated love that George had ever known. She dreamed about Nini, she worried about Nini, she sourced only the best foods, only the best toys, only the best clothes, for Nini.

Best of all was that Nini loved George.

Once, Solange's husband, the sculptor, arrived at the house and rode away with Nini. George was sick with worry, but Nini was returned to her within weeks, having told everybody she wanted to live with her grandmother. They resumed work on the garden. They told each other stories about the creatures who lived there, sleeping under the soil, snacking on seeds.

George took lovers and kept one of them, but seemed to care less than she once had about that sort of thing. She thought less about sex and more about the smooth, white shoots that erupted from crocus bulbs.

When I first saw signs that Nini was getting sick, I decided not to think too much about them. I sped up, eager to get past the illness and return to the garden. But the faster I went, the weaker Nini got, and when she died and George was once again reduced to a solitary, howling heap on the floor of her study, I thought, *It's not fair. It's not fair. It's not fair.*

George wrote a story. In the story, the narrator hears a voice, as if from nowhere. It is a voice she knows. A voice of a girl she loved, who died. The narrator asks herself if she is dreaming, or if this thing, this wonderful thing, is really happening. Is the dead girl speaking to her? She sets out in search of the girl, looking everywhere—it's a beautiful day, the sun is shining, the air is fresh and easy to breathe—until she comes across the girl. She can't believe it's really her. The girl wonders why the narrator is so surprised. The narrator explains: it is because the girl has died. The girl is supposed to be gone. In response, the girl laughs and says, "Dead? Only very rarely do children die here! I can see that you are not of this world and I do not know how you arrived here." The narrator has wandered, somehow, into a world in which the young live forever, and can speak and laugh and breathe the clean, good air.

I thought, *God, I love that story.* I read and reread it: the voice, the search, the child laughing, so unamazed by her continuing existence, so casual about the length and tenor of her life.

When George was an old lady, she couldn't work in the garden anymore, but she dreamed about plants more than she did about people.

A hot-air balloon was named after her.

It was summer when the pain in her stomach started, and she was seventy-one. It was all very matter-of-fact: she was dying. She summoned Maurice and Maurice's children to her. Told them to be good. Told them to move her bed towards the window so that she could see the sun. Told them to—

And then I couldn't see any more.

PRELUDE NO. 16 IN B-FLAT MAJOR, PRESTO CON FUOCO

The piano arrived first and a few days later came the fire set-ters, like a call and response, sound and echo. I was in a daze, having gorged on the future in a frenzy, unable to control myself. I landed back in the present as though dropped from a great height and was surprised to see them all looking so young and so belea-guered. Solange: a child. Maurice: gangly, unsure. Chopin: as pale and watery as the almond milk he drank in lieu of Adélaide's.

George was smoking in the garden, staring out at the hillside below, which had turned, since they'd first arrived, from yellows and greens to a narrow spectrum of grays. Goats scaled the ter-races, bleating tremulously. A farmer, far below, was swinging an ax against the trunk of a dead olive tree. I took in everything about George: the smoke curling up from her mouth and fingertips, the way the fine hair around her temples lifted up in the wind, the crease in the skin between her eyebrows. She was alive, she had so much more life to get through, she had so many years ahead of her before she would reach her garden, before she reached a day where she and Nini were stuffing moss between stones to make a miniature cave and she would notice how impossibly small Nini's fingernails were and nothing was wrong and there was no sense that anything was about to go wrong.

We heard the piano approaching several minutes before it entered the square outside the Charterhouse. The sound was the braying of two furious, exhausted donkeys. It was the wheels of the cart hammering the cobblestones under the Pleyel piano's great weight. It was the laughter and shouts of the gaggle of locals—teenagers and interested wives, mostly—who had gathered behind the cart to watch the spectacle.

George heard the commotion from outside and passed through the rooms without saying a word to the others. She marched down the corridor and then out of the building. She waited as the racket approached, smoking and leaning against the wall. She seemed calm, calmer than I'd ever felt her, the metronome stuck on *no*. When the crowd came into view, and the piano wobbling atop the cart, her mouth widened into a grin, a real grin, so broad she almost dropped her cigar.

She turned to haul open the Charterhouse doors and almost danced down the corridor back to the cell.

"Chopin!" she called, sliding through the door and across to his room. "Chopin! My Chopinet!"

He looked up, unsmiling. "What?" he said. His tone: irritated, a warning not to disturb him, not to be too loud or too close.

"The piano is here," said George.

Chopin shook his head and looked away from her. "No, it's not."

"Come and see."

"No," he said. He pouted. "I won't." He shook his head. Crossed his arms.

Childish, I told him. *Stop it.*

Then the piano really did arrive and he did stop it. As the men entered the cell and loudly steered through the main room towards Chopin's, he sat up a little. As the piano emerged, entire and enormous, through his doorway, he seemed so surprised he looked as though he might throw up. He turned a little green. He looked around for something to be sick in. And then he stared at the piano again—his own, real, familiar piano—and the nausea passed, in its place a sensation of enormous strength.

He stood up. He couldn't take his eyes off the instrument, wincing when they grazed the wall, or when they thudded into a chair as they staggered across the floor. He made unconscious little brushing motions with his hands whenever anyone touched the piano. He waited for the driver and his men to off-load their cargo in the center of the room. He waited for George to offer them water, coffee, and for them to glance warily at Chopin and decline. He waited as they shuffled off, shooing out the local children who had been waiting in the corridor. The cell door closed behind them.

He approached the piano slowly, as though worried it might not recognize him. He reached out a hand and stroked the side of it. He took a breath before lifting the lid, stroking the keys.

George and Solange and Maurice were all silent.

"It's here," said Chopin.

"Play something," said George.

He played the earliest preludes, the ones he had worked on when the family had first arrived and things had not yet gone wrong, when the compositions really were preludes to something else: little beginnings. The Pleyel piano was untuned after the journey and Chopin winced on occasion, but there was sinew in each note now. Chopin's hands melted into the keyboard as he played, as though he and the piano were made of the same substance, as though he and his music were not so different after all. Rising chords reaching up, up, up to the peak of the Valldemossan hill. A crunchy, uncomfortable section with a thick, strong melody cutting through it, reassuring and unwavering. Skittering, jittery patterns, jumping high to low, skipping between rocks, between light and shadow, between orange trees in the garden. He seemed to have gone back in time and become the man he was in his memories: bigger and firmer. Or forward in time, somehow: he looked like the man he would become when he got well.

And while he was playing, all the things that irritated me about Chopin seemed to subside. There was no denying how much he irritated me: he was petty; he was self-pitying. He never seemed to notice how George, my George, labored over him and for him, how she cut short her sleep to tend to him, how often in the night when she was sitting with her writing, he would intrude on her mind and she would tumble into a well of dark, worried thoughts about him. He appreciated none of it. He was like a little child, only seeing that his needs were not being met. But that all seemed to dissolve when he was playing the way he played the new piano, as though the music happened despite, not because of, him.

Chopin's feelings, when he was playing, were big, good, worthy feelings. Feelings like: *Love.* Feelings like: *Courage.* Feelings like: *I am a ghost alone in the world but there is a kind of loveliness in how melancholy I am.*

Chopin, when he was playing, was a man you could fall in love with.

And astonishingly, wonderfully, it stayed like this for days.

He sat up straight and his fingers moved over the piano like the beating wings of an insect. As though in response, the rest of the family seemed to resolve themselves. They began to feel hungry, to notice that María Antonia's meager portions had not been satisfying them. George began to laugh with Solange, and as she did, they remembered that they used to laugh together. Maurice found that he felt less bitter towards Chopin, was even grateful, at times, for the music that accompanied his reading. Even Amélie seemed pacified by the piano. She let her shoulders drop from their usual position near her ears. Sometimes, when she was cleaning the cell, she would stop what she was doing and lean against the doorframe of Chopin's room to listen. Her fingers drummed against her skirt.

Chopin worked and worked, and when he was not working he was humming the melodies he had been writing. He was finishing up, he told them. He was nearly done, just the final touches. He was playing everything through, just to check.

And then there was a morning, a few days after the piano arrived, when he was finished. The last prelude was done. He called George and the children into his room to listen; Amélie, who had come to bring him his almond milk, stopped in her tracks when he started to play and, distracted, lifted the cup to her own lips and sipped. The piece was breathless, opening with urgent chords and disintegrating almost at once into frenzied fluttering up and down the length of the keyboard, both hands chasing but never quite catching each other. There was a sort of mania to the speed of it, as though Chopin felt he was running out of time, as though he had to cram everything left unsaid into that final minute of music.

I felt a wrench in the silence that followed. There was something about Chopin's music that lodged itself between your teeth—where teeth had been—or slipped through your ribs—where ribs had been—and became a new part of your body—where body had been. There was something about it that gave you a body to borrow, if you didn't happen to have one, and let you live in it, briefly, extraordinarily. I couldn't bear the thought that it might be over.

Chopin bent over his papers and began scribbling notes as frantically as he had played. George leant towards Maurice and murmured, "I was wrong thinking we had to leave. Look at him."

"Look at what?" said Maurice, the old irritations creeping back. "He's the same as ever. He'll keel over at any second."

"He's not. He's better," said George. Her mind was racing. She was imagining the weather turning, as it surely would any day now, how the garden and the sky and the hillside would all soften and brighten in the spring. She was thinking that they could grow things for themselves. They could get another goat to keep Adélaide company and maybe even a sheep or two, and when Chopin sold the preludes he would get some enormous sum of money, enough to cover their expenses in Mallorca for another year, maybe more. She could even, perhaps, afford to hire a tutor for the children so that her time would be more her own and she would be able to write more and therefore earn more and therefore write more and so on.

The future was running away with her, or she was running away with it, peeling off from the trajectory I'd seen: a glossy alternative life in a Valldemossa where the sun always shone and nobody minded they were there.

"We can stay here as long as we like," she said, louder than before, and Amélie looked as though she might burst into tears. "Until the summer, or next winter, maybe longer. We could stay for the rest of our lives. Don't you want to stay here forever?"

George felt giddy, unable to sit still, and the sensation of hunger that had been growing over the past few days became unignorable: she wanted to feast on things, to celebrate, to devour the world and all its possibilities. They could stay as long as they liked in Valldemossa, and to prove it, she thought, she would go shopping. She would make the villagers take her money no matter how hard they tried not to.

"I'm going to buy food," she said, and left the cell before any of the others had a chance to question her.

The market when she reached it was not especially busy, but there were enough people that George was taken aback when she saw them. She was used to the limitations of the Charterhouse, the same few familiar faces. Here, confronted by strangers, un-familiar words shouted from stall to stall, and cooking smells, her body softened, resolve wavering slightly. She sidled around the edge and lurked. She seemed to think she was being discreet, though everybody had noticed her the second she arrived; they were all, to greater or lesser extents, keeping an eye on her move-ments. She crouched down in the shade between two buildings, smoking and rocking on her heels, observing the comings and goings of sellers and shoppers like a rival trader, eyeing up the competition like a stray cat, prowling behind a butcher's shop.

She was preemptively annoyed with everyone she saw, but I couldn't help delighting in the strangeness of my neighborhood through her eyes: sunlight very bright and the smell of garlic on the air and everybody looking a little harder around the edges. The language sounded like crisp nonsense in her ears. She was earnestly noticing all of it.

The Sacristan walked, with his sister in tow, across the far side of the square. They paused while the sister haggled for some coffee beans, and then proceeded on their way. I half considered following them—I'd been negligent in my efforts to ruin his life since George arrived—but while I was dithering I felt George startle, so I stayed put.

The fishmonger, a silver-haired man who undercharged everybody, had arrived. He was slapping sea bream down on a slate, laying out eels and combing his fingers through them to make them neat. The smell of salt and seaweed and the ocean caught George's attention. Dark, grinning monkfish and luminous, sharp-finned bonito fish and two enormous, bulbous, tangled squid, white and marbled, gelatinous, ghostly. George had never seen such things in her life. She could not look away. She breathed deep, hungry breaths. Saliva prickled at the base of her tongue.

She thought: *Fresh fish would be good for Chopin.*

She thought: *What is that thing, tentacled and slimy?*

She thought: *I'm going to make him sell it to me.*

She stood up. She took a final drag of her cigar, then dropped it and ground it underfoot. I thought she had never looked finer than she did in that moment, squaring her shoulders and stealing herself to approach the fishmonger.

"How much for this fish?" She asked in French, and did not let her voice waver on the word *fish*, though she had no idea if it was accurate.

The fishmonger, intuiting her meaning, shook his head and flapped a hand as though to shoo away a seagull. "It's not for sale."

"How much is it? I want to buy it. I'm going to buy it." She got out her money and waved it at the vendor. "How much?"

"No," he said. "No."

What she did next was certainly not right, certainly not fair, certainly not advisable. She didn't even think of it in advance, just did it, which meant I was as astonished as everyone else. She reached out and grasped the squid around its middle (it was cold to the touch, and softer than she was expecting; it squelched in her grip) and took it. It slid off the table, tentacles swaying so it looked reincarnated.

George slammed a coin on the table and marched away, tingling with pride and relief.

She wasn't to know how much the squid cost. He had refused to tell her, after all. She wasn't to know that of all the things she could have made off with, this was the most expensive, the item that really did cost a stratospheric amount, was considered a great delicacy, immensely special. She wasn't to know that the amount she'd put down would not have bought a single tentacle.

And there she was, the foreign woman from the Charterhouse, stealing a squid in broad daylight with no shame whatsoever, parading through the village with the spoils of her crime. People gawped. Whispering began. Grew louder. Became a sort of howl.

"That woman!" the fishmonger cried. "That woman has stolen my squid."

"That woman needs to be taught a lesson."

"That woman is no woman at all."

Of course it wasn't just this that brought the fire starters to the Charterhouse. Everything was already in motion by then. It had started before the squid, before the rumors about Chopin's health, before, even, the first missed Mass; it had started the minute George and her family arrived in Valldemossa and revealed themselves to be who they were: strangers and strange and strangely insouciant about their strangeness. The villagers were ripe for riling up, and George had been riling them for weeks, and nobody should have been surprised, least of all me, at what came next.

For a while longer, though, George was oblivious. The light began to fade as she ascended the path to the Charterhouse, swinging the squid, breathing in its sharp salt smell, reliving her victory against the fishmonger. She had felt powerful and proud in a way she hadn't since they'd come to Valldemossa. She had felt more like herself again and she was hungry for more: more victory, more eating, more George. Her stomach rumbled. As she approached the doors she paused and heard the faint sound of Chopin's piano, drifting out from the windows of the cell into the garden and across the cold, dusky air towards her.

GEORGE REMEMBERS

Imagine falling in love without music.

George can't. Has never done it. Or at least, if not without music, then without noise: the background crackle of gossip at a party, footsteps crossing the floor a little too eagerly, violin scales stuttering from a stranger's window as your beloved approaches on the street. Here, in this badly lit salon, where George is feeling restless and hungry and absentminded, there is suddenly music— she has never heard anything like it before—real music, piano music, dense and light and quick. She lets the sound happen to her; it is like getting caught in a storm.

She hasn't seen the man at the piano before. He is slight, a little hunched, with hair that bounces when he plays. She moves to the front of the room so she can see his hands on the keys, firm and broad-knuckled and moving very quickly. Spiderlike, she thinks. Spinning something.

Who's that? she asks the woman next to her.

George thinks about her husband, suddenly; she tries not to so often, but now she is thinking about him, about falling in love with him and the sensation she had at the time of im-

mense relief, of exhalation. Love as solid ground. Love as safe
harbor. And then, when she did not love her husband anymore
and that sort of love no longer seemed safe, she found Jules,
and felt the same way about him, although less so; there was
a little more anxiety alongside it second time around, a little
more risk. With Marie there was really no sense of relief at
all, no security, only exhilaration, although the affair never
seemed to quite get off the ground and soon Marie's attention
drifted to other lovers. There have been people since Marie too
and the sensation of love each time has continued to shift away
from relief and towards alarm.

This is how she feels now, observing Chopin at the piano as
he plays the third movement of the sonata: scared.

Who's that? she says again, and the woman beside her repeats
what she just said: it is Frédéric Chopin, Polish composer, friend
of Liszt, very particular, very sickly, probably a genius.

George tries to catch Chopin's eye as the evening progresses.
She has always been interested in genius. But somehow his attention is never on her. He leaves the piano, starts talking to Liszt,
turns aside to cough into his gloves. George watches. He is talking
to a woman now, nodding and smiling and performing a humor-
less laugh. George switches positions, maneuvering into a new
conversation so that she is directly in Chopin's line of sight. She
tries to be interested in other people and their conversations and
finds that she isn't.

She coughs loudly. She calls out brashly for someone to
bring her more tobacco. Stamps one foot, then the other. She
swears Chopin is flinching, directly angling his body away
from hers so that all she can see is the spread of his shoulders

under his shirt, his ear, an occasional hand waved to emphasize a point.

Why won't he look at her? It is as though she repels him.

For months, George tries and fails to attract Chopin's attention at parties. It is nothing sinister, her desire to speak to him: she is interested in him and she can't understand why the feeling would not be mutual. She is extremely interesting, after all. She has published eleven novels now—twelve if you count the one with Jules's name on the cover—and is much talked about. Most of the time she is fending off admirers. She is thirty-two, though people mistake her for younger. She is, she thinks, surveying her reflection in the dark windowpane, good looking. On the other side of the glass is the city, and somewhere in the city is Chopin, ignoring her.

She writes to friends who she thinks might know Chopin. She writes, first, cautiously, that she enjoys his music, that she would be interested in fostering an acquaintance. Over time, she gets looser: he looks so ill, so frail, she writes; she plans to take care of him. He needs the support and love of someone who can nurture his talents. Who better than George?

She feels ravenous. She feels irritable. When she is alone, she lies down, eyes closed, and tries to recall whatever it was he was playing the first night she saw him. All she can summon is some subpar tinkling melodies of her own creation, childish and obvious. She remembers what the music felt like, by turns teasing and surging (in essence, orgasmic), but the details are gone. Her memory is awful; she's not even sure she can picture his face, though she thinks about it—the idea of it—enough. What is it, then, if not the face, if not the music, that she's clinging to?

Sometimes, she thinks, *you just know that someone has something to do with you.*

One of the friends writes back: are you in love with him or do you want to eat him?

Another: I have spoken of you to him but he seems not to notice, or to prefer not to notice. I believe he is engaged to a Polish girl.

George writes: Where will he be, at parties and such? Small events only. I have no luck meeting him at these big gatherings. Tell me where I can run into him.

Eventually, there is good news. Chopin is hosting his own soiree, where he and Liszt will play duets, and she is invited. She is so gratified she forgets to send thanks.

George does not know what to wear to Chopin's party. She surveys jackets, trousers, waistcoats, skirts. If she wears a dress she will look like every other woman; if she wears a suit, just like every other man. There is always the Turkish costume, she thinks, as a joke. But then the thought is lodged, and she wants to see it; rummages through discarded clothes until she finds it at the back of an old trunk; crumpled but still bright, a long silk coat with embroidered shoulders, voluminous trousers that gather at the ankle, slippers with toes that flick upwards like tongues. Further excavation yields the little red hat. She wore the outfit once, years ago, in a play, and has not thought of it since.

She tries it on. She imagines walking into the room in it. She imagines saying *hello, hi, yes, very well thanks, how are you;* wonders if anyone would comment, and if so whether that would be a good or a bad thing.

Then Maurice wanders in looking for a book. He finds what he was looking for, leafs through it, then looks up and says, absentmindedly, *You look nice.*

It is settled then. She'll go to the party in her Turkish costume and if this doesn't get the composer's attention, she thinks—well, there is no way that this will not get the composer's attention.

When Chopin does, that evening, turn his eyes on George—at last, at last—she notices they are pink-rimmed, as though he has been crying or recently asleep. He extends a hand, crisply gloved, and says, *Madame Sand.* There is something about the emphasis he places on *Madame* that makes it sound like a question, though she does not know what, exactly, he is asking.

Yes, she says.

If falling in love were still relaxing, perhaps she would relax now. The work is done. It might take time, might be messy and complicated—there is an engagement with a Polish girl to be broken off, after all—but George knows that, eventually, Chopin will fall in love with her. She knows this as though she has already seen it happen. They have something to do with each other, she feels sure, and what better thing to do with each other than love? Yet what it feels like is being a key on Chopin's piano, ready and taut, waiting to be pressed.

She is nervous. She forgets to eat. Smokes more. Drinks more coffee.

She listens to him play and tries to commit it to memory. Nocturne, op. 27, no. 2 in D-flat major: trilling and sad, notes tumbling like gravel underfoot on a steep path. The jarring surprise of the A natural that seems like a mistake at first, then holds its nerve until it earns its place. Flurries of ornamentation played slowly and deliberately: urgent, whispered asides. She thinks, *I will remember this.*

Chopin lets her sit across the room from him as he plays.

And then he lets her sit by the piano.

And then she is beside him on the stool, watching his hands draw sound from the keys.

Chopin says, *I don't know what to make of you.*

George says, *Don't make anything of me.*

He is suspicious of her clothes, her smoking, the way she talks. She thinks: *I am the A natural in Chopin's D-flat major.*

Chopin lets her come to his apartment for dinner, and then lunch, and then breakfast.

When he is unwell, he allows George into the room to bring him broth, and turns even Liszt away. He coughs until he retches. Blood spatters on the handkerchief, the palms of his gloves. Some days he is so ill he looks shrunken, wide-eyed like a child, and George is so overcome with love she almost wants to breast-feed him.

His engagement to the Polish girl ends, as George knew it would, though he doesn't explain why.

Nocturne, op. 32, no. 1 in B major. Sudden pauses. Stop and start. Tentative and inevitable. The sound of someone working something out, growing certain, bolder, more tender and definite— definite enough to, one day, reach back from the keyboard and find George's hand resting by her thigh on the stool. He grasps it. She interlaces her fingers with his.

BURN IT ALL DOWN

María Antonia was beside herself at the sight of the squid. She slid it from George's arms and cradled it as though it were a monstrous, faceless baby. Solange was thrilled, squealing and reaching out to touch the tentacles draped over María Antonia's elbow. The smell, now that it was indoors, was sweaty and sharp; it drew Maurice away from his book. He pressed the squid's flesh with a finger and sniffed.

"What is it?" he asked.

"Squid," María Antonia said. She beamed. She forgot to limp. She was already thinking of cooking it, slicing open the body and scoring the inside of the flesh. Olive oil. Garlic. Lemon zest. She would serve it with red peppers and onions. If she started now, she could squirrel away a large portion before the family was hungry. They knew nothing about anything after all, least of all good food, and wouldn't notice what was missing. She envisioned a plateful of sharp, salty squid; she considered the way the flesh would resist and then succumb to her teeth.

"Are we going to eat that, Mama?" asked Solange.

George said, "It's food. Of course we'll eat it," and then glanced questioningly at María Antonia. "It *is* food?" She mimed eating. "Yes?"

María Antonia considered saying no. She twisted her lips. A flicker of conscience. She nodded. "Very good food," she said, and then when George still looked uncertain, spoke louder: "Yes, food, yes."

"We're celebrating," said George. "We're going to stay in Vall-demossa. We're celebrating."

They were all so intrigued by the squid, so wrapped up in their plans, that they didn't notice Amélie slipping out of the cell. They didn't hear her footsteps as she ran down the corridor, nor the door heaving shut behind her when she left the Charterhouse.

It was beginning to get dark as Amélie followed the path down to the village. I wasn't sure where she was going and she didn't know either. She was too angry to know anything. The village seemed emptier than usual; it was freezing and people were huddled indoors. Her steps were heavy and loud. The sound bounced between the buildings and amplified. She ran towards the market square, only slowing when her breaths became rasping. She had been panting, gasping in the cold air. She bent over, hands on her knees, and tried to collect herself.

Those bastards, she thought. *Those lying, sickly, selfish bastards.* They had told her they were going home. George had promised her they were going home. It had all been decided; it should have been a matter of days before they packed up and left. George had promised her.

Calm down, Amélie, I said. *Hey, Amélie. Listen to me. Calm down.* I wanted to tell her about the future. I wanted to tell her it was all right. They were definitely leaving. They were going to Marseille. I had seen her there, opening the door of the big house by the water, telling the visitors her master and mistress were indisposed, possibly dead. It was going to be wonderful.

But her thoughts were loud and angry and she wasn't listening to me.

When she saw the crowd approaching, it took a moment for it to register as strange: it seemed so true to her own feelings that there would be an angry mob ahead of her, as though her thoughts had left her head and taken human form. A cluster of bodies filled the width of the street, torches aloft and a low, angry thrum running through them. She realized, then, that this was something beyond herself and hostile. She felt a jolt of fear. Before the light reached her, she ducked into an alley, pressed herself against a wall, and waited for them to pass.

News of the squid incident had spread fast through the village. It was a spark falling on dried grass. The villagers were ready for it, had been ready for a while, and soon the place was ablaze. Was it not enough that these people had come to the village with strange customs and clothes and a strange language? Not enough that they were heathens? Was it not enough, even, that they were sick, infectious, had brought consumption with them? Now the foreigners were stealing from them, too. It was intolerable. It was insulting. They could not bear it any longer. Their anger had a coagulating effect. People emerged from their houses with torches; they gathered together in the market square; they found themselves moving, without discussing it, in the direction of the Charterhouse.

The torches gave off a low, unstable light that made the path and the plants and the buildings all look insubstantial. They passed by Amélie's hiding place without even a glance into the dark, and I left her and joined the crowd. As we moved, more and more people drifted into the fray. They were angry and excited but none of them could explain exactly what was happening. Whenever anyone found themselves at the front of the group, they stepped back and waited for someone else to move past them. They were in need of a leader.

If the Sacristan had been at home, where he belonged, he would never have become involved. The route did not take us by his house. But instead, we came across him as he was leaving the house of Margarita and Jaume and their daughter, Fidelia, and at once I was on high alert. He slunk out with his head bent down. He moved the way a man moves when he doesn't want to be seen. He seemed alarmed to find himself in the midst of an angry rabble of torchbearers.

"What's going on?" he said.

"Is Jaume there?" someone asked, and the Sacristan shook his head.

"Nobody's home." Which made no sense.

And then Fidelia appeared at the doorway, peering out at the street.

Oh, you bastard, I said. *You perverted, horrid, sick bastard. Fidelia? She's fifteen years old!*

And it wasn't that I loved Fidelia in particular, or cared for her more than I did for other people. And it wasn't that I knew for certain that whatever she'd got up to with the Sacristan would be terribly damaging; perhaps no harm would come to her and she would think of it in later life as an odd interlude, a private anecdote. It was the repetitiveness that made me angry, the tedious pain of seeing the same thing over and over again. I thought about the Sacristan's smirk when he said that thing about protecting the virgins in the Charterhouse paintings. I thought about Ham and all the other men who preceded the Sacristan, and how angry I had felt about them too, and all the centuries of anger made me feel, in that moment, tired to the point of rage.

You bastard, you bastard, you bastard, I said. I looked at Fidelia, who was red-cheeked and smiling a strange, brave smile, as though she was sure of herself, as though she was sure she had done the right thing. I thought about the Spanish refugee's daughter, spherical and confused. I thought about me. About what happened to me.

The group of torchbearers was milling around waiting for someone to urge them on, and the Sacristan was making some quick calculations. It was his fault that the foreigners were at the Charterhouse at all. If the villagers remembered this too clearly, their rage might turn on him. Wouldn't that be inconvenient? And mightn't there be questions, once they thought to ask, about what he had been doing leaving Jaume's house when only the young daughter had been home? And if there was to be a scene, and it appeared that there certainly *was,* wouldn't it be better to be at the front of it, to take charge of it, to be viewed not as the enemy, but as the solution?

He stepped forward. He said that he too felt enough was enough, that the foreigners needed to go. Somebody handed him a torch. He took his place at the front of the group, and they proceeded, as though nothing horrendous had happened, as though the Sacristan was an acceptable man.

The group picked up speed as we neared the Charterhouse. People began to shout. Their faces looked stark and weird in the torchlight, and everything around us was dark, and I found that I was angry, very angry, possibly angrier than I had ever been in all the hundreds of years of my existence. It was as though all the rage of my centuries of ghosthood returned to me at once, and I was angry at the Sacristan and angry at the villagers and angry too about Ham and all the other men and all the other bad things I'd seen happen and not been able to prevent. The fishmonger led a chant of, "Foreigners out!" They pushed open the Charterhouse door and poured into the corridor. In the confined space, the shouting was louder, deafening, thudding off the hard surfaces. I was screaming along, in time with the chant, *You bastard! You bastard! You bastard!*

All the same, it was an accident. The Sacristan made to approach the door of Cell Three, torch aloft, face set, looking entirely righteous. Was he going to set the door alight? Was he going to knock first and politely let them know that he was going to set the door alight? He hesitated.

I felt my way through his brain, his throat. I tickled his larynx and made him cough. I prodded his liver and squeezed his kidneys. He bent forwards a little. Felt peculiar. Felt unsteady. And then I looked him right in the heart and I raged. Pummeled and slapped and screamed *You bastard*, and it just happened. Everything froze. The arteries shut off. The blood stilled in the tubes. The heart wriggled, spasmed once, twice, and one last time. Then it stopped.

The Sacristan slumped and then fell. People ran to pick him up, but there was nothing to rescue. He was already gone. The feeling of dying was familiar, of course, and it had calmed me to go through it with him: the sensation of taking off, the tightening of vision, burgeoning and immense outrage just about to explode into a scream when—nothing. I slid out of his body. I took myself off, away from the group. I was satisfied and very, very ashamed.

I've never done that before, I said. There was nobody to tell. *I swear, I swear, I've never done that before. I didn't know it was even possible. I didn't know I could do that.*

There was commotion around the Sacristan, and then there was more, because the door of Cell Three had opened and George had stepped out. She took a slow drag from a cigar as she looked at the uncertain faces of the Valldemossans. They had stumbled over each other trying to step back when she appeared, and now stared at her, mouths clamped shut and hands over their noses. George glanced at the cluster of people bent over the Sacristan. They were swatting and thumping and breathing on him, as though that might bring him back to life. Then she turned back to the group with the torches.

She felt more afraid than she ever had in her life. She had led her family to a place of danger and now it was all going to go up in flames. They might die like this, she thought, at the hands of the torchbearers, and though she did not fear her own pain, she feared the pain of her loved ones so much she thought she might faint. Her fingers trembled around the cigar and her breaths were coming too fast and too shallow for her to inhale properly.

"You can all go home," she said. "We're done. We're leaving."

She tried to look as though none of this mattered to her, as though the villagers holding torches were of no relevance to her decision.

"We were always going to leave," she said.

The villagers did not move.

George took a quick step towards them, and again they shifted back. "Go now," she said.

When they didn't move, she sucked her cigar and blew a cloud of smoke in their direction. It drifted through the air towards them and they ran from it as though it was a gunshot.

I REMEMBER

When it starts, I tell nobody. It's not too bad in any case, contractions quick and light and lots of time in between. I don't tell my mother, who is downstairs singing to herself and pouring out her evening measure of wine, and who I now realize has known all along that I've been lying about Ham. Look at the size of me now. There's no hiding it, no time for her to plan my wedding to a boy she has glimpsed once, from a distance, and never spoken to. What else could she do, I suppose, except nod and smile and say it would be all right when I strung her along with assurances Ham never gave. I wonder what is coming my way in the next few hours: a baby and what else? My mother must have thought it through. She must have a backup plan.

Ham is never going to marry me. The baby is never going to not come. These two facts are clear and sharp. I wait until my mother is distracted, calling out of the back door towards a friend passing by—a draft enters the house, thick with the smell of the pigs—and then I scurry outside.

It is dusk. The Charterhouse looks black up on the hilltop. The sky is that kind of bright, dark blue that makes the edges of everything look severe. I hold up a hand and see my fingers outlined, crisp and black, with watery little stars in between them. Somewhere below me in the village, someone is singing an obscene song about hunting boar. Footsteps down an alley. I pass my sister's house, where she and Felix are eating, or arguing, or doing whatever else married people do. For a moment, I falter; I could knock on María's door, explain everything, tell her to send for someone. I could turn around and go back home, let my mother take care of everything. She knows, after all, what to expect.

But then I think of Ham, think that this is, after all, as much to do with him as it is to do with me. It isn't right that he should or could be oblivious when this is happening. He will love the baby, won't he? It is natural to love your own baby. He might love me a little more too once he's seen what efforts I am going to because of him. He is never going to marry me, but he might respect me. A contraction comes on, hard enough to make me bend double on the path, and I tell myself it is fine, that other women are babies for making such a fuss about this. I wait, and when it passes, I climb the hill a little faster.

My waters break as I am hammering at the Charterhouse door. The liquid turns the flagstones of the threshold black. The man who answers takes one look at me, at the puddle between my legs and the drip-drip-drip still falling from my crotch and vanishes again, leaving the door ajar. I hear him calling for the apothecary. When I poke my head inside, I see him scurrying along a stone cloister and around a corner, still shouting. I take a step inside, and then another, and when a contraction hits I find that I am screaming, *Ham! Ham!* in a voice I've never heard myself use before.

And then there he is, wide-eyed and pale, shuffling towards

the doorway and glancing over his shoulder as though worried he is being followed.

He grips me by the elbow and steers me back the way he has come, hissing, *Be quiet, be quiet, be quiet,* as he leads me down corridor after corridor, past dark passage after dark passage, and then, finally, to a door that he pauses at and opens and bundles me through. The pain comes again and I make a sound like an angry goat.

Sit, says Ham, pushing me towards a little stool.

I grit my teeth. Shrug his hand off my back. *I don't want to sit,* I say, and then I resume my bleating.

Ham looks stung. Withdraws from me a little, as though the thought of touching me is obscene, as though he has never, would never.

What do you want, then? he asks. *If you don't want to sit, what do you want?*

I labor for hours. The night passes and the light comes. In bursts, I remember where I am, that I am in Ham's room in the Charterhouse, that I am in a place where women should never be and have never been and it strikes me as hilarious to be here, now, when I am at my most feral, bellowing and grunting and bleeding on everything so unapologetically. Ham paces around, grabs his hair a lot, offers water and damp cloths, once thrusts something that looks like stewed fruit in my direction, and I snarl at him until he leaves me alone. I am aware at some point that he has lit a candle and is reading in the corner, and it strikes me that this is what his life is like, that this is what he does when I am not there in his room, having his baby. It is also, apparently, what he does when I am in his room, having his baby.

Are you sure you don't want me to get the apothecary? Ham

says. *It's just you're not really supposed to be here, and there could be trouble for me if they find out. But I will get the apothecary if you want me to.*

I begin to bear down sometime in the middle of the next day, when it is bright outside and a screeching bird has set up watch on the windowsill. I can feel the baby sinking somewhere so deep it feels that it must, surely, be outside of me now, but when I put my hands down to feel for it, there's nothing, only empty space.

I notice that Ham's room smells musty, of unwashed linen.

Soon, the only smell is blood, rusty and hot.

There is a time, maybe half an hour, maybe longer, when I panic, when I see all at once what is happening and that there is nothing to be done to stop it and yet I want to fight it, want to do something, want to make it right again. *Ham,* I say, *Ham. Get the apothecary. Get my mother. Get my sister.* He is kneeling by my side, his face gray, eyes red from sleeplessness, and he does nothing. *Get my mother,* I say. *Get my mother. I want my mother.* They must be wondering where I am. They must be looking for me. Ham doesn't move. I try saying it louder, screaming it, and then realize I haven't said anything at all, that I have been wordlessly grunting this whole time and this is like a dream in which I need to run and find that I can't, that my legs won't move the right way.

I put all my energy into producing his name. One more time: *Ham,* I say.

He starts. *Yes?* he says. *Yes?*

And then the panic subsides and of course it is too late, there is nothing to be done, and the rest of the labor I spend giving up the ghost with as little fuss as I can. There is so much blood everywhere there can surely be none left in me, though when my daughter finally appears, pink-blue and waxy, she is accompanied by a small red gush. I watch in astonishment as her shoulders twist, first one and then the other, to release themselves from my body and find that I am looking at myself, my own vagina, from somewhere else in the room; Ham peering between the lattice of his own fingers and then reaching out, shakily, to guide my daughter further away from me into the world. She cries. Ham jumps at the sound, as though surprised to find anything living amongst all this death.

My body is flat, deflated, limp, red in places, gray in places, very dead, and my daughter's is writhing now, lithe, alive, she is taking a great gulp of air and screaming, and in my initial confusion I think perhaps I am experiencing a resurrection, that I am her or rather that she is me, that what I am feeling, the lightheadedness and weightlessness and disorientation and smallness and lostness are the feelings of a baby just born.

PARIS

It never occurred to me that I would not go with them. It all happened very quickly, and I didn't have time, I suppose. George stepping back into the cell and saying, "We have to leave." The pale faces of Maurice and Solange. "The Sacristan is dead on our doorstep," said George. "They want to burn us to the ground." Running to the courtyard to scoop up Adélaide from the corner where she had slumped, carrying her out to the garden, setting her down beside the pomegranate tree. Adélaide lifting her head, sniffing the air coming in off the hillside, sidling up to the wall, and then leaping over it without looking back. The sound of her landing and trotting away into the dark. Amélie returning sometime after three a.m., drunk and distraught, to be told by María Antonia that they were all leaving in the morning.

I just did it. I went with them. In the morning, as the family fiddled with their boxes and paid the donkey boy three times the usual fare and fussed over Chopin with blankets, I looked around me at the Charterhouse, the square, the path down to the village, and thought, *So long.*

Valldemossa was home, and had been home to everyone I'd ever cared about before George. I'd kept close watch over my daughter, who grew up in my sister's house with her cousins, and on her children and their children and so on, all the way down to Bernadita. And I'd loved Constanza, had loved loving her, but she, like all my family, was gone. The Charterhouse, which had been the source of all my trouble when I'd been alive, and so much entertainment and purpose since I'd died, was a living map of my memories. I could pin one to each flagstone in the cloisters, each brick in the wall, the doorstep. It was in many ways, I thought, too full of me by then. It had become burdensome. It was time for a change.

So when George and her family climbed up onto the back of the cart with all of their belongings, I said, *So long,* and went with them. First to Palma and then onto the ship with the pigs. I saw everything: the ocean from the middle as opposed to the edge, and then from the other side. Marseille. The house by the water. I tasted French apple tart in Solange's mouth, and thought it was the most delicious thing of all time, of all places. That was before I reached Paris.

In Paris I tasted champagne. George drank a lot of champagne.

Of course, I knew everything that was going to happen to them. I had made the mistake of already seeing it all. But I also thought: *Let's go through this again.* Let's see how it feels when taken at the crushing, trudging pace of ordinary life, so incredibly slow, ponderous, deadening, and with so many astonishing moments in between.

And when I tell this story you might think, *Weren't you just a lovelorn hanger-on, clinging to people who were more interesting and more alive than you, just to feel something?*

To which I'd say, *Oh, yes, absolutely.*

And when Chopin was dead, and when George was dead, and Amélie and Solange and Maurice after that, what did I do? Where did I go?

Oh, everything. Everywhere.

I ended up here, talking to you.

Occasionally, and very briefly, I think you hear me.

ACKNOWLEDGMENTS

Thanks—

To Rebecca Carter, my agent at Janklow & Nesbit, whose integrity and insight give me courage.

To Emma Parry at Janklow & Nesbit in New York for her vision and her faith in me.

To Sophie Jonathan, my editor at Picador, and Sally Howe, my editor at Scribner, who saw in my work the best version of itself, even when I didn't.

To the many people at Picador in the UK and Scribner in the US, including Gillian Fitzgerald-Kelly, Orla King, Alice Dewing, Nicholas Blake, Dan Cuddy, Susan Brown, Tristan Offit, and many others, who made possible the existence of the book currently in your hands.

To MacDowell, where I found just the right balance of peace and chaos, and to the friends and artists I met there; to Lauren Sandler for her immense generosity of spirit.

To the Society of Authors' Somerset Maugham Award, which funded my research trip to Valldemossa.

To Antonio and his pug, Luna, for making my stay in Valldemossa a delight, and for producing books from thin air.

Acknowledgments

To Laura Marris, for continued transatlantic guidance and inspiration.

To Amanda Walker, Claudia Gray, and Grace Shortland, always.

To Margaret and Richard Stevens, for patience, wisdom, and support.

To Ambrose Williams, for his joy.

To Eley Williams, who makes my life delicious, enduringly.

ABOUT THE AUTHOR

Nell Stevens is the author of *Bleaker House* and *The Victorian and the Romantic*, which won the 2019 Somerset Maugham Award. She was shortlisted for the 2018 BBC National Short Story Award. Her writing has been published in *The New York Times*, *Vogue*, *The Paris Review*, *The New York Review of Books*, *The Guardian*, *Granta*, and elsewhere. Nell teaches Creative Writing at the University of Warwick and lives in London with her wife and son. *Briefly, A Delicious Life* is her first novel.